PURSUED FOR THE VISCOUNT'S VENGEANCE

W0009959

To my fellow Quayistas (you know who you are),
for the love, friendship, support and
understanding that only other writers can give.

Chapter One

So here was his quarry. Miss Deborah Meltham.

Standing at the side of the assembly room, away from the glitter of the chandeliers, Gil studied the lady as she went down the dance with her brother. There was a decided likeness between the pair although Randolph, Lord Kirkster, was taller and fairer. Gil had to admit he was a handsome young buck, fashionably dressed and with his thick, waving hair brushed back from his pale brow. He was also a graceful dancer, but there was an air of indifference about him, a restlessness to his face, as if he wanted to be elsewhere. The epitome of a Byronic hero, thought Gil, his lip curling, and already as dissolute as the poet himself. He turned his attention to the lady.

Beneath the plain round gown of green muslin her figure looked good, but she was very slim. Petite. Not at all his style. A mirthless laugh shook him at the irrelevance of the popular saying. He had never shown preference for any lady, for he was convinced that soldiers should not marry and he was a soldier. Or he had been. Having sold out, he supposed that at some point he would take a wife, but it would be a marriage of convenience for both parties. There was no need for the heart to be involved. In his experience love meant only loss and unbearable pain.

What he was planning now had nothing to do with marriage or courtship. It was to fulfil an oath he had taken and was the only way to assuage the grief that threatened to devour him. Since leaving the army last summer he had withdrawn from society, a prey to his grief and determined upon revenge. Which was why he was so interested in Deborah Meltham. He turned his attention back to her.

Her features were regular and he supposed she might be quite pretty, if she dressed her hair more becomingly, instead of having it scraped back so severely into a knot. She wore no jewels and her dress was high necked and long-sleeved. A dowd, Gil decided, coldly assessing her. Not at all attractive. But at that moment Lord Kirkster spoke, she looked up and a sudden smile transformed her face. The lively animation in her countenance and the decided twinkle in her green eyes forced him to revise his opinion. Reluctantly he admitted that she was more than pretty.

He felt a sudden contraction in his chest, a jolt of unwelcome attraction. Beneath that puritanical dress and severe hairstyle she was quite beautiful.

'So it should be no hardship to court her,' he muttered.

He pushed aside a tremor of distaste. He had never before seduced a woman, although in more than a decade of military service he had seen other men do it, dozens of times. He had no time for such knavery, nor for romance: in his opinion there was no room for such emotion in a soldier's life. Not that there had been any shortage of women willing to throw themselves at him and he had taken some of them to his bed, but only those who understood the rules, who knew he offered nothing more than dalliance. The liaisons never lasted long and when it ended Gil always provided a generous settlement to soften the blow.

This, however, was different. He would take no pleasure in it, although it must be done. He raised a hand to his cheek, rubbing one finger lightly along the fine, jagged line that ran down to his jaw. The scar might cause some small difficulty, especially since he was using neither his title nor his wealth to entice the lady. Well, time would tell.

The music ended and he watched Miss Meltham leave the floor on her brother's arm. The looks they exchanged confirmed that they were clearly fond of one another. Her disgrace, her downfall, would hit the young lord hard. From all he had learned Gil was convinced that the only way to be avenged upon the man was through his sister. The fellow had already gambled away most of his fortune and seemed to care little for the fact. It was only his sister who was keeping him from bankruptcy and disgrace. Deborah was the only thing Kirkster now cared about. Gil turned away from the dance floor, trampling his scruples. It had to be this way. Merely forcing a duel upon Kirkster would not be punishment enough. He must be made to suffer as Gil had suffered. Although if the scoundrel should call him out for ruining his sister, then Gil would take pleasure in putting a bullet through him.

And Deborah Meltham?

Again Gil stifled his conscience. It was only a whisper, easily pushed aside. His years as a soldier had inured him to much greater suffering than anything he was likely to inflict here. After all, it was not as if he planned any real harm to the woman, nothing more than a bruised heart and loss of character. And he would not force her. She would come to him willingly, but her seduction would be his revenge upon her brother. An eye for an eye. A seduction for a life. Two lives.

Or three, if you counted the unborn child.

Deborah's spine tingled as she went down the dance. He was here again, the stranger in the shadows, watching her. She had never seen him clearly, but she was aware of him, it was as if she could physically feel his presence. As the dance ended and she accompanied her brother from the floor she glanced across the room. Yes, there was the tall figure of the man she had noticed around the town several times in that past few weeks. He kept his distance and was always just turning away whenever she glimpsed him, or disappearing into a doorway. He was plainly dressed, but he carried himself with such assurance that she was sure he must be a man of substance.

Not for the first time she thought of telling Ran, but what could she say, that she had noticed the stranger on several occasions? The man had not accosted her; she had never caught him ogling her. Indeed, he had never been that close to her, but somehow her body knew when he was in her vicinity. She sensed him, like a wild animal sensed danger.

Randolph would only laugh if she told him that. He

would dismiss it as female fancy. Perhaps it was. She squeezed his arm.

'Ran, they are striking up for another country dance. Shall we not return to the floor?'

He shook his head. 'By no means. I have done my duty and stood up twice with you. Now I mean to go to the card room.'

'But you are such a good dancer. Would you not like to stay for one more measure?'

He grinned at her. 'No, dear sister, I would not. I am determined on cards.'

Knowing his good mood could evaporate in a twinkling, she did not argue but said cheerfully, 'Very well, I will come, too, and watch you. That is, if you do not mind.'

'Not at all, but it will be dull work. Would you not prefer to dance?'

Deborah had been burying her own preferences for so long that she did not even hesitate.

'Not without you.'

'Come along, then, Deb. You shall be my good-luck charm.'

She tucked her hand in his arm, but she knew from the intent look upon his face that he had all but forgotten her existence, even before they entered the card room.

Deb watched the play, discreetly waving away the waiter when he would have refilled Ran's glass. She knew there was not much to fear when her brother was playing cards here. The gentlemen gathered around the table had known her and Randolph since they were children. Sir Geoffrey would not allow the stakes to grow too high and old Mr Appleton would call a halt to the game if her brother's losses became too great, so it was only Ran's drinking she needed to keep in check, because that could lead to more dangerous cravings. However, when he called for another bottle she did not embarrass him by publicly remonstrating. The best she could hope for was that he would grow weary of the game and escort her home very soon.

She remained at his side, obliged to hide her chagrin as the evening progressed. The more Ran drank the wilder his play. As the losses mounted she saw his frown deepening, but she knew better than to protest when he threw down yet another losing hand. Instead she fluttered her fan.

'Heavens, I vow 'tis close in here tonight, anyone would think it was high summer rather than March. Dear Brother, I do not know how you can concentrate, I feel quite faint with the heat.'

'Do you? Go on home then, if you wish. Take the carriage, I will follow later.'

Forcing a little trill of laughter, Deb leaned closer and touched his arm, saying affectionately, 'La, I cannot go without you, Ran, you know that. I should not rest until you are home safe.'

He shrugged her off with a scowling look.

'I have agreed to live in this benighted place,' he muttered. 'Is that not enough for you? Must you also dog my every waking minute?'

'Ran, that is not—'

His chair scraped back.

'If you will excuse me, gentlemen. My sister is fatigued and must go home.'

Beneath his smiling words Deb knew he was furious, she could see it in the set of his jaw and the white knuckles of the fist tucked against the tails of his coat.

'Of course, my boy, of course.' Old Mr Appleton waved him away before picking up a fresh pack of cards. 'Away you go now. You can have your revenge 'pon us next week, eh?'

'That I will, sir. Come along, my dear.'

Outwardly, Ran was all care and consideration, but when Deb took his outstretched hand there was no gentleness in his grip. No matter. She would bear with his mood, as long as he came home with her. Silently and with her smile fixed in place, she accompanied her brother out of the assembly rooms.

'Will your lordship be requiring the carriage?'

'No, Harris, I am going to walk in the town today.' Gil threw a quick warning glance at his valet. 'And do try to stop calling me "your lordship". I am plain Mr Victor while we are in Fallbridge.'

'And if you will forgive me saying so, my—sir,' Harris corrected himself, 'we've been here a sight too long already.'

Gil was busy tying his cravat and pretended not to hear. That was the problem with old retainers, one could not reprimand them for stating an opinion. And John Harris was more than a servant, he had been a sergeant in Gil's regiment. They had faced death together on several occasions, most recently on the bloody battlefield of Waterloo. John would obey any of Gil's commands without question, but it did not stop him from making it plain when he disapproved of a course of action. And he clearly disapproved of Gil's latest plan.

'Do you want me to come with you?' Harris asked now. 'If this Kirkster should get wind of who you are he could be dangerous.'

'My dear John, the fellow doesn't know me from Adam and will not learn my identity until I am ready.' He could not resist adding, 'Unless your gabbing gives our game away.'

'Well I don't like it and so I tell you. Why you can't just call the man out and put a bullet through him I don't know.'

The neckcloth was tied to Gil's satisfaction, but he continued to stare into the mirror.

'That would be too easy a death for him. I want him to know what it is to have someone close to you suffering and not be able to help them.'

'Well, it ain't like you, sir, that's all I'm saying. You've always been one for plain dealing, but this, well, I don't like it.' Even without looking around Gil knew Harris was shaking his head as he spoke. 'Plain simple justice I could understand, but not this havey-cavey business.'

'If you don't like it, John, then you are free to go back to Gilmorton and wait for me there.'

'And have your mother worrying even more because you was on your own? No, my lord, that I won't do. I'm your man and I'll be here to the end. Whatever that may be.'

His loud sigh and gloomy words banished Gil's scowl. He turned, grinning, and put a hand on the valet's shoulder.

'And I am glad to have you with me, John, truly. Now, you stay here and see what gossip you can pick up about Kirkster and his sister in the taproom, while

I sally forth to sample the pleasures of Fallbridge on market day!'

It was a sunny morning and the walk from the inn to the market a short one. Gil had chosen his clothes with care, a plain coat of russet-coloured wool over buckskins and boots, eminently suitable for a country gentleman, although a knowledgeable eye would know at a glance that the coat had been made by one of the finest tailors in London, the glossy top boots purchased from a certain establishment on the corner of Piccadilly and St James's Street, while his curly brimmed hat, impeccable cream waistcoat and snowy linen were clearly the mark of a fashionable man.

Gil had been in Fallbridge for two weeks, making himself familiar with the area, but he was in no hurry to approach Lord Kirkster or his sister. He had seen Kirkster a couple of times in local taverns and at last night's assembly at the Red Lion, but Deborah Meltham was regularly out and about in the town. She appeared to be well respected in Fallbridge and spent most of her time on charitable errands or visiting neighbours. Occasionally he would see her purchasing a few household necessities before walking back to Kirkster House, the substantial family mansion just outside the town on the Ormskirk Road. She rarely visited the milliner or the haberdasher and Gil concluded she had little interest in frivolities such as hats or ribbons.

She always walked alone, without even a maid, and there was something very contained about her, reserved, as if she had made a conscious decision to keep the world at bay. Gil wondered if she was lonely and was obliged to push aside a stab of sympathy. If that was the case, she would be all the more receptive to his overtures, when he made his move.

A sudden chill ran through him. He ascribed it to the gusty wind, which made him grab at his tall hat to prevent it flying away. He kept his head down and quickened his pace, heading for the town centre, where the tall buildings would offer some shelter from the wind. As he turned the corner into the high street he almost collided with someone coming the other way. A woman, he realised as he took in the neat little boots and plain skirts made of serviceable dimity. They both stopped, but he heard a soft 'Oh' and saw a brown-paper package drop to the floor.

'I beg your pardon.' Instinctively he bent to pick it up, only raising his eyes as he handed over the parcel, and it was at that moment he found himself looking into the face of Miss Deborah Meltham.

Deb had been lost in her own thoughts, hurrying to return the shawl her kind friend Lady Gomersham had loaned her and get back to Randolph, but the near collision brought her to a sudden halt. She was murmuring her apology even as the gentleman scooped up her parcel. It was then, as he straightened and looked at her, that she recognised him.

Manners were forgotten. Deborah stared at the man as he handed back her package. He had been a shadowy figure for some weeks, but fate had given her this opportunity to study him and she took it. She observed every detail: the near-black hair, the slate-grey eyes set beneath curving dark brows, the unsmiling mouth and strong cleft chin. The lines of his lean face were too angular to be called handsome, but they were further disfigured by a thin scar that ran down the left side, from temple to chin.

All her suspicions were confirmed when he met her eyes. His was not the look of a man who had just bumped into a stranger. The intensity of his gaze made her tremble inside and set her pulse racing, but the next instant he had stepped back and was smiling politely as he tipped his hat to her and strode on. Deb clutched her parcel and remained frozen to the spot, trying to quieten her pounding heart. She must not turn back. She must not stare after him. Summoning all her willpower, she forced herself to walk on around the corner and out of sight, but for the rest of the day she carried his stern, unsmiling image in her head. The Man with the Scar.

Well, that was unfortunate. Gil walked swiftly away, cursing his bad luck. It had not been his plan to become acquainted with Deborah Meltham until he had learned a little more about her. He needed to be sure of his ground if he was to woo her successfully. He had never set out to do such a thing before and had intended to plan his every move as he would a military operation, to ensure he achieved the required result.

Gil frowned, thinking of her reaction to their un-expected meeting. At first there had been the shock and embarrassment natural to such an encounter, but when she raised her eyes to his face there had been something more. Recognition. Damnation. He had been careful to keep his distance, to remain in the background while he had been observing her, but it was clear that he had not been careful enough. After this chance encounter he could no longer put off his plan, so he had best get on with it. His eyes searched the town square and, spotting his quarry, he moved in.

'Sir Geoffrey, good day to you.' Gil touched his hat, smiling pleasantly, and when the man looked blankly at him he added, 'James Victor. You may recall we met in the card room last night.'

'Ah, yes, Mr Victor. Good day, sir, good day.' The older man beamed at him. 'I remember you now! Here on business, if I recall.'

'No, no, not business exactly. I am minded to buy a property in the area.'

'And there's nowhere better, sir, as I can vouch for!' Sir Geoffrey turned to accompany him on his way. 'So, what have you seen so far?'

Gil mentioned a couple of houses, asked a few questions and it was not long before this had the required effect.

'Well if you are serious, young sir, then perhaps you should meet some more of your prospective neighbours. My wife is holding a little party tomorrow night. Nothing fancy, you understand, just a few card tables, perhaps a little dancing. Gomersham Lodge, at the end of Mill Lane.'

'I'd be delighted to come, only… Lady Gomersham will not object to a stranger turning up at her drawing room?'

'Not a bit of it, always pleased to have another gentleman in attendance…' Sir Geoffrey's pale eyes twinkled merrily '…and if you can be persuaded to stand up for a dance or two she will be even more delighted!'

Gil allowed himself to be persuaded, exchanged a few more words with Sir Geoffrey, then went on his way, well pleased with the morning's work. He had seen Lady Gomersham's name scribbled on the package he had picked up for Miss Meltham, so it was more than likely she would be at Gomersham Lodge tomorrow.

It only occurred to him later, when he was shaving himself and staring into the looking glass, that the one thing he had not seen in Miss Meltham's clear green eyes was repugnance. She had hardly appeared to notice his scar.

Chapter Two

Deborah was relieved to find her brother at the break-fast table the following morning and apparently in good spirits. She greeted him with a kiss on his cheek before taking her seat beside him.

'Lady Gomersham has invited us to the Lodge for supper this evening.' She kept her voice light, trying not to sound too eager. 'Shall we go, Ran?'

'If you wish to do so.'

'Well, I do,' she replied. 'Lizzie has just returned from her trip to London, where she has been staying with her aunt. I saw her yesterday, when I called at the Lodge, and I must say she was looking very smart in her London fashions. I dare say she will put us all in the shade.' She ended with a little laugh, watching her brother for the slightest flicker of interest. Elizabeth Gomersham was only two years younger than Randolph and at one time they had been good friends, but now he showed no enthusiasm at all at the prospect of seeing her again.

'These provincial parties are always so dull. Can you not go on your own?'

She framed her answer carefully.

'I could, of course, but we have known the family for ever and Lady Gomersham is always asking after you. I know she would be delighted if you could attend one of her little gatherings.'

He shrugged carelessly.

'Oh, very well. As long as the brandy is tolerable I shall not object.'

With that she had to be satisfied. She could only hope that his mercurial mood would not dip too badly during the day, for if it did he was very likely to cry off from the engagement.

Gomersham Lodge was a neat but substantial property within easy walking distance of the George, where Gil was putting up, but for the sake of appearances he ordered his carriage to take him to the door. While he was changing into the dark coat and knee breeches that were obligatory for formal evening parties, he asked his valet to tell him what he had discovered about the Melthams.

'It's just the two of them, my lord, Lord Kirkster and his sister. The family has had a house here for a couple of generations. The locals is mightily close-lipped about 'em, too. Protective, I would say, as these places can be about those they consider their own. The family came originally from Liverpool and made their money in the sugar trade, so I'm told. Their father died four years ago and it appears the new lord doesn't take his responsibilities quite as seriously. The widowed Lady Kirkster moved here with her daughter, but soon followed her husband to the grave, and Miss Meltham has lived in Fallbridge ever since.'

'No sign of a suitor for the lady?'

'None was mentioned. She's four-and-twenty, my lord, so she's lost her chance by now.'

'Not necessarily.'

Gil spoke more sharply than he had intended, irritated that society should consider a young woman to be past her best at such an age. She was a very attractive young woman. Or rather, many men would think so, he corrected himself.

When Gil arrived at Gomersham Lodge Sir Geoffrey was looking out for him and immediately presented him to Lady Gomersham, a plump, jolly woman who greeted him warmly and bade him go off and enjoy himself. His host seemed intent upon making him known to everyone in the room and, since that was his avowed reason for being there, Gil endured it patiently until at last Sir Geoffrey drew him towards a couple standing in one corner of the room, Miss Deborah Meltham and her brother, Lord Kirkster.

Once the introductions were made Gil referred to his previous encounter with Miss Meltham.

'So careless of me not to be paying more attention to where I was going,' he ended, smiling. 'I trust your package was not damaged when you dropped it?'

'No, sir, not at all. Pray think no more about it.'

Her hand fluttered and she plucked at the shoulder of her gown, not meeting his eyes. Did the scar on his face repulse her after all? Perhaps she had been too startled yesterday to pay it any heed. He was aware of the differing reactions to his spoiled face whenever he was introduced to someone new. A few were fascinated by it, many affected not to notice, but the way they averted their eyes told its own story. Gil had learned to live with that.

He cared nothing for the opinions of others. He had more than a few physical scars as well as some that no one could see. A decade of military service had pitched him into some of the bloodiest battles of the Peninsular War. It had been a cruel time and any sensitivity had been forced out of him. One had to be tough to survive. The hard shell he had built around himself was intact and he intended that it should remain so. The only thing he cared for now was family, which was why the news that greeted him upon his return to Gilmorton Hall last summer had been so difficult to accept. Which was why he was going to be revenged.

It was a pity, then, if Deborah Meltham disliked his scarred face, but not an insurmountable problem. Gil fixed a suitable smile in place and listened to his host explaining his presence in Fallbridge.

'Mr Victor is looking to buy property in the area—' Sir Geoffrey broke off as the bustle of another arrival caught his attention and with a hasty apology he moved away.

'You could have Kirkster House, with my blessing,' said its owner, giving a laugh that held only bitterness.

'Randolph, hush.' His sister's smile was strained. 'My brother is funning, of course. Fallbridge is a very pleasant place to live, Mr Victor, I assure you.'

'Do you spend much time here?' Gil asked politely. 'Is it your only home?'

'I have lived here for some time, but my brother joined me only last year.'

'And already it feels like an eternity.'

'We spent every summer here as children,' Miss

Meltham hastily broke in to cover Lord Kirkster's muttered words. 'The rest of the time was spent at the family home in Liverpool.'

Not by so much as the flicker of an eye did Gil show how much this interested him.

'And do you still have that house?'

She looked away. 'Yes, but I do not go there now.'

'What my sister means is that Duke Street is not grand enough for her any more,' said Kirkster.

'And when were you there last, my lord?' asked Gil, at his most casual.

'I made Duke Street my home when I left Oxford, until I came here to join Deb. There's a dashed sight more to do there than here, I can tell you!'

Gil raised his brows, looking politely interested and giving Kirkster time to tell him more, but Miss Meltham forestalled him.

'If Mr Victor is looking to move to Fallbridge, I am sure he would prefer to hear what the town has to offer.' There was a slight flush on her cheek, as if she were embarrassed by her brother's ungracious speech. 'There are clubs and societies for every taste, sir. If your interest is history the Antiquarians meet regularly and I understand the Debating Society is very lively, not to mention the weekly balls at the Red Lion.'

Her eyes flickered up to his as she mentioned the balls and Gil knew she had seen him there.

'Ah, yes, I looked in at the assembly rooms the other night,' he said easily. 'I played a hand or two in the card room.'

'Cards!' Lord Kirkster looked up at that. 'Are you any good?'

'I am considered a pretty fair opponent, I believe.'

'Indeed? Then perhaps we should go now and put that to the test.'

'My dear brother, you cannot monopolise Sir Geoffrey's guest in that way. Why, Mr Victor has only this minute walked through the door! Besides, you promised Lizzie Gomersham you would dance with her. If you will excuse us, Mr Victor.'

Gil watched her walk off with her brother, noting the way her silk skirts flowed and swung with every step. Had he imagined it, or had she been unwilling to discuss their house in Duke Street? She had certainly brought the subject back to Fallbridge pretty quickly. Perhaps she knew something of her brother's life in Liverpool. His lips thinned as anger rose in him. Those activities would certainly not reflect well upon the family name. He noticed Sir Geoffrey bearing down upon him. Time to play the innocent visitor again, so Gil dragged up a smile and turned to meet his host.

Once Randolph had danced with Lizzie Gomersham, Deb persuaded him to partner her for a Scotch reel and a country dance, but after that he lounged off to play whist at one of the card tables that had been set up in the adjoining room. He would be safe enough, she knew, but it was still difficult to relax when he was out of her sight and her eyes kept straying to the door as she wondered if she should join him.

She jumped at the sound of a smooth, deep voice at her shoulder.

'Would you do me the honour of dancing with me, Miss Meltham?'

'Mr Victor! Thank you, but I—'

'If you are going to say you do not dance, then I

shall not believe you,' he said, smiling. 'I saw you standing up with Lord Kirkster.' The smile faded. 'Perhaps my scar offends you.'

'No, of course not.' She felt obliged to look into his eyes, to show she was telling the truth. 'Sir Geoffrey said you were a military man. Is that how you came by it?'

'Yes. An encounter with a French cavalry sabre at Salamanca. I am grateful it was such a neat cut and not deep enough to do much damage.'

She shuddered. 'You were very fortunate, I think.'

'Indeed I was, Miss Meltham. But we are straying from the point. I invited you to dance.'

Deb hesitated, then saw the glint in his grey eyes. Laughter, or a challenge? She could not be sure.

He said softly, 'Perhaps you are afraid to dance with me.'

It was the truth. The attraction she felt to this man frightened her. She had never felt such a strong affinity before. Not even with the man who had courted her. Who had said he loved her and then proved himself worthless in the most devastating way.

She shook off the memory. Mr Victor was smiling at her, causing her insides to flutter in alarm. However, she was not about to admit it and her chin went up.

'Afraid? Why should I be afraid, here amongst friends?'

His lips curved upwards into a smile that caused a flutter of excitement deep within her.

'Quite.' He held out his hand. 'Shall we?'

Tentatively she lifted a hand and her fingers were immediately held in a firm grasp. It was surprisingly comforting, as if he had drawn her inside a protective shield. As if she need fear nothing while he was beside her.

One dance, no more.

She was dancing with a stranger. She could not deny the lift of her spirits to be on the dance floor, nor the *frisson* of excitement to be dancing with someone other than her brother. For years she had denied herself this pleasure, but all the old familiar feelings had returned almost as soon as the music started. The intoxication of skipping and twirling around the floor with an admirer, someone whose gaze made her feel as if she was dancing on top of the world.

Deborah tried to rein in her happiness, but it was impossible. No matter, she told herself, giving in to the temptation to smile at her partner as they held hands and moved down the dance. She was older and wiser now. Her head could not be turned in such a short time. But, oh, the way the blood fizzed and sizzled through her veins when he spoke to her!

'You dance very well, Miss Meltham.'

His voice was deep and warm, wrapping itself around her like velvet.

'I fear you flatter me, sir. I am out of practice.'

'Then we should remedy that. Will you not dance a second time with me?'

The music was ending and he was holding on to her hand, smiling down at her. Warning bells clamoured in Deborah's head. This was too much, too soon. She had seen that look in a man's eyes before. It meant nothing. No, she thought, worse than nothing. If she allowed herself to believe he was sincere, it meant trouble.

She pulled her hand free.

'Thank you, but I, I am not inclined to dance again.'

With a formal little smile she backed away before turning and walking off. Her spine tingled, she was sure his eyes were upon her. He had looked surprised, almost shocked, at her words, as if he could not believe she would refuse him. She lifted her head a little higher. No doubt he thought she was desperate for a partner. He did not realise that she dressed in this drab way to avoid such attentions.

Once bitten twice shy, she reminded herself. But that did not stop her surreptitiously watching him from the side of the room. Her eyes followed him as he moved off to join Sir Geoffrey and she watched as their host introduced him to Mr and Mrs Appleton. She was guiltily aware of feeling pleased that he did not ask anyone else to dance.

'Dear heaven,' she murmured, 'what a pathetic creature I am, to be so smitten by a man after one dance.'

Feeling rather lost and even a little sick at this shocking revelation, she made her way to the dining room, where refreshments had been set out. She helped herself to a cup of punch. She did not think she should drink it, but at least it looked as if she was doing something. Lizzie Gomersham came bouncing up and Deb summoned up a smile for her.

'I saw you dancing with Mr Victor,' said Lizzie, filling a punch cup and drinking it in almost one gulp. 'I stood up with him, too, but thankfully I was already promised to another partner after that and could make my escape before he asked me to dance again.'

'Why should you want to escape?' Deb asked her, mystified.

Lizzie's eyes widened. 'That horrid scar! I vow,

Deborah, I could not help but stare at it and I almost missed my steps. Did it not upset you?'

'I barely noticed it.'

Deborah had been too intent upon his eyes, glittering in the candlelight. And on the glinting smile that seemed to be for her alone. Just thinking about it now sent her stomach swooping. Lizzie continued to chatter.

'Papa said I must try to ignore it because Mr Victor was a soldier. He told Papa he was wounded while fighting in Spain. Of course, as soon as Mrs Appleton heard that she insisted he come to her charity ball tomorrow night. She said she was sure he would want to support the Military Widows' Fund and, of course, what could the poor man do but agree?'

'What indeed?' murmured Deborah, although in her opinion, the gentleman would do nothing he did not wish to do. There was a steeliness about him, a dangerously ruthless air. It made her shiver just to think of it and she was obliged to give herself a little shake.

'It is quite wrong to judge a person by appearances,' she said, as much to herself as to her young friend.

'Well, to be truthful, I soon grew used to the scar,' Lizzie confided. 'In fact, when I look at him now I think it makes him look quite piratical. Like the Corsair, which you must admit is very romantic.'

Deb decided she did not want to think about the man at all, scar or no scar.

Mr Victor did not approach her again that evening, but Deb was still aware of his presence in the room. She knew a moment's unease when she saw him talking to her brother, but they did not disappear together into the card room, so whatever the man was about she could acquit him of wanting to fleece her brother of what was left of his fortune.

Perhaps she was indeed being fanciful. Perhaps he had not been watching her those times she had seen him in the market, or at the assembly. Fallbridge was a small town, so it was inevitable that one should see its inhabitants out and about. And yet, she could not quite dispel the feeling that all was not as it seemed with Mr Victor and on the short carriage ride back to Kirkster House she asked her brother what he thought of their new acquaintance.

'Victor? Why, nothing. He declined to play cards with me this evening, did you know that? Told me he preferred to listen to the music! He seemed a dull dog. Why should I think anything at all of him?'

'Oh, no reason.'

'Have you taken a fancy to him, is that it?' Ran sat forward, as if trying to see her face in the darkness. 'Shall I make enquiries, find out if he is an eligible *parti*?'

'No, no, of course not. Do not be so foolish.' She forced herself to laugh and speak lightly. 'It is just so unusual to have visitors in Fallbridge, that is all.'

'Well I think it would be a very good thing if you were to make a play for him,' he said, throwing himself back into his corner. 'It might give you something to think about rather than fussing over me.'

She heard the petulant note in his voice and did not reply. She was familiar with his quick changes of mood and knew a wrong word now would spark an argument. Tonight had been a good evening. Ran had been on his best behaviour, he had not drunk too much, nor gambled too heavily and she allowed herself to hope that he was indeed improving. But when they arrived at the house she was dismayed when he did not follow her up the stairs, but went off to the drawing room, calling to Speke, the butler, to bring him a bottle of wine.

As charity balls went, this was a small affair. Gil stood at the side of the room, watching the dancing. Appleton had told him that, cleared of furniture, the drawing room could accommodate four-and-twenty couples at any one time. Gil tried to appear impressed, but his overriding feeling was that he had wasted another evening. Last night at Gomersham Lodge had been a disaster. He had rushed his fences and Deborah Meltham had shied off like a frightened colt. He had told himself he would do better this evening, but he had been here for over an hour now and there was no sign of her.

He should leave. He had no wish to stay here, being polite to these good people when his heart was so full of blackness. He pushed through the crowd towards his hostess, ready to make his excuses, but as he drew close a sudden flurry at the door heralded a late arrival. Mrs Appleton turned and Gil was close enough to hear her delighted cry.

'Deborah, my dear, what a delightful surprise, I had quite given you up!'

And there she was, in the doorway. Her silk gown was very simple, but with its high neck and long sleeves, it gave a slender elegance to her petite figure and the rich plum colour enhanced the creamy tones of her skin and made her green eyes glow with an added vibrancy. Gil's eyes went swiftly around the room, surprised that the other men present were not staring in admiration at Deborah Meltham. Was he the only one who could see the passionate woman behind that cool, elegant façade?

She was saying something to Mrs Appleton, who dismissed it with the wave of her hand.

'Pray do not apologise, Deborah. You are here now, that is all that matters. And here is Mr Victor, in need of a partner for the next dance.'

'I am indeed,' put in Gil, bowing. 'If Miss Meltham would do me the honour.'

There was a wary look in her eyes when she lifted them to his face and he was tempted to give her a reassuring smile. Instead he raised his brows and gave her a challenging look. It worked, her chin went up.

'Miss Meltham always supports our good causes by purchasing a ticket, but she rarely attends.' Mrs Appleton laughed, unaware of the tension sparking around her. 'Tonight we are all honoured.' She stepped aside, putting a hand on Deborah's back as if to push her forward. 'Hurry now, my dear, there is another set forming and they have room for you and Mr Victor.'

Still holding those green eyes, Gil put out his hand. Silently she took it and he could not be sure which of them trembled as his fingers closed around hers. The music started and they danced the first few movements in near silence. Deborah replied with no more than a word to Gil's attempts at conversation. She was unsmiling, guarded, as if she was afraid to enjoy herself. They made their way down the dance and then it was their turn to stand and watch the others.

'Is it such a penance to stand up with me?' he asked

her, knowing that for the moment they could not be overheard.

Immediately her eyes flew to his, then she looked away again.

'I beg your pardon,' she said. 'I told you last night, I am out of practice. Dancing with anyone other than my brother, I mean.'

'And why is that? Does your brother object to gentlemen paying you attention?'

'No, of course not. Although he is—can be—very protective of me.' They were moving again and she said, 'Forgive me, I must concentrate on my steps if I am not to stand upon your toes.'

He said innocently, 'Is that why you came, then, to practise your dancing?'

Her lips twitched. 'Perhaps it was.'

Or perhaps she came to see me.

The faint blush on her cheek suggested that might be the case. She was smiling, more relaxed in his company, so he forbore to tease her and they finished the dance so much in harmony that he risked asking her to stand up with him for another.

'Purely for the practice,' he added solemnly.

She chuckled. 'Are you sure your toes will stand a fresh assault?'

He grinned. 'Oh, I think so.'

She laughed, blushed, but she remained with him for the next dance and after that she allowed him to take her in to supper.

It was not until later, when he was back at his rooms at the George, Gil realised that for all the time he had spent with Deborah Meltham at the Appletons', he had not once thought of revenge. Even when she had told him her brother could be very protective, a point he should have noted, as it played perfectly into his plans. But those plans might well come unstuck if he allowed Deborah Meltham to get under his skin.

He had spent dark, grief-ridden months working out a way to destroy Kirkster, only to discover that the fellow was doing that himself with his drinking and his gambling. Gil was convinced now that the only way for him to inflict pain on Kirkster was by ruining his sister and he would not let anything stand in his way.

Deborah was in the morning room, writing up her accounts, when Speke came in.

'There is a gentleman to see you, Miss Meltham. A Mr Victor.'

Deb's pen spluttered at the butler's words and she blotted the page, giving herself time to compose herself before she replied. The gentleman was only making a courtesy call after their dancing together last night. Nothing out of the ordinary about that. For a panic-stricken moment, Deb wished she had not given in to the temptation to go to the charity ball. The butler coughed, reminding her that she could not delay much longer.

'I have shown him into the drawing room, ma'am.'

'Thank you, Speke. Where is Lord Kirkster?'

'His lordship has not yet left his room.'

No hope of a chaperon, then. It was nearly noon and this information suggested Ran had drunk himself into a stupor again, which was another reason she should not have gone out. With a sigh she rose and shook out her skirts before going off to meet her visitor.

Speke left the door open once he had shown her into the drawing room. Which was as it should be, Deborah knew, to observe the proprieties, and this sign of the old butler's regard helped her to greet her visitor calmly.

'I am sorry my brother is not here to see you, Mr Victor.'

She gave a disarming smile, hoping it would distract him from the faint smell of stale wine that pervaded the room.

'No doubt he is busy out of doors.'

'Yes.'

No need to tell him the truth, that in all likelihood her brother was still sleeping off last night's excesses. In her mind she could see Randolph falling unconscious in his chair and dropping his full wineglass on to the carpet. She had witnessed it herself too many times to doubt that is what had occurred.

'I am on my way to view a house. Lagallan Manor.' He waved a hand, as if to apologise for his riding coat. 'I thought I should stop to pay my respects.'

'That is very kind. Will you not sit down?'

'Thank you.'

She took a seat and watched as he carefully placed his hat, gloves and riding crop on the side table before crossing the room and lowering himself into the chair opposite. There was strength and a lithe grace in every movement, she noticed. But then he had been a soldier, he was no idle fop.

'Forgive me.' His eyes flickered towards the open door. 'You have no lady living with you?'

'I live here alone with my brother, sir.' One hand

fluttered. 'At four-and-twenty I am beyond the age of requiring a chaperon.'

He inclined his head silently and she was grateful he did not try to flatter her with insincere disclaimers.

'So, you really are looking for a property, Mr Victor.'

'Did you not believe me?'

'Fallbridge is a small market town, the society is not…fashionable.'

'I am not so hard to please and I found the company last night very enjoyable.'

There was nothing she could do to stop the blush rising and staining her cheeks. She was sure they must be crimson. Heavens, had she forgotten how to accept a compliment? As if to spare her embarrassment he turned to look out of the window.

'The countryside around here is very fine; I should like to explore more of it. Of course, it always helps if one has someone local as a guide.'

He paused and Deb's pulse leapt as she recognised that he was waiting for her to offer to accompany him. She might suggest they ride out together, or even to drive. It was such a long time since she had gone on an outing purely for pleasure. There could be no harm in it, as long as they were accompanied by a groom. It was very tempting, but she resolutely kept silent.

He was watching her and she looked away. She thought she heard him give a faint sigh.

'But I am taking too much of your time, Miss Meltham.'

'Not at all,' she said politely, but she rose and walked with him to the door and they stood for a moment, so close she might have reached out and touched him. The alarming thing was that she very much wanted to do just that.

'I believe there is another ball at the Red Lion next Thursday, Miss Meltham. I thought I might look in. Will you be there?'

Deb hesitated. She had resisted the temptation to go out riding with him, but why should she not enjoy herself, just a little? She smiled.

'Yes, sir. I will be there.'

Chapter Three

Gil stood before the looking glass, putting the finishing touches to his neckcloth. It was Thursday and he was going to the assembly at the Red Lion. He was going to see Deborah Meltham. A tingle of pleasurable anticipation rippled through him at the thought and his fingers fumbled the knot. Confound it, this was not intended to be an enjoyable encounter! With a muttered oath, he tore off the crumpled muslin and began again with a fresh cravat.

It is not too late to change your plans.

No. There was no other way. The law could not help him and killing Randolph Meltham would be too easy, the scoundrel must suffer as Gil had suffered. As his mother was still suffering at the loss of two of her children. Gil's conscience might try to appeal to his finer feelings, but he reminded himself that he had none. Not any more, he thought bitterly. Years of warfare had seen to that. But he had to admit that if there was a way to have his revenge without involving Deborah Meltham, he would choose it.

He tucked away the ends of his cravat and stood

back to survey the result. Perfect. As was his plan. He was a soldier and once resolved on a course of action he must stick to it. Whatever the consequences.

He delayed his arrival at the Red Lion until there was only a trickle of latecomers entering the rooms. He saw Deborah immediately. She was standing on the far side of the room, talking to the Gomershams. He suspected she had been watching for him, for as soon as he walked in she looked up. Even from this distance the pleasure in her face when she saw him was clear.

Like a lamb to the slaughter.

He fought off the thought by reminding himself that it was *his* sister who was lying in the family tomb. *His* brother who had been slaughtered trying to defend her honour. He crossed the room, but it took time to reach her—first there were new acquaintances to be acknowledged, greetings to be made. At last he was there, standing so close he could see the pulse beating at her throat and smell the fresh, flowery perfume that she wore. She had not yet looked up at him, but she knew he was there, for there was a faint blush mantling her cheek and one hand had crept up to her shoulder in the same nervous gesture he had noticed on previous meetings.

He said, 'I came, you see.'

She looked up then and her shy smile hit him like an iron fist in the chest, winding him. He realised with a shock that he would find it only too easy to woo her. Beside them, Sir Geoffrey was chuckling loudly.

'Well, well, sir, you have not come here to talk with the likes of me tonight. I do not doubt you are here to dance, so off you go now with your pretty partner.'

Deborah was laughing and blushing at the same time and as Gil led her on to the dance floor he thought he had never seen her so animated. Even the gown, covering her from neck to toe, and her neatly coiled hair did not detract from it. It was no hardship to suggest they remain on the floor for a second dance.

When she did not answer, his fingers went instinctively to his cheek. Immediately her face softened and she put up a hand to draw his away.

'It is not so very bad, you know,' she said gently. 'And it is not the reason I hesitated. There has been talk, you see. After we danced together twice at the charity ball.'

'But it is perfectly acceptable to stand up for two dances, Miss Meltham.'

She glanced down at her hand, still held firmly in his grasp.

'People here are not accustomed to seeing me dance with anyone save my brother, or our close neighbours.'

'They should be pleased to see you enjoying yourself.' His fingers tightened around hers. 'There is only one question for you to answer, do you *want* to dance again with me?'

She looked at him, a smile lilting on her full red lips. 'Yes, sir, I would like to, very much.'

'You are not merely feeling sorry for me?'

'Not at all.' Her eyes twinkled. 'Lady Gomersham told me that at the last assembly any number of ladies were asking for an introduction to you.'

His mouth twisted. 'Some women find scars fascinating.'

'That is where gentlemen have the advantage,' she replied as they took their places in the set. He saw her hand briefly touch her shoulder. 'For them a scar is a badge of honour, to be worn with pride and no one would think ill of them. It is a very different matter for a woman.'

He was surprised at the note of bitterness that had crept into her voice. He wanted to know why, but the music struck up. Deborah was smiling again and the moment for confidences was lost.

They danced together for their two dances, then Gil stood aside. Unlike the previous assembly, when he had seen her retreat to the benches and refuse to dance with anyone save her brother, this time she accepted another partner with seeming pleasure. Indeed, she was looking so pretty he was not at all surprised that gentlemen were lining up to dance with her and at the break he had to act quickly to ensure he could escort her into supper.

'Is your brother not here this evening?' he asked as she tucked her dainty hand into his arm.

'No.' A faint shadow crossed her face. 'He is indisposed this evening. I came here with Sir Geoffrey and his party.'

Contempt stirred. The fellow was probably too drunk to attend. No one was willing to speak out of turn against the young Lord Kirkster, but Harris had gleaned enough from the taproom gossip for Gil to be sure that the man was far too fond of his drink. When he had called at the house Gil had noticed the unmistakable smell of wine in the drawing room, the ring marks of carelessly placed glasses on the sideboard, and Deborah's demeanour suggested she knew of her brother's weakness. Did she also know he was a callous seducer?

They had reached the supper room and Gil pushed aside his dark thoughts as he escorted his partner to a small table where they might converse uninterrupted. It was time for him to charm her into submission.

The Gomershams' carriage dropped Deborah at her door and once she had ascertained that her brother was not waiting up for her, she almost flew up the stairs to her room. It was as much as she could do not to be impatient with her maid as she helped her to undress, for all Deb wanted to do was to slip between the sheets and blow out her candle. Not to sleep, but to be alone and go over the events of the evening again and again.

She could not recall the last time she had enjoyed herself so much. She had forgotten what it was like to dance with a gentleman, certainly she had never danced with anyone like Mr Victor. He made her feel like a princess. His conversation at supper had been sensible and intelligent. He had made no attempt to flirt with her and she was very thankful for that, because she would have had to check any attempt at intimacy. Instead they had talked of, oh, she had no idea now, but it had ranged from books and art to music and travel.

How the evening had flown. And then he had stood up with her for two more dances. Perhaps she should not have allowed it, perhaps it might cause talk in Fallbridge, but it was worth it. For a few hours she had felt like a normal young woman again. She had forgotten Randolph—she had even forgotten her first love, the man who had blighted her life for ever. Forgotten everything except the joy of being admired by a handsome man.

Deborah turned in the bed and snuggled her cheek against her hand, unable to prevent a smile growing inside her. He *was* very handsome, despite the scar on his face. When he looked at her it was as if she was the only woman in the room. Restlessly she shifted again until she was lying flat on her back and gazing at the far wall, where the moonlight glinted on the polished brass of the candleholder. Her spirits were still soaring and she wanted to hold on to the feeling, to stay awake all night and go over every look, every word they had exchanged and bury them deep in her memory for ever.

She could not remember falling asleep, but when she opened her eyes it was morning and the sun was pouring in through the unshuttered window. The feeling of well-being remained. Never had the sun shone so brightly, never had she heard the birds singing to joyously. Smiling, Deborah slipped out of bed and rang for her maid, eager to enjoy every moment of this beautiful day.

Deborah decided to walk to Gomersham Lodge and thank Lady Gomersham for taking her to the assembly. The visit was not strictly necessary, a polite note would have done as well, but Deborah felt too restless to stay at home. Randolph had come downstairs, bleary eyed and complaining of a headache, but it was clear she could do little for him, so she left him to the tender administrations of his butler and sallied forth into the sunshine.

Fallbridge was bustling with life and Deborah

greeted her acquaintances with a cheery smile. If she was disappointed that she did not see a certain person in the town she would not admit it, even to herself. Just because one danced a few times with a gentleman and went into supper with him did not mean they were anything more than acquaintances, as she explained when Lady Gomersham quizzed her on her conquest.

'Mr Victor seems a very pleasant man, Deborah, and if he is keen to settle in Fallbridge, who knows…'

'My dear ma'am, we know nothing about him,' Deb protested, laughing.

'True, but he is staying at the George, which is not cheap, and Sir Geoffrey thinks he is a very good sort of man. I could ask him to make enquiries, if you wish.'

'No, no, I pray you will not do that,' said Deb, hastily. 'I assure you, I have no interest in the gentleman at all.'

If her hostess did not quite believe her, Deb was thankful that she was too polite to say so.

'Well, I was pleased to see you enjoying yourself last evening, as I am sure all your friends were,' was all Lady Gomersham said, nodding so that her greying curls danced around the edges of her lace cap. 'You spend too much time worrying about that brother of yours.'

'But there is no one else to worry about him,' Deb argued, a small cloud dimming her sunny spirits when she thought of Randolph.

'Lord Kirkster is a grown man now, my dear. You should look to your own happiness.'

The look on the older woman's face said as clearly as words that she thought Deborah should not allow the chance of getting a husband to slip through her grasp. But Deborah would never marry without love and she was determined not to risk her heart again. Once was quite enough. Just the memory of it made it necessary for her to repress a shudder.

'I am perfectly happy, ma'am, thank you.'

And she was, Deb told herself as she took her leave. She loved her brother deeply, and she had promised Mama she would look after him. There could be no happiness if she did not honour that promise.

She thought again of the assembly, of dancing with the stranger. No, *not* a stranger, not any more, but she would not allow herself to be carried away by day-dreams. The elation she had felt last night was the fleeting sort and she knew better than to make too much of it.

However, when she turned into the High Street and saw Mr Victor striding towards her she could not help a little kick of excitement and a quickening of the pulse. They could not avoid one another, even if they wished to do so. He stopped and tipped his hat.

'Miss Meltham.'

The warm smile in his eyes sent her heart skittering in her chest and she felt so breathless it was a struggle to greet him.

'Are you running errands this morning?' he asked her.

'I called upon Lady Gomersham and now I am going home.'

'Then I will escort you, if you will allow me.'

Instinct warned Deborah to make some excuse, but she ignored it. She inclined her head in tacit acquiescence and he turned to walk beside her.

What harm can it do? she reasoned. They were merely walking together; they were not even touching.

But, oh, how she wanted to touch him! How she wanted to rest her hand on his sleeve and feel the strength of his arm, as she had done last night. But the conduct permissible in the ballroom would be frowned upon in the public street, so she had to be content to walk beside him.

The streets were busy and it seemed to Deborah that all her friends and acquaintances were out of doors, smiling and nodding when they saw her. She returned their smiles, knowing that gossip would be rife by the morning.

'You are very well known in Fallbridge, Miss Meltham.'

'It is my home, sir.'

'But you have a house in Liverpool, too, do you not? I should have thought that would have been your preference. After our conversation over supper the other night I know your lively mind enjoys the arts and theatre.'

She did not reply and he asked her what had influenced her to live in this small market town. She considered her words carefully before answering.

'When Randolph and I were children our time was divided between here and the house in Liverpool. Mama loved Fallbridge, but Papa still had some interest in the shipping company that our grandfather started and was obliged to be in Liverpool for several months of each year. We always went with him. It was very different from Fallbridge and we did not have the freedom of the country, but the house was so large Ran and I could spend hours playing hide and seek, from the attics to the cellars.' She laughed. 'I have no doubt the servants thought us a veritable nuisance!'

'It sounds like a very happy childhood.'

'It was.' She stopped, swallowing a sigh as she wished it was possible to return to those carefree days.

'And now you live alone with your brother?'

'Yes.' She nodded.

'And your mother?'

'She died just a year after Papa. She had been in poor health for a long time.'

'I am very sorry. Who—?'

He broke off and she looked up at him, brows raised.

'Yes? What were you going to ask, sir?'

'Forgive me if I am impertinent, but did you not need a chaperon, if your mother was so ill?'

'A widowed aunt had lived with us for years and continued to do so for a while after Mama died. Now, of course, I have Randolph.'

She said no more. He did not need to know Ran had insisted they live alone, that he was too ashamed to have anyone other than Deborah know of his addictions.

Mama had always planned for Deb to make her come-out in London under her aunt's aegis and they would take Ran with them. But that had been postponed because of Papa's ill health and when he died Deb had given up her dreams of a glittering presentation. By then Ran was already drinking and gambling to excess and she had been afraid to expose him to the temptations of the capital. She had always hoped that at Oxford he would make new, more sober friends and grow out of his excesses. A vain hope, she realised now.

'And now you live here most of the year.'

'Yes.' Should she say more? 'You may think it odd that a young man like my brother would choose to live in such a small out-of-the-way place. Randolph suffers from, from ill health. It is better that we live quietly.'

'I see.'

There was such a wealth of sympathy in the two words that Deb was tempted to tell him everything, to unburden herself of the cares and worries that beset her. But, no. He was little more than a stranger, after all, and Randolph did not like her discussing family matters.

'Your brother is lucky to have such a devoted sister.'

'Anyone would do as much.' She added lightly, 'And Fallbridge really is a very agreeable town. We have everything we need here for entertainment. The countryside is very fine, there is some hunting to be had in the season. And we are not ten miles from the coast.'

'Yes, I have noticed you have the benefit of bracing sea air,' he commented as the wind made a sudden snatch at his hat.

Deb laughed. 'Very bracing!'

She put a hand up to her face. Several wisps of hair had escaped and were curling about her face. She tried to tuck them back under her bonnet.

'No, don't do that.' Her fingers stilled. He added softly, 'It suits you.'

Her cheeks flamed and she walked on quickly, unable to think of a suitable reply.

'Do you know,' he continued, in a conversational tone, 'I have made myself familiar with the local rides around here, but I have not yet been to the coast.' He stopped and turned to face her. 'Do you ride, Miss Meltham?'

She should walk on, but her feet had stopped, too. 'Yes, I do.'

'Do you have a groom to accompany you? If so, there could be no impropriety if we were to take a little trip together. Will you not take pity upon a poor stranger and ride out with him?'

Deborah hesitated. They would be gone from breakfast until dinner. It was unthinkable. She determined to say no, but then she looked up to find him smiling down at her and she could not speak at all.

'Say you will come with me,' he murmured. 'I promise I will look after you.'

Physically, perhaps, but that was not what was worrying her. Deb was aware of her growing attachment to Mr Victor. It would be wiser not to see too much of him. And yet...

Ran was engaged to go shooting with Sir Geoffrey and a party of friends at the beginning of the week. They would make an early start and he would dine at Gomersham Lodge, so Deborah would have the day to herself.

'I might be free on Monday,' she said slowly.

His smile deepened. 'Monday it is, then. I shall call for you.'

She shook her head, suddenly panicked. 'I do not know; it is not certain I shall be able to come.'

'Then you may send word to me at the George.' He hesitated. 'Will you not take my arm for the remainder of the journey? No one would take it amiss, I am sure, for the wind is much stronger now we are clear of the town and I am afraid it might blow you away.'

* * *

What was she doing?

Deborah handed her cloak to Speke, but instead of going upstairs she went into the morning room and ran to the window, just in time to see her escort striding out of the drive. When he was no longer in sight she turned away with a sigh. He was handsome, kind and gentlemanlike.

And dangerous.

She shook her head, as if to clear the doubts. It was not really dangerous, it was only a ride, after all. She would take her groom, who could be relied upon to look after her. She would enjoy a day's riding in agreeable company. It was nothing more than that.

Having made her decision, Deb went off in search of her brother, but by the time she went to bed she had still not told him of her forthcoming excursion, and as she drifted off to sleep she knew she would not disclose it to him. Not until after the event.

Monday morning dawned to a heavy mist, but by the time Gil reached Kirkster House it had burned off and the day promised to be fine. As he trotted up the drive he saw Deborah Meltham riding out of the stables on a neat bay mare, a groom following at a respectful distance behind her. She was wearing a dark green riding habit and her hair was firmly clipped back beneath the matching hat, but the severity of her outfit only enhanced her trim figure.

She was looking serious as she came up to him and he said without preamble, 'Are you having second thoughts, Miss Meltham?'

The way her green eyes flew to his face told him

he was right. Part of him hoped she would tell him she had changed her mind, that she would not go with him, but he knew he would be bitterly disappointed if she did that and not just because it would be a setback to his plans.

She leaned forward to pat the bay's neck. 'We go out rarely now, so it will be good take Bramble for an airing.'

She had not really answered his question, but he let that go. He turned his horse and came alongside her.

'Is she fast?' he asked, nodding at the mare.

'Fast enough,' she said and Gil noticed the sober look had been replaced by a definite twinkle. 'We ride cross country most of the way, so you shall see for yourself.'

They turned west from the gates of the drive and headed away from the town. He was at pains to set her at her ease and within a very short time Deborah was chatting to him as if they had known one another for years.

It did not take long for him to learn that Deborah was an accomplished horsewoman and when they reached a stretch of open ground it seemed the most natural thing in the world to set the horses racing. The chestnut gelding had the advantage of size and strength over the mare, but for most of the way they were neck and neck, Gil just pulling away for the last few hundred yards. When he reached the hedge that separated them from the lane he drew rein and waited by the gate for Deb to come up to him. When she did, her cheeks were flushed and her smile was as wide as the sky. He could not help grinning back.

'Did you enjoy that?'

'Very much.' She watched him as he manoeuvred his horse around to come alongside her and said, 'You do not need to do that.'

'Do what?'

'I have noticed that you keep to the left of me, so I do not have to look at the scar on your face. I am not offended or repulsed by it, Mr Victor, believe me.'

She was smiling at him, nothing but warmth and kindness in her green eyes, and he felt something stirring inside of him, as if there was a chink in the armour he had built around his heart. She had touched softer feelings that he had kept buried for years.

'Gil,' he said suddenly. 'Call me Gil.'

'But your name is James.' Her brows drew together. 'You are James Victor, are you not?'

He was already cursing himself for inviting her to use that familiar name. He had not intended to allow her such intimacy, but he was not so much in control as he should be in her presence. He would need to be more careful.

'Gil is what my family and close friends call me,' he said, recovering quickly. 'I should be honoured if you would use it, too.'

'I cannot. It would not be seemly.'

She turned the mare and went ahead of him on to the lane, but he knew it was more than a physical distance. She had withdrawn from him. He brought his horse alongside her and began to talk of mundane matters until their previous rapport was re-established, and after that he was careful to say nothing more that might upset the easy camaraderie.

Gil knew he had been at fault. When they had raced

across the turf he had forgotten his ulterior motive in befriending Deb Meltham. He found himself wishing that they could just be friends, that he had not set himself upon this path. But he had chosen his route and he could not change it now. He must approach it like any other military operation. Sometimes one's duty was unpleasant, yet it must be done. But it was difficult, when she looked at him with those large trusting eyes and all he wanted to do was to protect her. He hardened his heart. She would be hurt, there was no help for it. In any battle there were casualties, it was the nature of war.

Chapter Four

◈◈◈◈◈◈

They rode westwards, the sun climbing higher in a clear blue sky. Deborah stopped on a slight ridge and pointed.

'Look, there in the distance is the town of Formby, and do you see the sandhills? Beyond them lies the sea.'

There was an excitement in her voice and the lively anticipation in her face amused Gil. Seeing his smile, she laughed.

'I have not been to the coast for years. When we were children Ran and I used to come here with Papa. The greatest treat was to call upon one of the local families, where we would dine on shrimp before we returned home.'

He waved her on. 'Lead the way then, Miss Meltham. I am anxious to see it for myself.'

They set off again at a brisk trot, but Deborah's mood began to dip as she contrasted those happy carefree memories with her brother's life now. Even to be out enjoying herself today seemed wrong, when Ran was so unhappy. And last night she had come very close to despair.

When Randolph had joined her after dinner he had gone straight to the side table and poured himself a brandy from the decanter.

'What?' he demanded, looking up and catching her eye. 'Why do you look like that?'

'Have you not drunk enough? Doctor Reedley said—'

'Damn the doctor and damn you!' The outburst seemed to sober him. He passed a hand over his eyes and said more quietly, 'I beg your pardon, Deb, I know you are trying to look after me.'

'You are all I have left, Ran.'

He frowned at her, then took the brandy in one gulp and refilled his glass. He sat down, cradling the glass between two hands and staring moodily into the amber depths.

'You should leave me,' he said abruptly. 'Go and make a life for yourself somewhere far away.'

She smiled lovingly at him. 'And just where would I go? What would I live on? An income of fifty pounds a year will scarce support me.'

'I could make you an allowance.'

Her smile slipped a little, 'How will you do that, when the estate is already mortgaged to the hilt?'

She pressed her lips together to avoid saying anything more. For all his faults Ran loved her. She knew that. It was the knowledge of her family's love that had helped her survive those dark days when she had given her heart to a man, only to have it trampled and broken. She had sworn then she would devote her life to her family, but with Mama and Papa both dead, there was only Randolph. He might be weak, and flawed, but he was the only man she was prepared to trust and to love. She crossed the room and dropped to her knees beside him.

'I promised Mama I would look after you,' she whispered.

A lock of fair hair had fallen over his brow and she reached up to brush it back. He did not look up.

'I am beyond redemption, Debs.'

The hopelessness in his tone tore at her heart, but if she showed him sympathy it would only increase his self-pity.

'No, no,' she said bracingly. 'You will come about, in time.'

'Time!' He laughed bitterly. 'And meanwhile I must remain here, mouldering away in this dreary, forsaken little town.'

'We discussed it with Dr Reedley, do you not remember, Ran? We agreed it would be best for you to live here quietly.'

'No, you and Reedley agreed it, not I! You want to keep me here, a prisoner. Can we not live in the Liverpool house? At least at Duke Street I was close to all my friends!'

It was those friends who are responsible for your present state!

Deb closed her lips tightly to prevent the words escaping. With an oath Ran pushed himself out of his chair.

'I am sick of it, do you hear me? Sick of this place, where everyone knows our business, where they all look down their noses at me.'

'That is not true, Ran.'

'Oh, isn't it? Playing cards for penny points, Sir Geoffrey Gomersham wanting to show me the prize bull he has added to his estate—as if I cared about such things!'

'Well, you should,' she said sharply, her patience breaking. 'This estate is your responsibility now and needs you to take an interest.'

'Hah, what odd notions you have, Sister! Let the farmers take an interest in the land. As long as they pay their rent I do not *care* what goes on here!'

She had watched him lounge away, staggering a little as he left the room. No, she thought sadly. Ran cared nothing for Kirkster or its people. Their people. He saw it only as a purse to dip into whenever he wanted money. That purse was nearly empty now, but an even greater worry to Deborah was Ran's health. Doctor Reedley had been blunt.

'If Lord Kirkster continues with his mode of life he will not live the year out. Keep him here, quiet and sober, and he has a chance.'

But how was she to do that? She could not physically restrain him and sometimes she thought her brother was hell-bent upon self-destruction.

'Deborah, what is it, has something upset you?'

Gil's voice broke into her despondent thoughts and she gave a little start.

'I was thinking about my brother.'

'I see.'

She shook her head. 'No, how could you?'

'You could tell me.'

She closed her eyes, suddenly exhausted by carrying the burden of it on her own. She wanted to share it, at least a little of it, and Gil's tone was so calm, so kind, it invited confidences.

She said, 'Ran was just eighteen when Papa died. He was really too young to take responsibility for his inheritance, but his guardian was a distant uncle, who saw no profit in his putting himself out for his nephew. Wild friends and wilder living soon swallowed up the funds from our modest estate. I did not know how low Randolph had sunk until I visited him unexpectedly in Duke Street and he confessed the whole. That was when I persuaded him to come and live with me at Fallbridge and close up the Liverpool house. It is an attempt to retrench. I know full well that Ran is doing it only for my sake. But that is not the worst of it.'

She saw Gil recoil and raise one hand as if to silence her, but the next moment that hand was reaching across and covering hers in a brief, comforting grip. 'I beg your pardon,' he said quietly. 'I did not mean to stop you. Do go on, my dear.'

She shook her head, realising how close she had come to unburdening herself fully, but these were not his problems. And Randolph would not wish her to tell anyone that through his own actions he had destroyed his health so comprehensively.

'I should not have said so much. It is unforgivable to disclose my family's problems to you or anyone else.'

Gil's heart contracted when he heard the distress in her voice. What had she been about to tell him? That Kirkster had seduced an innocent schoolgirl and then killed her brother in a duel? He did not want to hear her say it, even though it was the truth. For one wild moment he had a craven impulse to turn his horse and gallop away, but he couldn't do it. He could not leave Deborah now. He swallowed, clearing his throat of the constriction that threatened to choke him.

'You can tell me, Deborah. If it will help, you can tell me anything you wish.'

Somehow he managed to meet her eyes, even to smile, although he hated himself for it. But she was shaking her head and dashing away a rogue tear.

'No, no, I must not burden you with such things. And it is not so very bad, after all. We shall come about, I am sure.'

She turned the conversation and Gil answered mechanically, the conjecture in his brain almost too much to bear. Did she know that her brother was a libertine? Did she condone his behaviour? He did not want to believe it, he thought her too good, too honest for that, but he could not be sure, because she was clearly unhappy about her brother. He would find out, but not now. Not today. Today he had invited Deborah to ride out with him purely for pleasure and he would do his best to make sure she enjoyed it.

Another mile riding cross-country brought them to the sandhills and Deborah led Gil to a narrow track that ascended the embankment. The path wound its way through a thick carpet of star grass, which she told him the locals were obliged to plant, to keep the hills intact and protect the farmland. When she reached the crest of the hill she stopped and he brought his horse up beside her. The embankment dropped away to a sandy shore, and beyond it the rippling waves of the sea.

'The tide is coming in,' she said, 'and with it the breeze. Be careful of your hat, sir.'

He grinned at her. 'You need not worry, it is a snug fit.'

They rode down to the beach, eventually coming

to a small cottage nestled into a dip in the sandhills. A few small nets were drying on the outer walls and a thin spiral of smoke was issuing from the chimney. On impulse Gil jumped down and went to the door, returning moments later to suggest Deborah should dismount.

'The widow who lives there is cooking shrimp and has offered to feed us. Will you join me?' He added, to persuade her, 'I shall pay the old dame well for her trouble, certainly more than the shrimp would fetch at market.'

He saw the laughter in Deb's eyes, but she hesitated and looked back at her groom, who shrugged.

'I'll look after the horses, Miss Deborah. Just as long as you don't go out of sight.'

'No, of course not. We can sit upon the log that has been washed up yonder.'

Kicking her foot free of the stirrup she hesitated for a heartbeat before she dropped down into Gil's waiting arms. The faint flush on her cheek told him she was as conscious as he of the risk she was taking. His hands moved to her tiny waist to support her. They almost spanned it and it took all his willpower not to draw her closer and steal a kiss from those full, inviting lips. Instead he stepped to one side and pulled her arm through his.

'Come along then, ma'am, I shall escort you to our seat.'

They had barely made themselves comfortable when the old woman brought them two small bowls of tiny pink shrimp, still hot from the pan, and slices of rye bread to mop up the juices. They chattered and giggled like schoolchildren as they enjoyed their impromptu meal and Gil wondered if it was sitting in the fresh air that made it taste so good, or the company.

'Delicious,' declared Deborah, when they had finished. She handed her bowl to Gil and dabbed at her mouth with the small square of lace that was her handkerchief. 'I hope you enjoyed it, too.'

'Very much.'

He bent to put the bowls on the sand, reluctant to take them back to the cottage, for that would mean moving away from Deborah and breaking the magic of the moment. When he sat up again he found she had turned her laughing face towards him, totally at her ease. Some of her hair had escaped from the confines of her bonnet and the wind whipped it across her cheek, the errant strands gleaming the deep golden-brown of liquid honey. How could he ever have thought her drab, he wondered as he reached out to push aside a stray curl.

The jolt through his arm as he touched her skin was like a lightning strike, heating his blood and setting his pulse racing. She was very still, her eyes wide and fixed on his, trusting, inviting. He tucked the curl gently behind her ear, then he cupped her face, drawing her close and planting a gentle kiss upon her mouth. She trembled, but did not pull away. Her lips parted, inviting him to deepen the kiss.

Lord, it would be an easy seduction. A wave of self-loathing washed through him at the thought of his carefully constructed plan for revenge and the chink in his defences widened. After a decade of bloody warfare, he had believed himself capable of anything, but not this. He drew back, hating himself. Her eyelids fluttered and she looked at him, eyes dilated like deep, dark pools where a man could drown himself. His thumb grazed over her cheekbone.

'I did not intend to do that.'

His voice was not quite steady. He felt the pressure of her cheek against his fingers as she leaned into him, gazing into his face as if seeking the answer to some great problem. Despite his own dark thoughts, whatever she saw there reassured her and he detected the barest quiver of a smile curve her lips.

'We are fortunate my groom did not see it. He has been with me since I was a child and would have no hesitation in ringing a peal over me.' Her eyes flickered towards the beach. 'Thankfully the horses are blocking his view.'

Gil swallowed, his thoughts racing. If the groom had not been so near he could have kissed her again and again and then perhaps led her into the sand dunes and made love to her, with the sound of the sea whispering around them and the gulls wheeling and crying overhead. But it would have been *his* seduction, his downfall, as well as hers.

He gave himself a mental shake. What was he about, to be prey to such maudlin thoughts? He was growing soft. He must remember the vow he had taken while standing by the tomb, to see the blood of his sister and brother avenged or die in the attempt. He must not allow anything to sway him from his purpose.

He heard her sigh. 'It is time we were heading back.'

She moved away from him, her hand going to her left shoulder in the nervous little gesture he was beginning to recognise. Gil gathered up the dishes and returned them to the cottage. When he came back to the horses Deborah was already in the saddle. Very wise, he thought grimly, to have the groom throw her up rather than risk his hands upon her again. He scrambled up on to his own horse and accompanied her back over the sandhills.

They rode for several miles in silence, each lost in their own thoughts. Gil glanced several times at Deborah. Just once she met his eyes and gave him a faint smile. She appeared to be quite composed and he was at a loss to understand her. Outrage he could have dealt with, or blushing, maidenly distress, but it was as if she had accepted what had occurred. Even welcomed it. He glanced back to check that her groom could not overhear them.

'Miss Meltham, Deborah.'

She silenced him with the wave of a hand. 'Please, there is no need to say anything.'

'I think there is. I should not have presumed—'

She turned her head and fixed her frank green eyes upon him.

'I am not a child; I could have prevented you.'

'Are you sure of that?' Her dark lashes fell, screening her thoughts from him. He said quietly, 'Will you allow me to see you again?'

Suddenly he found himself praying that she would refuse and send him about his business. She could still save herself, even if he was powerless to do so. It was as if he had taken a step off a cliff and was now hurtling towards destruction.

She did not reply immediately and he was half-hope, half-despair, as to what her answer might be. At last she spoke, choosing her words with care.

'Forgive me if I am presumptuous, but I must make you aware that I have no thoughts of, of marriage. Not as long as my brother needs me. I would not wish to raise false hopes.'

'Do you wish to cut the acquaintance?'

'I would not want you to be hurt, sir.'

Oh, Deborah, if only you knew!

'I will take that chance.'

Gil schooled his features into a smile while all the time a roaring anguish filled him. It was too late to turn back now. The souls of his sister and brother cried out for revenge and she was to be the weapon.

'Very well, then, Mr Victor, I would be very pleased to see you again.'

The pleasure and relief in her face sliced into him like a sabre, but somehow he kept his smile in place and managed to converse with tolerable composure as he escorted her back to Kirkster House. They parted at the gates and he watched her ride away along the drive. When she reached the arched entrance to the stables she turned and raised her crop to him in a final salute.

Still smiling, Gil touched his hat, but once he had turned away the smile disappeared and by the time he walked into his rooms at the George his thoughts were so black that he could not even find a civil word for his man.

Harris regarded him with raised brows. 'The day did not go well, my lord?'

'Everything went perfectly.' Gil scowled as he tore off his gloves and threw them down on a chair. 'The plan is proceeding better than I could have hoped.' He shrugged himself out of his coat and walked towards the little dining parlour.

'And shall I send for your dinner, sir?'

'No. No dinner.' Gil stopped, his fingers curling around the edge of the door until the knuckles showed white. 'Fetch me up a couple of bottles of claret. And one of brandy. And then I do not want to be disturbed!'

Chapter Five

Deborah was pleased to take a solitary dinner that evening; it gave her an opportunity to consider all that had happened during the day. As she pushed her food around her plate she thought how much she had enjoyed herself with Gil. She smiled. She must never call him by that name, of course, but she would think of him as Gil. She had been able to converse quite naturally with him, as if they were lifelong friends instead of new acquaintances. She had even been able to tell him about Ran and he had understood that her brother was a wild young man who was far too fond of his cards and his wine. It was not after all such an unusual story, but he had shown neither disapproval nor sympathy, either of which she would have resented. Instead their discussions had ranged widely and she had found herself in perfect accord with him.

Until he kissed her.

That had changed everything. She could no longer pretend that she thought of him as a mere acquaintance, or even a friend. She wanted him, as a husband. A lover.

Sighing, she put down her fork and pushed her plate away, her appetite quite gone. She was worldly enough to know she would be ruined if she became Gil's mistress and would he even want her, once he knew how damaged she was? Her hand crept to her shoulder. He might turn away in disgust.

Even more foolish, then, to imagine he might want to marry you, Deborah Meltham.

Foolish indeed, she replied to the voice in her head. And there was no question of marriage. She had already made up her mind that she could not, *would* not contemplate marriage as long as Ran needed her. She hoped that as her brother matured he would settle down, perhaps even take a wife, a woman who would love him and care for him. Then Deborah would be free to make a life for herself, but there were no signs of that happening in the immediate future. Or ever. She pushed the dismal thought firmly aside. Ran was only two-and-twenty, plenty of time for him to fall in love.

But you are already four-and-twenty. Your chances of finding a husband are diminishing with each year that passes.

'Then so be it,' she told that bothersome voice in her head. 'I shall remain a spinster and I shall *not* repine for what I have missed. I shall have my honour and my self-respect, despite the temptation.'

Temptation. That idea immediately brought her thoughts back to Gil.

Gil. An unusual epithet. She must ask him how it came about, when they next met. A tiny flicker of hope warmed her. They *would* meet again and she would enjoy his company, for as long as she could before he moved on, as he was sure to do, since she could offer him nothing more than friendship.

Over the following weeks, she saw Gil almost every day. If the weather was not good enough for them to ride out together, they met at some party or the assembly rooms. They behaved with the strictest propriety, even in the odd moments when they were alone together. Gil was the perfect gentleman, as if that kiss had never happened, but Deb could not forget it, and neither, if she were truthful, did she regret it.

Her brother was surprisingly cordial towards their new acquaintance, even inviting him to join them for dinner, where Ran proceeded to drink heavily. Deborah's spirits fell when he ordered Speke to bring another bottle.

'Not on my account,' murmured Gil.

He spoke cheerfully, no censure in his tone, for which Deborah was grateful, but her brother merely waved his hand.

'Well, that is up to you,' he said dismissively. 'I want another glass of that claret. M'father filled his cellars with some damn fine wines, but they're nearly all gone now. I could send to Duke Street, see if there's some left there.'

'You forget, Randolph, we brought the remaining bottles to Fallbridge earlier this year,' Deborah reminded him, blushing faintly for her brother.

'Now the war is over it should be easier to obtain more French wines,' observed Gil.

'Yes, we might take a trip to the Continent ourselves,' she said. 'What do you say, Brother, would that not be entertaining?'

But Ran was not listening, he was waving his glass at Speke who had returned with a fresh bottle of claret.

Deborah glanced apologetically at Gil, but he merely smiled.

'Perhaps I should go—' he began, but that brought Randolph's attention back to him immediately.

'No, no, you can't leave yet. You must stay and take a glass of brandy with me.' He flapped one hand. 'Time for you to withdraw, Deb, leave the men to talk.'

She looked despairingly at Randolph, but Gil had already risen and was standing behind her, ready to hold her chair.

'Miss Meltham?'

She could remonstrate, but Ran was beyond caring for her censure now and it would only cause a scene. She allowed Gil to escort her from the room. She had no doubt he had seen many young men in their cups before, but it distressed her that he should witness her brother's crass folly.

Gil held open the door for her, saying as she passed him, 'Pray wait for us in the drawing room, Miss Meltham. We shall not be long, I give you my word.'

She nodded and went out, grateful for his understanding, but unhappily aware that after this evening it would be impossible for him to dine at Kirkster House again.

Gil closed the door but did not immediately return to his seat. The butler was silently moving around the room, putting fresh glasses on the table and replacing the claret with a decanter of brandy.

Kirkster waved his hand at Gil.

'Come and sit down, Victor. Something I wanted to say to you.'

Gil slowly came back to the table. His host was slumped in his chair and Gil wondered if he had slipped into unconsciousness, or if he still had enough wits about him to keep quiet until the butler had withdrawn. Apparently Kirkster was not quite so drunk as he first appeared, because he remained silent until they were left alone to enjoy their brandy, then he pushed himself upright and fixed Gil with a bleary eye.

'I hear you are going to take a house in Fallbridge,' he said at last.

'I am considering it.'

'And you are becoming mighty friendly with Deborah.'

Gil kept his face impassive. 'Not beyond the bounds of propriety.'

'M'sister is the only thing in this dam' world that I care for,' Kirkster went on, slopping brandy into his glass and spilling even more of it on to the table. 'Her happiness means everything to me. If anyone was to hurt her they'd have me to answer to. D'you understand me?'

'Oh, yes,' Gil replied. 'I understand you perfectly.'

Kirkster took a gulp and put his glass down with exaggerated care.

'Reason I invited you here, to make sure you knew that. Breaks my heart if I see her unhappy. She's a treasure. An angel.' He was slurring his words and almost incapable of holding up his head by this time. 'She knows everything about me. Everything and still she loves me. What's that if not angelic? I don't deserve her.'

'No,' Gil murmured drily, 'no, you do not.'

He regarded the drunken figure across the table with contempt. The fellow was almost beyond feeling anything. If he was going to have his revenge he must act and soon.

A wave of revulsion rose within him, as much for himself as Kirkster. He pushed his chair back, his own brandy glass untouched.

'Shall we join your sister in the drawing room?'

Deborah was sitting by the hearth when they went in, but Gil suspected she had been pacing the room and had flown to the seat when she heard their approach.

She smiled, a little too brightly. 'I asked Speke to bring in the tea tray very soon. We do not keep late hours here.'

Gil nodded silently. Kirkster had said Deborah knew everything about him. If that was true then she was as depraved as her brother, but he could not believe that. And yet he wanted to believe it, for it was the only thing that made his plan for revenge palatable. The loss of her reputation and Kirkster's suffering, in exchange for the lives of his brother and sister.

Gil maintained a conversation with Deborah, but they were both of them aware that Randolph was still drinking. He became by turns rowdy, aggressive and maudlin and he ended the evening by falling into an unconscious stupor in the drawing room.

Speke had just come in with the tea tray and Deborah asked him to fetch Lord Kirkster's man to help him to bed.

Gil pushed himself to his feet. 'I think I should be going now.'

'Yes.' She rose. 'Yes.' She waved one hand towards her brother. 'I—that is…'

Gil stopped her with a smile.

'In my army career I have seen it happen many times to young men. I am only offended on your behalf and I am sure you would much rather we both put it out of our minds.'

He took her hand, felt it tremble like a frightened bird in his grasp.

'This is very unfortunate,' she said, the words coming out in a rush. 'I had thought Ran was getting better—indeed, he has been showing definite signs of improvement! He joins me for breakfast most mornings now, he even took me driving the other day and he can sometimes be persuaded to accompany me to an evening party.'

'Then I have caught him on an unhappy relapse,' he said. 'It does happen, you know. Pray do not let it upset you.'

She nodded, her lip trembling as she made an effort to control her emotions. It was as much as he could do not to pull her into his arms and kiss away the tears that were threatening. Instead he asked her cheerfully if she would still ride out with him the next morning.

'Yes, sir. If you still wish it.'

'I do,' he assured her. 'I wish it more than ever.'

With that Gil kissed her hand and left the house. Everything was falling into place. He just wished he felt more comfortable about it.

Three days later Gil had made all the arrangements and he was determined that by the end of the day he would have put his plan into action. He was engaged to join the Gomershams' riding party to Hoyland Water. Several heavy storms during the past week had swollen the local rivers and it was anticipated that would make the waterfall even more beautiful than usual. Deborah had told him she and her brother were engaged to join the party and he hoped at some point to find a quiet moment alone with Deborah and issue his invitation.

When he trotted up Mill Lane he saw a little group of horses and riders gathered outside Gomersham Lodge. Instinctively his eyes sought out Deborah, feeling the now familiar rush of pleasure at the sight of her. She was escorted by her brother and they were talking to Mrs Appleton and her elderly husband, whom he had met at one of the assemblies. He knew it would not do to single Deb out, so instead he turned aside and touched his hat to Lady Gomersham, who was looking at home upon a sturdy hack. She returned his salute, but left it to her husband to ride forward to greet him.

'Ah, there you are, Victor,' cried Sir Geoffrey in his bluff, good-natured way. 'You are the last of our little party, so we can set off now.'

'I hope I have not kept you waiting,' he said, his smile encompassing them all.

'Not at all, sir, not at all,' declared Sir Geoffrey. 'Lizzie has only just mounted up, so you are in good time. And it promises to be a very fine day, although there is a chill wind blowing. Best not to tarry.'

The little party set off, accompanied by Sir Geoffrey's groom. As they reached the end of Mill Lane, Lord Kirkster brought his horse alongside Gil's. It was the first time they had met since the dinner at Kirkster House and from the younger man's demeanour Gil guessed immediately what he was about to say.

'I wanted to beg your pardon for my behaviour the other night,' said Kirkster, as soon as civilities had been exchanged. 'I was not quite myself.'

'I am not the one to whom you should apologise,' Gil replied shortly.

'If you mean Deborah, I have already made my peace with her.' He looked a little shame-faced. 'It was she who said I must speak with you and make amends.'

Gil maintained his stony expression, but inside he was raging. He wanted to grab Kirkster by the throat and ask him how he intended to make amends for ruining his little sister and killing his brother. He was tempted to forget his plan and issue a challenge this minute. To call the fellow out and demand Kirkster name his friends.

A movement caught his eye. Deborah was watching them. How could he make such a declaration here, in front of Sir Geoffrey and his family? It would be all around Fallbridge by night and Deborah would be tarred with her brother's disgrace.

And is what you plan for her any better?

He pushed that thought aside.

'You have made your apology, then,' he said to Kirkster. 'We shall speak no more of it.'

The young man looked relieved. He smiled, touched his hat and rode off to join Lizzie Gomersham, and the pair of them were soon laughing and chattering as if they had not a care in the world. Gil watched them. If he did not know the truth he would have thought Kirkster nothing more than a heedless young fool. Too fond of his drink, perhaps, but not a bad man. But he knew the extent of Kirkster's perfidy and was determined he would make him suffer for it.

'You look very grim, Mr Victor.' Deborah had ridden up beside him and was looking at him, anxiety clouding her eyes. 'I hope you can find it in your heart to forgive my brother for, for his drunkenness the other night.'

Immediately the frown disappeared from his brow. As always in her presence, he felt better, more complete, as if she was a part of him. Whenever they were together he could feel the bond between them growing and strengthening. It made what he had planned even more difficult, but he would not think of that, he would merely enjoy her company. For now.

'I told him we would say no more about it,' he said lightly.

The anxious look fled and she smiled. 'I am glad.'

She looked as if she wanted to say more and he quickly changed the subject.

'This promises to be the finest day we have had for a while and I am determined to make the most of it.'

'We all are,' declared Lady Gomersham, dropping back to join them. 'This will be a most delightful outing. Deborah, my dear, Mrs Appleton was asking me the best way to dress crab and I recalled the last time we came to you for dinner you had a particularly good method for this, and I wondered if you would come and explain it to her...'

Gil caught Deborah's laughing look of apology as she allowed her hostess to draw her away. For himself he felt only relief. His conscience was becoming troublesome and he roughly thrust aside the prickle of unease. It would be folly to give up the solemn vows he had made over his sister's body for a woman he had known only a matter of weeks.

It took the party a couple of hours to reach Hoyland Water, a small pool set within rocky woodland. On the far side of the pool a lichen-covered cliff reared up and from it a waterfall tumbled noisily. Their view was partially screened by surrounding trees and Sir Geoffrey suggested they leave their horses with the groom and walk the short distance along the narrow path to the water's edge.

As Gil jumped down he noticed that Deborah and her brother were making no effort to dismount, but were talking earnestly together. Rather than follow the others towards the water Gil remained by his horse, adjusting the stirrup and listening to their conversation. Deborah was holding her brother's arm and speaking in a low, urgent voice, but Gil heard every word.

'You cannot leave now, Ran. What will the others say?'

'I neither know nor care. I must return to Fallbridge. I have remembered I promised a fellow I would meet him there today and I will not let him down.'

'And no doubt you will say you have to meet him at an inn! Do not lie to me, Ran. Why have you not mentioned this before? I believe it is merely a ruse to go back.'

'I told you, Deb, I forgot all about it! Damnation, can a fellow not be allowed to make up his own mind on these things?' He pulled his arm free and wheeled his horse, saying as he trotted away, 'Tell them what you like, but I am leaving. I am not needed here. The Gomershams will see you home safe, I am sure.'

Gil was about to move away, not wanting Deborah to know he had overheard their conversation, but at that moment she caught his eye, such a look of distress upon her face that he could not ignore it. He crossed the short distance to stand beside her horse.

'Your brother is unwell?'

'He has remembered an appointment.'

She looked uncomfortable so he did not press her for more. Instead he put up his arms and she slid down into them, clearly grateful for his support. Gil knew that a man bent on seduction would hold her a little longer, perhaps even steal a quick kiss. Instead he quickly set her on her feet and stepped away.

'We had best catch up with the others, Miss Meltham.'

They walked together to the little lake, neither speaking, but Gil was aware of an unhappy tension between them. As they cleared the trees and the water was fully in view, Deborah spoke with a cheerfulness that did not quite ring true.

'There, sir. Was that not worth the ride?'

'It was indeed.'

He could not bear it. He moved away from her, his thoughts black as pitch. He was a villain to even consider hurting her as a way to be revenged upon Kirkster. The fellow was not worth half the affection his sister showered upon him. He should never have come here.

Even as he smiled and spoke with the other members of the party his thoughts were racing, trying to find a way out of the dilemma he had made for himself. Deborah cared for him, he was aware of that. After all, it was what he had set out to achieve. What he had not intended was that he would feel anything for her. He briefly put a hand up to his chest, feeling the hard edge of the locket that he wore beneath his shirt. He could not break his vow and leave his siblings unavenged. The knowledge that he had not been able to protect them was almost unbearable and it was only the thought of vengeance that had supported him through the bleak months of grief and distress. How could he live with himself if he gave up now?

How could he live with himself if he did not?

Chapter Six

For the next hour he kept his distance from Deborah. The plan must be carried out, he was determined upon it, but every moment he spent in her company made it more difficult. Therefore he must keep away from her until there was an opportunity to speak to her alone, without fear of being overheard. Outwardly he remained calm; he was attentive to the other members of the party, accompanying them as they walked around the lake and climbed the steep path to the top of the cliff, where he agreed that the views were breathtaking, although he barely noticed the beauty of the prospect. Sir Geoffrey invited everyone to come a little closer to the edge of the cliff and see for themselves just how high they had climbed.

Obediently Gil stared down at the green-blue waters of the pool, his mind full of dark, painful thoughts.

'I hope you are not thinking of jumping in,' remarked Sir Geoffrey, coming up beside him. 'Where the falls crash down the water is full of tumbled rocks and the rest of the pool is no more than knee-deep.'

'As the children know well,' remarked Lady Gomersham. 'They all used to play here a great deal when they were younger. Shall we take the path down the other side now? Before we ride back, we can visit the spot where we have picnicked often and often.'

There was a general agreement. Gil saw Deborah looking towards him and he quickly turned to Mrs Appleton to offer her his arm on the descent. He resolutely kept his gaze away from Deborah, but he could imagine her disappointment. It could not be helped—he must keep his distance, painful as it was for him to deny himself her company.

They reached the water's edge again and after thanking him for his assistance, Mrs Appleton moved off to join her husband. Gil was so lost in his own thoughts he barely heard the others reminiscing about earlier trips to this very spot, of summer picnics and moonlit rides.

He felt a touch on his arm.

'Have I offended you?' He looked down to see Deborah beside him. 'You have been at pains to stay away from me.'

'No, no, I was merely—' He stopped, despising himself for even thinking of lying to her. 'I did not want to show you too much attention. It would give rise to speculation.'

Her brow cleared, but for once her smile did not brighten his day.

'Ah, I see. Do you think it would *give rise to speculation* if we walked back to the horses together?'

'Yes, I do.' He glanced past her to make sure there was no one to hear them. 'I have been paying you too much attention, Miss Meltham.'

She looked stricken. 'Do you mean you, you regret the time we have spent together?'

'Yes. *No*.' By heaven he was making a mull of this! 'You are a single lady. Unchaperoned.'

Walk away, Deb, now. Do not let me do this to you.

'But I am no ingénue, Mr Victor.' Her green eyes regarded him steadily. 'I am aware that in seeing you so often, walking with you, riding out with you, I have strayed a little beyond the bounds of propriety, but it was done with a full knowledge of the consequences. If you are tired of me then I will understand. I was merely concerned that I might unwittingly have said or done something to offend.'

'Tired of you! Deb—'

He was interrupted by a scream and a shout. Looking up, he saw everyone crowded at the water's edge. Deborah was already running towards them and he followed her. Lady Gomersham was shrieking and as they drew near Gil saw that Sir Geoffrey and Mr Appleton were helping Lizzie Gomersham from the water. She was laughing and declaring that she was not in the least hurt, but her skirts were sodden and discoloured with muddy water.

'I went too close to the edge and slipped,' she was explaining to her anxious parents. 'There is no harm done, truly.'

'No harm? You are soaked to the skin, child!' cried Lady Gomersham.

Sir Geoffrey was already stripping off his coat and wrapping it about his daughter.

'We must get you home immediately before you catch your death of cold.' He began to hurry her along the path towards the horses, the others following.

'Yes, yes, we must get back,' cried Lady Gomersham. 'The wind is getting up and now you have given up your coat, Sir Geoffrey, I am anxious that you, too, might catch a chill. Oh, how I wish we had never come here!'

They reached the horses and Gil helped to put Lizzie in the saddle, her wet skirts clinging heavily about her and making it difficult for her to mount. By the time he looked around Deborah was already on her horse and moments later they were all trotting back to the main road. The groom pointed out that the quickest way to Fallbridge was to turn left and then cut across country, coming to the town from the north.

'But that would be quite out of Miss Meltham's way,' Mr Appleton pointed out.

'No need to worry about that,' said Deborah quickly. 'I know my way home from here and if Sir Geoffrey will allow the groom to go with me I shall be quite content.'

'I will, Miss Meltham, with pleasure, but I would prefer one of the gentlemen to accompany you instead. Victor, perhaps you will go with her, see her home safe?'

'Yes, yes,' said Lady Gomersham, momentarily withdrawing her attention from her daughter. 'Do say you will go with her, Mr Victor. I know it would not be a chore for you, since you ride together regularly.'

It was a sensible suggestion. Quite logical, but Gil wished with all his heart it had not been made. He considered asking Mr Appleton to take his place, but the fellow was not a young man and he was already tired from the day's exertion.

'Really, I have no need of a chaperon,' put in Deborah, her chin up. 'A groom's company will suffice perfectly.'

Her tone caught Gil on the raw. She was clearly referring to their earlier conversation.

'Nonsense, my dear.' Lady Gomersham dismissed her arguments with an imperious wave. 'Mr Victor does not object, I am sure. And it is not so far out of his way, after all.'

All eyes were on Gil. He could only smile and agree that he would be delighted to ride with Miss Meltham. Sir Geoffrey pronounced everything settled and the party split up, although it was clear to Gil that Deborah was not happy with the arrangement. She rode beside him in stony silence for the first part of the journey, until they were obliged to stop while he opened a farm gate. Then she addressed him with cutting formality.

'Pray feel free to ride on, Mr Victor. I would not inflict my company upon you.'

'I have assured Sir Geoffrey that I shall see you home.'

'Even though you do not wish to do so.'

No, he did not wish to do so. Yet this was his opportunity and he must take it.

'You mistook me earlier. I want to see you, to be in your company, but I am thinking of your reputation.'

She did not look convinced.

He could not stop himself. He said, 'I do not wish to hurt you, Deborah.'

'I told you at the outset I expected nothing from you.' Her head dropped a little and her voice softened as she added quietly, 'Except perhaps friendship.'

He felt as if a giant hand was squeezing his heart. How could he even offer her that?

'I think there are things you are not telling me,' she said slowly. 'You have some deep sorrow in you. I wish you would share it with me, Gil.'

Her perception startled him, but he recovered quickly.

'There is nothing to tell.'

Deborah saw the shadow in his eyes and her heart went out to him. Somehow he had withdrawn from her today and she was surprised how much that hurt her. She felt in some inexplicable way that he was trying to protect her, but she did not understand. She said now, 'I do not believe that. Is it because you were in the army? Is it something in your past, too painful to relate?'

'Something like that.'

'We all have our own sorrows. Mine is my brother.'

She wondered suddenly if it was Ran's wildness that had offended Gil. After all, he was her brother and it did not reflect well upon her.

She said impulsively, 'Pray do not think too badly of him.'

His face darkened. 'I think he is a very wild young man.'

'He has been led astray. Perhaps you think I would say that, out of loyalty, but I truly believe it. As a boy he was the best brother anyone could have. I think, I believe Ran would have been better off at home rather than at school. He could then have learned from Papa's example and possibly followed his principals more nearly. I hoped Ran would be better at Oxford, but he allowed himself to be influenced more than he should by others.'

'The law would not take that as a defence.'

'The law?' She looked at him in surprise. 'Why should you say that? My brother is not a criminal. He has done nothing illegal in his life, I would stake my own life on that. He may have acted wrongly at times, but no worse than many young men.'

'You truly believe that?'

'Yes, I do.' Her hand crept to her shoulder. 'Others have done much worse.'

She did not wish to dwell on that and shuddered, shrugging off her painful memories. They had nothing to do with this.

'Randolph has hurt himself more than anyone else,' she told him. 'But I am hopeful that now he is living at Fallbridge things will improve. Now he has me to look after him. He is very fond of me, you see, and will make the effort, for my sake.'

'Yes, he told me at dinner the other night that your happiness is paramount with him.'

She gave a little smile. 'Of course.'

It was only partly true. Deb knew Ran's affection for her was genuine, but when he was in the grip of his depression, or befuddled by drink or laudanum, it was beyond her ability to reason with him. And even today, she suspected it was his craving for wine that took him back to Fallbridge.

Gil watched the changing emotions flickering over her countenance. He knew Deborah well enough now to know her every mood. She worried about Kirkster, as well she might. She thought she could save him from himself, but privately Gil doubted it. It would not be long before he was too far into a life of dissipation and drunkenness to care about anything.

And then there would be little point in revenge.

Revenge. Gil had put that word from his head these past few weeks, cravenly refusing to think of the reason he was in Fallbridge and why he was courting Deborah Meltham so assiduously. It was too easy to tell himself that he was merely relieving her of her cares for a few hours. But every time he looked at her, every time she smiled at him, he felt the desire stirring. It would be easy to take her to his bed.

The difficulty would be leaving her afterwards.

'I have hired a house,' he said suddenly. 'A neat little place called Sollom Hall, do you know it? It lies a few miles to the east of Fallbridge. It is fully furnished and staffed, the family has had to retrench, the father is in poor health and they have removed to Harrogate for the next few months.'

'No, I do not know the property, but most likely it is not in this parish. It will be more comfortable for you than remaining at the George, I suppose, while you look for a house of your own.'

'I would like you to see it. Are you free tomorrow? I could drive you there.'

Even as the words left his mouth part of him was willing her to refuse. To save herself.

'Tomorrow morning I have no engagements.'

She smiled up at him and he knew the trap was sprung.

'Excellent, I will call for you at ten. In my curricle.'

'I shall look forward to it.'

'So you are off on another pleasure jaunt.' Randolph came down the stairs just as Deborah was pulling on her gloves. 'With Victor, I suppose.'

'Yes. He is taking me out in his curricle.'

The scrunch of wheels upon the drive announced Gil's arrival.

Ran kissed her cheek. 'You had best wear your cloak, then. It looks like rain.'

'I shall.'

As he turned away she caught his arm. 'Would you like me to stay and keep you company today? I would happily cry off; I am sure Mr Victor would understand. We could ride to Long Acre; the steward tells me the improvements there have now been completed.'

'What, and risk a drenching? No, no, my dear, off you go and enjoy yourself. I am going into Fallbridge later. George Appleton is come home from his travels and I thought I might call upon him.'

With that he gave her shoulder a brotherly pat and she watched him lounge off to the breakfast room, her spirits lifting. She was pleased that Ran was mixing more in local society and her heart was lighter than ever as she went out to meet Gil.

He drew up on the drive and as soon as the groom was holding the horses he jumped down and ran around to greet her.

'The hood is up, you see, in case it comes on to rain. I have already felt a spot or two in the air.'

He was smiling and her heart missed a beat. She gave him her hand and his fingers closed about hers in a strong, comforting grasp as he helped her into the curricle. It was a low-slung racing model and the pair of powerful greys were moving restlessly in their harness, eager to be away.

'Here, I have brought a rug for you,' he said. 'I do not forget that it is not yet May.'

She sat very still as he placed the rug over her lap and tucked it around her skirts. Her heart swelled so much that she could not breathe. It was years since anyone had looked to her comfort in such a way. His hand brushed her knee and even though there were several layers of cloth between them she felt it keenly. Her mouth dried and her skin tingled. She clenched her hands together tightly, determined to remain calm. This was merely a drive in the country, nothing more.

She concentrated on steadying her breathing as he took his place beside her and gathered up the reins. He sent a swift, piercing glance in her direction.

'Nervous? You are quite safe, I promise you.'

She managed a smile. She did not doubt his driving ability, but *safe*? How could she be safe, when her body reacted so violently to him? He only had to look at her and she felt herself melting with a desire that threatened to overwhelm her. Deb knew beyond a shadow of a doubt that she would never be safe in his company.

The horses sprang into their collars and they were off. Deborah kept one hand in her lap, the other gripping the edge of the seat, not out of fear for the cracking pace, but to stop herself bumping against Gil as the curricle rocked and swayed. Then he reached out and covered her hand with his. He gave her fingers a brief, reassuring squeeze and she felt the tension easing out of her body. He knew. He understood what she was feeling. She relaxed, allowing her shoulder to touch Gil's arm, to feel the muscled strength of him and revel in his nearness.

With the hood up and separating them from the groom riding in the rumble seat, she felt emboldened to speak.

'Do you think it foolhardy of me to come with you today?'

He did not pretend to misunderstand her.

'Yes. But I am extremely glad you did.'

He guided the curricle around a bend and she leaned into him, revelling in his strength and support. She smiled.

'So, too, am I.'

Sollom Hall was a small, stone-built mansion in the old style, with leaded windows and a studded oak door. It was buried deep in woodland. Gil told her that it had originally been a hunting lodge, which explained its isolated position. They were admitted by a rosy-cheeked maid in a snow-white apron, who showed them into a parlour where wine and fancy cakes had been set out on the table.

'Would you like refreshments first, or to go over the house?' he asked, taking her cloak from her shoulders.

'Oh, a tour of the house, if you please. With its gables and tall chimneys, it looks like something from a fairy story.'

With a smile he took her off to show her the main reception rooms before leading the way up the wide oak staircase and throwing open the doors that flanked the landing, so that she might inspect each chamber.

'And this is my room,' he said, standing back that she might enter.

Deb went no further than the doorway. All ideas of fairy tales had fled, replaced by wanton thoughts that made her heart beat far too fast as she gazed at the heavily carved tester bed with its rich damask hangings. In her imagination, she and Gil were already lying there, naked. He was kissing her deeply, hungrily, and she was kissing him back, running her hands over his strong, muscled shoulders, pulling him closer, inviting him to caress her body.

He was standing very close, she could feel his presence, her spine tingling with the nearness of him. If he touched her, if he put his arms around her and kissed her now, that scene she imagined could become reality in a matter of minutes. And she was shocked to realise how desperately she wanted it to happen.

Hastily she stepped around him and back on to the landing, biting her lip. Gil closed the door and stood for a moment, looking at her, and Deb had no doubt that he knew what she was thinking. Their minds were too attuned for him not to be aware of it. The longing she felt, the desire for him to hold her, to kiss her, was so strong it was almost overpowering and she knew it was his restraint and not hers that was keeping her safe.

'Let us go back downstairs.'

Gil spoke softly, but she heard the tremor in his voice. He, too, was struggling for control.

She preceded him down the stairs, hoping her legs would hold her up and not daring to speak until they were once more in the little parlour with its polished wainscoting and heavy furniture.

'It, it is a very pleasant house,' she said, as he poured her a glass of wine. 'A little dark, perhaps, but that will be because of the small windows and so many trees around about.'

He glanced out of the window.

'Also, it has clouded over.' Thunder rumbled ominously in the distance and he grimaced. 'I am glad I told my tiger to put the curricle in the stable. I doubt I shall be able to show you the gardens today.'

As if to confirm this, rain began to patter at the glass. It grew darker as the rain increased to a torrent. Deb put down her glass and walked over to the window, just as the lightning flashed. It was immediately accompanied by a clap of thunder that made her jump.

'Are you frightened of storms like this?' he asked, coming closer.

'No.'

But he still took her in his arms. She leaned her head against his shoulder, breathing in the comforting smell of him, hints of soap and wool and leather mixed with the clean spicy scent of his skin and something else, something very masculine.

His embrace was indescribably comforting, but she was aware of other, more disturbing sensations: her rapid heartbeat and shallow breathing. The ache between her thighs. Desire was unfurling, dangerous and irresistible, taking control of her body.

She looked up, but even as she thought of entreating him to let her go he lowered his head and captured her lips with his own. His mouth was warm, the kiss demanding and Deb responded hungrily. His arms tightened and she clung to him as he teased her lips apart. For a few dizzy moments she allowed his tongue to explore her before responding in kind, following his lead while the blood pounded through her body.

Without breaking off the kiss, he sank down on the window seat and settled her on his lap. Deb was not so innocent that she did not know when a man was aroused, but it did not frighten her, she was excited by the thought. She felt malleable, liquid in his arms.

She wanted him to possess her and when he broke off and raised his head, she felt almost unbearably bereft.

She remained with her head against his shoulder, gazing up at him. The storm had passed and the rain had settled into a steady downpour. Lightning still flickered in the distance, but the thunder was little more than a menacing rumble.

'I should take you home,' he murmured, easing her gently on to the cushion beside him.

'Yes.' His arms were still around her and she clung to him, unwilling—unable—to move away. Not yet.

'Or you could stay.' He kissed her hair. 'Stay and dine with me.'

Her insides liquefied at the thought. To stay and dine—as well put a lamb into a lion's cage and expect it to be safe. And she did not *want* to be safe.

'I cannot.' She spoke on a sigh, turning her face into his coat. 'We are engaged to dine at Gomersham Lodge tonight.'

'Tomorrow, then. I will send the servants away for the night and my man will wait on us. We may be quite discreet.'

The madness was receding. Deborah pushed herself away from him and sat up very straight, sliding one hand around her waist while the other crept to her left shoulder.

'I cannot do that. I must not.'

'But you want to. Your kisses tell me so.'

She swung around to look at him. 'You knew this would happen.'

He cupped her face. 'It was inevitable, if you were here with me. Alone. And I should warn you it might well happen again, if you come to me tomorrow. I cannot resist you.'

His eyes were dark, unreadable, and she gave a shiver.

'You are very...frank,' she said at last.

He let her go, a shadow passing over his countenance, and with a sudden, impatient movement he got to his feet.

'You must think carefully, Deborah. You must be very sure before you come back here. I will tell you now, I cannot marry you.'

'Y-you have a wife?'

Impatiently he shook his head. 'No, nothing like that, but I want you to know, I cannot offer you marriage. Whatever else I may do, I will not deceive you on that point.'

He spoke roughly, as if he was angry, but instinctively she knew it was not with her. She rose and went to stand before him.

'You know already that I cannot marry while my brother needs me.' Amazed at her own daring, she took his hand and cradled her cheek against the palm. 'As for tomorrow, there is nothing I want more than to come here and dine with you.'

He held her gaze, his own eyes sombre, searching, then he gave a little nod.

'Very well. I shall send my coach for you. Now, we had best get you home.'

They travelled back in silence, save for the rain pattering on the curricle's hood. Deborah was still reeling from the tumult of emotions that he had roused in her and she wondered if Gil felt it, too. No one had ever made her feel so alive, or so reckless. She was fully aware that to dine with a man, without a chaperon, would be quite ruinous to her reputation. She also knew that to be alone with Gil, in his house, she would be at his mercy, should he wish to seduce her. And the dreadful truth was she *wanted* him to do so. What had she to lose, as long as they were discreet? He had assured her no one need ever know of it and perhaps the memory of a few hours spent in his company—in his arms—might help to warm the cold, empty years she saw stretching ahead of her.

When they reached Kirkster House and he handed her down she peeped up at him, but his lean face was inscrutable.

'Until tomorrow,' he murmured, raising her gloved fingers to his lips.

She nodded wordlessly and stood in the rain while he climbed back into the curricle and gathered up the reins. He looked across at her and Deb thought he was going to speak to her, but after a frowning moment he whipped up his team and drove away, his groom scrambling nimbly up behind him.

Deborah prepared carefully for her dinner at Sollom Hall. She discarded several gowns before finally deciding upon her dark red silk. Tiny seed-pearl earrings were matched by a single string around her neck, although they were covered by the fine muslin fichu she used to fill the low neckline of the gown. As she sat before her looking glass, adjusting its folds, her hands stilled. Tonight, if what she suspected would happen—what she *wanted* to happen, she reminded herself—Gil would undress her and there would be no hiding her body from him. For a moment she allowed herself to imagine his look of shock. He might shudder and draw away, repelled. Worse, he might pretend it did not matter, but she would know. She had endured enough lies and pitying looks over the years. She always knew. She hoped, prayed that Gil would not reject her, but her desire for him was so strong that for the first time in years she was prepared to take the risk.

She was so distracted by her thoughts that she barely noticed the unusual activity outside her door and thought nothing of it, even when she made her way downstairs shortly after five o'clock and Speke informed her that his lordship was in the drawing room with a guest. She went in, expecting to see George Appleton or perhaps Sir Geoffrey, but when she saw her brother's visitor her heart plummeted with dismay.

Sir Sydney Warslow turned and made her an elegant bow. Of all her brother's acquaintances, Deborah disliked and distrusted him the most. He was a few years older than Ran, classically fair and many considered him handsome, but not Deb. She saw only cruelty in his blue eyes and insolence behind his smile. He was smiling now as he came towards her. She moved away quickly, unwilling to give him her hand.

'Miss Meltham,' he drawled, raising his quizzing glass to observe her. 'As charming as ever and even more beautiful. But alas, I fear this finery is not for me.'

'How could it be, when she had no idea you were calling?' said Ran with a laugh. 'Deb is dining out. Damme if I haven't forgotten where you are going, m'dear?'

She managed a smile. 'An old friend and her husband, whom you do not know, Randolph.'

How easily the lies tripped from her tongue. She held her breath, afraid he would ask for more details, but he was already moving towards the sideboard.

'But you'll take a glass with us first, Deb, won't you? We are having claret, but you might prefer something else. Ratafia, perhaps, or sherry?'

'Nothing, thank you.' She turned a cool gaze upon their visitor. 'My brother is correct, Sir Sydney. I had no idea you were in the area.'

'I was passing this way and thought I would call upon my old friends,' he said smoothly.

'Yes,' Ran interjected. 'And I've invited him to stay here for a few days. We have much to catch up on.' He glanced at Deb and continued, a note of defiance in his voice, 'I promised you I would not return to Duke Street, but I suppose I can invite my friends here, if I wish.'

'Of course, it is your house.' Deb struggled to speak politely.

'And a man must be master in his own house, ain't that so, Randolph?'

Warslow made the comment laughingly, but Deb knew he was angry at the way she had persuaded Ran to remove from Duke Street, away from the influence of his so-called friends.

She put a hand to her shoulder to adjust the fichu at her neck.

'My friends are sending a carriage for me, but perhaps I should not go, after all.'

'Pray do not alter your plans on my account, Miss Meltham,' said Warslow easily. 'After all, I shall be here for a few days yet, plenty of time for us to become reacquainted.'

She suppressed a shudder.

'Aye, go and enjoy yourself,' said Ran. He handed a glass to Sir Sydney, then crossed the room to stand before her. 'You have been in alt about this visit all day and you deserve a treat. You need not fear for me,' he said, smiling. 'I am well now, I promise you.'

She gazed at her brother. He had looked and sounded so much better the past few days, surely she could trust him? And it was only for a few hours after all.

'Don't be anxious for me, Deb,' he said, kissing her cheek. 'A good dinner and a few games of cards is the intention for this evening.' He looked towards the window. 'There is a chaise pulling up on the drive now. Off you go and enjoy yourself, my dear. You spend too much time worrying about me.'

She was late. The heavy cloud made the day seem more advanced than it really was, but when Gil looked at the clock he saw that it was nearly six. He found himself hoping, nay, praying that she would not come. He wanted her, there was no denying it, but not like this, not as a weapon of revenge against her brother. He strode restlessly up and down the room, raking his fingers through his hair. Randolph Meltham had the blood of Gil's sister and brother on his hands and he must pay for it. Gil had come to Fallbridge seeking vengeance and, in the white heat of an anger and grief that had sustained him through the past several months, seducing Deb Meltham had seemed an ideal solution. A neat sort of justice.

He stopped before the fireplace and reached out to grip the mantelshelf while he stared into the mirror. What sort of ogre had he become that he could even contemplate such a thing? He fixed his eyes on the jagged scar; it was but a minor consequence of his years as a soldier. A decade of fighting had shown him the very worst side of mankind, but he had not realised until now just how much it had dulled his sensibilities and made him indifferent to the suffering of others. Perhaps it had been a necessary defence, to get him through the horrors of war, but he was no longer a soldier. He could no longer use that excuse.

Deb Meltham had made him understand all this, had given him back some semblance of humanity. And he planned to repay her with seduction! It eased his conscience not one jot to remind himself that he had told her to think carefully, that he had left the decision to her. A constriction, like a band of iron, gripped his chest. If she came here tonight he knew he would take her to his bed. He would not be able to help himself.

From the moment they had met Gil had known it would happen even though he had tried to ignore it. The attraction between them was too strong to be resisted. She might give herself willingly, but he could offer her nothing. The honourable course of action would be to marry her, but how could he do that, knowing his family's blood was on her brother's hands? Yet how could he live with himself, knowing he had ruined her? No, if she came here tonight he knew they would destroy one another.

He was just uttering up a prayer of thanks that she had stayed away when he heard voices in the hall.

Swallowing, he turned, praying it was not too late to avoid disaster.

Deborah stood before him now, clasping her hands tightly together as the footman withdrew, closing the door behind him. She was wearing a red gown, the silk so dark it looked almost black in the fading light. As always, the sleeves came to the wrist, but unlike her other gowns this one had a low neckline, with a cream-muslin fichu covering her neck and shoulders. He thought with painful irony that she was a picture of maidenly modesty.

He said, 'I had almost given you up.'

'I beg your pardon; I was delayed by the arrival of a guest.' When he looked concerned she shook her head. 'He is a…an acquaintance of my brother's so it makes no odds that I had arranged to go out.' Her mouth twisted into an expression of distaste. 'In fact, I was relieved to be able to do so.'

'You do not like the man?'

'I do not like the majority of my brother's friends,' she said frankly. 'But this one…' She shook her head, as if to clear some nagging worry. 'Randolph has promised me they intend only to have a good dinner and enjoy a hand or two of cards. There can be no harm in that.'

'None at all.' Gil had been going to suggest she should leave immediately, but she was clearly relieved to be away from her brother and his friend and he could not bring himself to send her back just yet. He said, 'What did you tell your brother?'

'That I am dining with an old friend.'

'Ah.'

Her shy smile ensnared him. Gil decided he would

give her dinner and then send her home. It would be an effort, when the blood was already thundering around his body and she was looking so nervous that he wanted to take her in his arms and kiss away her distress, but he still had some control. He must prove to himself that he could behave with perfect propriety.

Chapter Seven

It was quite different, Deb realised, dining alone with a man other than her brother. Out of doors in the sunshine, enjoying a bowl of shrimp with Gil was one thing. Then they had been quite comfortable together, but sitting either end of the table in this small dining parlour with the candles burning and the curtains drawn against the darkening sky was very different. Deborah's appetite had quite gone. She pushed her food around her plate and tried to respond to Gil's attempts at conversation. He was trying to put her at her ease, she knew it, but all she could think of was what was to follow.

Occasionally she would look up and find him watching her. She recognised the desire in his eyes, contrasting starkly with his polite conversation, and it sent a tremor of anticipation through her. She was aware of an unfamiliar sensation deep inside. A fluttering lightness that made the breath hitch in her throat. He wanted her, she knew it. Just as she wanted him. The attraction was so palpable it crackled in the air between them even now. And when the meal was over he would make love to her. Nothing had been said, but she knew it had been implicit in his invitation and she was willing to risk everything to lie with the man who had filled her dreams for the past weeks. Her insides swooped. This overwhelming desire she felt for Gil shocked her.

She appreciated his honesty; he had offered her nothing, promised her nothing. In fact, at one point he had seemed to be warning her off, but it was not necessary. She wanted this as much as he. But first she must be equally honest. There was something she must tell him and, if he no longer wanted her, she would have lost nothing but her pride.

And perhaps her heart.

At last the meal was over; the covers had been removed and they were alone. Gil noted that they had eaten very little and neither of them had taken much wine. For his part, it had been deliberate—he needed all his willpower if he was to send Deborah away with her honour intact. Why she had abstained he did not know, but he suspected she was nervous.

He glanced at her now, the length of the table separating them. She was looking down, lost in thought. The candlelight glinted on her hair and there was a rosy glow to her cheek, but her mouth was turned down and she looked unnaturally solemn. The iron band around his heart tightened painfully. Now he felt sympathy *and* desire. Not a good combination.

It was time to end this. To send her home. He rose and moved away from the table.

'It is usual to invite one's guest to the drawing room after a meal, but in the circumstances—'

'Please, before you say anything else, let me speak,' she interrupted him. 'There is something I must tell you.'

She got up and came towards him, one hand touching her shoulder. After one fleeting glance at his face she looked away.

'I wanted you to know, before we go any further, that I am not, not quite as I seem.' She spoke haltingly, the blush on her cheeks deepening.

Now, what was this? Gil frowned. Could it be she was not a maid? He could hardly object, he had had lovers himself, but the thought that her heart might still be engaged was like a sabre thrust, followed by the realisation, bitter as gall, that he had no right to care. He raised his hand to silence her.

'Deborah, there is no need to tell me anything.'

'Yes, there is.' The words were little more than a whisper. Her fingers shook as they clutched at the creamy fichu. 'There is something you must see.'

As the muslin came away Deborah turned so that the candlelight fell on the left side of her neck and illuminated the skin, which was pitted and puckered with scars.

'The marks go down the arm to the elbow,' she told him, easing her gown off the shoulder to expose the tracery of fine lines that covered the skin, dying away at the swell of her breast.

Gil put out his hand as if to touch the scars, then pulled back.

'How did it happen?'

'It was a parting gift from the first—the only— man who professed to love me. I thought he wanted to marry me, but I was wrong. I was young and headstrong and I thought myself very much in love. He was a man of the world and I suppose I thought him handsome, at the time. He persuaded me to run away from Duke Street, to elope, but when we stopped at an inn that first night it was clear marriage had never been his intention. When, when I refused his advances he threw the contents of a boiling kettle over me. He was trying to ruin my face, but fortunately for me he was in his cups and he missed, so that it is easy for me to conceal my...disfigurement.'

Gil's throat clogged with a scorching mix of outrage and sympathy.

'Papa was very good,' she went on. 'He never reproached me, said I had been punished enough. It was all hushed up and he tried to find a suitor for me. He was willing to make a very generous settlement to anyone who would marry me. One or two came forward and pretended my scars did not matter, but I could see that they did. It was horrible to think they were prepared to marry me for the money, but even worse was the pity.' She shuddered at the memory, then gave herself a little shake. 'Our friends and acquaintances in Fallbridge knew nothing of the, the incident, so when I moved there with Mama, the staff who came with us were sworn to secrecy and it has never been mentioned. But perhaps you see now why I have avoided any man's attentions. Until now.' Her eyes fluttered to his for the briefest moment. 'I wanted you to know,' she said again. 'I needed to show you before...before we go any further. I did not want you to discover it later and, and recoil in horror at my ugliness. This way, I can leave now and we can, perhaps, part as friends.'

Gil could not move, could not speak, but his mind

was racing. Her scars did not repulse him—after all, he had plenty of his own—but he was aghast at the situation he was in. If he sent her away now, as he had planned, she would not believe he was acting out of conscience. She would think he was rejecting her. But if he did what he most wanted to do, if he took her to his bed, she would be ruined.

Either way she would be hurt, but reason told him rejection was better than ruin.

'I should go.'

She replaced her gown and as she turned from him the candlelight glinted on a teardrop suspended on her lashes. Instinct triumphed over reason and he reached out for her.

'No.'

She stopped, her back to him. He had his hands on her shoulders and slowly he pushed the silk from her left arm and kissed the damaged skin. She trembled.

'This is part of what you are,' he murmured, trailing a line of kisses over the scarring. 'To me it makes you even more beautiful.'

He turned her around to face him and saw that she was crying. He cupped her face, his thumbs gently wiping away the tears that coursed down her cheeks, then he lowered his head and kissed her. Her lips were salty and she resisted him for a moment, then a little shudder ran through her and she slipped her arms around his neck, kissing him back with a fervour that sent arrows of desire shooting through his blood. With a growl that was part-triumph, part-need, he lifted her into his arms and strode out of the room.

The hall was empty and the only sound was the whisper of Deb's silk skirts against his legs as he carried her up the stairs to his bedroom. She clung to him, her face buried in his shoulder, but he had no fear that they would meet anyone. There was only Harris in the house and he could be trusted to keep out of the way until he was needed.

Gil had ordered a fire to be kindled in his room against the damp chill of the late spring evening. That and the few candles burning around the room was all the light he needed to undress her. He went slowly, kissing each newly exposed area of skin. As he eased the gown from her left arm he took extra time to explore, to show her that he was not in any way deterred by the scars that covered her shoulder and arm in a delicate filigree.

She responded shyly, but without fear, helping him to remove his clothes and dropping them on to the floor where they mingled with hers in a colourful heap. Her touch inflamed his already aroused body. When they were both naked she reached for him, her eyes dark and luminous in the candlelight, her lips parted in an invitation he could not resist.

As their mouths came together Gil's heart kicked against his ribs. She leaned into him, breasts and hips pressing against his skin and he gave up all thoughts of making love to her slowly. He swept her up in his arms and carried her to the bed. She dragged him down with her and his mouth sought hers again, this time in a crushing kiss to which she responded with a hunger as fierce as his own. He swept his hands over her body and felt it arching up to meet him. His caresses moved lower, he slipped one hand between her thighs and they parted instinctively. She was hot, pushing against his fingers, and when he would have withdrawn she clamped her hand over his.

'Oh, pray do not stop now,' she gasped. 'Oh, Gil, I never thought, never knew…'

The way she breathed his name, the wonder in her voice, sent his spirits soaring to new heights, but that and the feel of her fingers trailing over his burning skin snapped the final shreds of his control.

Deborah gasped as he thrust into her, but it was more in joy than pain. She pushed back, following his rhythm as he went harder, deeper and ripples of excitement began to build within her. Then she was out of control, flying, falling, and clutching at the bedcovers. She cried out as her body shuddered in wave after wave of pure ecstasy that left her faint and breathless, and it was some moments before she became aware that Gil had pulled away and was finishing his own pleasure outside her body.

When he collapsed against her she lifted a hand and touched him.

'What is it?' she whispered. 'Was that, was I not good for you?'

'You?' He kissed her. 'You were wonderful, but I would not risk getting you with child. Rest now.'

He pulled her close and she snuggled against him, but she did not sleep, too filled with wonder at what had occurred, at the new and powerful sensations he had roused in her. It had been everything she had dreamed of and more. The only problem was, she wanted to experience it all over again. She stirred and his breath sighed against her neck.

'You are awake.'

He pushed himself up on one elbow to look at her. Suddenly aware of her nakedness, Deb went to pull the sheet over her shoulder, but he stopped her.

'I want to see you. All of you.'

She smiled. 'You make me feel beautiful.'

'You are beautiful.' He sat up. 'And when it comes to scars, you cannot compete with me. I have several on my back, too, but let's start with these.'

He took her hand and guided it over his chest, running her fingers over the bullet hole in his shoulder, made by a sharpshooter at Badajoz, the line across his chest where he had narrowly survived a cavalry charge at Busaco, and the jagged scar on his side incurred at Vitoria.

'And there's this one,' he said, taking her hand down to his inner thigh. 'That was caused by a piece of shrapnel at Vimeiro.' He grinned. 'Another inch or two higher and it might have been much worse.'

He eased her hand upwards and she gasped, her eyes widening.

'I am no expert,' she said, struggling to speak in more than a croak, 'but it appears to me that you are quite…intact.'

His eyes glinted wickedly.

'Oh, yes.' He rolled her on to her back and covered her in one smooth movement. 'I am quite intact, as you so elegantly phrase it. And I am quite willing to prove it to you.'

Deborah stirred and immediately Gil's arms tightened around her and he pulled her against him, kissing her neck.

She felt the smile growing inside her. He had said

she was beautiful. He had made her *feel* beautiful and in return she had given herself to him. She was no longer a maid, but that was unimportant, compared to the new-found happiness he had given her. Deborah had spent so long nursing her mother and looking after Randolph that she had forgotten what it was like to think only of herself and her own pleasure.

She kept very still, trying to memorise everything she was feeling; the blissful security of lying here, in Gil's arms, the warmth of his body wrapped around her, the whisper of his breath against her cheek. She carefully stored away each and every new, wonderful sensation and hugged them to her while the distant chime of a clock reminded her of her duty. She sighed.

'I should go. It must be near midnight.'

His sigh caressed her cheek.

'I heard the clock strike eleven not long since.'

'And I have just heard it chime the half-hour. It will take me some time to get back.' She sought out his lips for another of those long, lingering kisses that made her whole body ache for him, but at last she resolutely broke away and slipped out of bed.

The fire had died to a glow, but a solitary candle still burned and she began to dress. Gil propped himself on one elbow and watched her.

'Would you like me to help you?'

'There is no need. I deliberately chose garments I can manage without assistance.' She marvelled at her audacity to say such a thing. She was telling him quite clearly that she had intended to let him bed her. But he already knew that, she thought, another smile bubbling up inside her.

While she finished dressing he shrugged on his banyan and went off to order her carriage, saying when he returned that he would dress and go with her.

'I will ride beside the carriage, as an escort.'

'And how would that look, if anyone saw you? No, I am sure your coachman will look after me.'

He gave a menacing growl. 'He will answer to me if he does not.' He took her hand. 'Come along then.'

By the time they reached the hall the carriage was at the door. They stopped in the shadows and Gil caught her in his arms again. She could feel the hard strength of him beneath the silk of his dressing gown and she clung to him, suddenly unwilling to let go of this new-found happiness.

'Will you call upon me tomorrow?' she asked shyly.

'Of course.' He gave her a final hug, then picked up her cloak and placed it around her shoulders. 'Go now, before I give in to temptation and carry you back to bed.'

Quickly she ran down the steps and into the waiting coach. The steps were put up and they lurched away into the darkness. Deb settled back into the corner, pulling her cloak tightly around her as she tried to examine her feelings. She had given herself to a man. She should be alarmed, afraid, even perhaps ashamed of what she had done, but she felt none of these things. She felt...she felt alive.

But as the carriage drew nearer to Kirkster House, her thoughts became more sober. The past few hours had been blissful, but she knew that such times could never be more than a brief interlude. Now she must face the reality of the life she had chosen.

* * *

Chinks of light showed through the shutters of the drawing room when Deb arrived home, so she did not need Speke to inform her that her brother had not yet gone to bed. She tried not to feel anxious as she hurried across the hall. It was possible that they were engrossed in a game of cards, but as she opened the door her worst fears were realised.

Sir Sydney was lounging in a chair beside the fire, a glass of brandy between his white hands, but Randolph was sprawled on the sofa, unconscious. With a cry she flew across the room and dropped to her knees beside him. Almost immediately she saw the small bottle that had fallen from his nerveless hands.

She turned an accusing stare upon Sir Sydney. 'How did he come by laudanum? I keep none in the house.'

'I could not come to visit my old friend empty-handed.'

His smile made Deborah long to slap him.

'You are no friend, sir.'

His smile grew. 'You would like to turn me from this house, would you not, Miss Meltham? But you will not do it. I am your brother's guest. I will go when he demands it and not before.' He finished his brandy and crossed the room to put his glass back on the sideboard before turning to look down at her, his lip curling in a sneer. 'And he is not going to do that tonight, is he?'

Deborah remained on her knees beside her brother as Warslow strolled out of the room.

'Oh, Ran,' she whispered, gently pushing his fair hair away from his brow. 'You promised you would not do this.'

A few tears escaped her, but she wiped them away

and climbed to her feet. Randolph must be put to bed and she would have to summon Miller, his valet, to help her.

Suddenly the rapture and joy she had felt earlier in the evening seemed a lifetime away.

Chapter Eight

Once the carriage had pulled away from Sollom Hall Gil returned to his room, where he paced the floor until dawn, cursing himself for not sending her away the moment she arrived. Whatever he did now would hurt her and he was desperate to do as little harm as possible. But how?

He still had no answer to this question when the first grey fingers of dawn crept into the room. He plunged his face into the bowl on the washstand, but even the shock of the cold water brought no relief, just the growing conviction of his own perfidy. He had acted wrongly, he had taken Deb's virginity, ruined her in the eyes of society and by his own code of honour he should offer to marry her. But that was impossible.

Her seduction was to have been his revenge for the deaths of his brother and sister. Instead he had taken her to his bed for a complex mixture of reasons, but certainly not vengeance. He had wanted to comfort her, to prove to her that she was a passionate, desirable woman and also to satisfy some deep primal need that they both shared. They only had to be in the same room together to feel the connection. There was an awareness, an almost tangible bond between them, and because of that he could not walk away and leave her without some explanation. The devil of it was he did not know what he could say that would make any sense.

He could not tell her what her brother had done, he had already decided that for her sake he would forget his planned revenge. Kirkster was ill—Gil had seen enough young men destroy themselves with dissolute living to know the signs. The fellow was unlikely to live much longer, however assiduously his sister cared for him. And then she would have no one. The idea of Deborah being alone and unprotected was unbearable. Somehow, Gil needed to assure her that if she needed him he would be there for her, to help her in any way he could.

Any way short of marriage.

Deborah had no expectations that Randolph would leave his bed in time for breakfast the following day and, not wishing to sit down alone with Sir Sydney Warslow, she ordered Elsie to bring her breakfast to her room.

The months of patient persuasion and cajoling to keep Randolph from taking laudanum had been undone in just a few short hours. It did no good to regret that she had gone out last night. A few moments' rational thought told her that even if she had dined at home, Warslow would no doubt have waited until she left them to their brandy, or had retired to bed before he encouraged Ran in his destructive habit.

She closed her eyes, remembering the previous evening, the hours she had spent with Gil. There was a great deal of comfort in the memory and it lightened the darkness of her present situation. She had given herself to him, knowing full well what it could mean for her, but she could not regret it, nor did she doubt that he cared for her and she hugged that thought to her. He had warned her at the outset that he could not marry her, but since she had already vowed not to leave Ran she wasted no time wishing for what could not be. If they could share a little time together, she told herself it would be enough.

It was a lie and she knew it. Deep in her heart Deb was sure that she could never have enough of Gil. He had said he would visit and the thought that he might call early made her hurry through her breakfast and call for Elsie to help her dress.

After changing her mind three times, Deb decided upon the yellow muslin, embroidered at the hem and sleeves with acanthus leaves and tied at the high waist with a green sash. She then surprised her maid by asking her to put up her hair in a matching ribbon and allow it to fall at the back in soft curls.

'Why, miss, 'tis years since I did your hair in anything like that. I've been scraping it back into a knot for so long that I may well have forgotten how to do anything so fancy!'

Deb laughed and, catching sight of her reflection in the glass, she noted the way her eyes sparkled. She looked vivacious, even pretty, and felt a little rush of excitement. How many years was it since she had thought of herself as anything but Ran's older sister?

'For once I do not wish to look sober and serious, Elsie. I think it is time for a change.'

The maid gave her a searching look, but said nothing, and Deb wondered if Elsie thought she was trying to attract Sir Sydney Warslow. The thought gave her pause, but the idea of looking her best for Gil was too tempting to resist.

As soon as she was ready she made her way to Randolph's room, only to be informed by Miller, his valet, that he was still sleeping. She insisted on looking in on him, relieved that his breathing was even and his pulse more regular than it had been last night.

'He will be in the devil's own temper when he wakes,' said Miller, speaking with the frankness of a long-serving retainer. 'Best leave him to me, miss. By the time I send him downstairs he'll be as sorry as can be that he has let you down.' She nodded and as he followed her to the door he asked, in a voice devoid of emotion, 'Do we know how long Sir Sydney will be remaining with us, Miss Meltham?'

'No, Joseph, we do not.' She bit her lip and risked exchanging a speaking glance with the valet. 'A few days, perhaps.'

'Let us hope it is no longer,' he muttered. 'For all our sakes.'

Downstairs the house was quiet and Deb was informed that Sir Sydney had ridden out early. She felt her resentment rising. Why should he press the opiate on her brother, when he rarely used it himself? She did not trust him; Randolph's worst bouts of ill health had always followed Sir Sydney's visits to Duke Street and she thought now that perhaps the laudanum was a way to bind Randolph to him.

A grey depression stole over her as she thought of the difficult days ahead. In fact, the only glimmer of sunshine was that Gil had said he would call. She needed to speak to Cook about dinner and ran lightly down the stairs to the kitchen, where she interrupted a lively altercation between Cook and the housekeeper.

'I was just asking Mrs Woodrow to account for her having a bad two-pound note in her strong box, Mistress,' Cook explained, when Deb asked what was going on.

'And I told her I can't account for it,' retorted the housekeeper, her arms crossed over her ample bosom and two spots of angry colour on her cheeks. She turned an indignant gaze upon Deborah. 'I tell you, Miss Meltham, I knew how it would be once the Bank of England started printing more bank notes. Not as safe as coin, not by a long chalk.'

Deborah gave her a reassuring smile and turned back to Cook, asking her just what had occurred to bring about this discussion.

'Well,' said the good woman, slightly mollified, 'I'd set young Jane to scrubbing the floor this morning, miss, so rather than have her stop what she was doing I decided I'd go myself to the market, to fetch another leg of lamb, seeing as how we has a visitor staying. It was as I was passing the drapers that Mrs Alsop herself comes running out and asks me to step inside for a quiet word. Then she says as how Peter the footman had called there late yesterday to collect the new table linen and he paid for it with a bad two-pound note.

'She said if she hadn't seen me she'd have come to

the house to see you, miss, for she knew neither you nor the master would be passing forged notes. So of course, I paid her again and brought the note back with me, but when I tackled Peter about it he says it was what Mrs Woodrow here gave him from the cash box.' She shook her head, her round face troubled. 'I've known Mrs Alsop these twenty years past and she wouldn't diddle us, so if she says it was Peter as gave her that note, then I believe her.'

The housekeeper harrumphed loudly. 'And I wouldn't knowingly give him a forgery, madam, as you know full well.'

'Of course you would not,' said Deborah soothingly. 'It has clearly been passed off on us and in all likelihood quite unwittingly.'

'Well, there's always lots of strangers in Fallbridge on market day and I was out shopping, so 'tis possible I picked it up then,' admitted the housekeeper. 'But I swear to you madam, 'tis such a good copy I couldn't see anything wrong with it at all, when Cook first showed it to me.'

'Aye, it was a very good likeness,' Cook agreed. 'Mrs Alsop said she wouldn't have noticed, only her boy, who's apprentice to the printer, happened to be in the shop and took a look at it. He said the watermark wasn't right and nor was it, miss, for Mrs Alsop had a proper note there and we compared the two.'

'And where is the note now?' asked Deborah.

'I burned it,' replied the housekeeper. 'Begging your pardon, madam, but I was sore afraid of what would happen if we was caught with it in the house. I've known people be clapped up for less. The penalties are very severe for even handling a forged note.'

'Quite right, too,' said Cook, nodding. 'It was good of Mrs Alsop to point it out to us so discreetly. Fair shook me up, it did, to think that such a note should come from here. And I dare say it isn't what you're used to either, Mrs Woodrow.'

'No, indeed. I am all of a lather over it, I can tell you,' agreed the housekeeper.

She then invited Cook to join her in her parlour and take a dish of tea, at which juncture Deborah knew this token of peace should not be ignored. She generously told Cook she would come down later to discuss the menu for dinner and escaped upstairs. She was free now to await Gil's visit, but her hopes were dashed when she received word via the butler that Mr Victor's man had called to say his master had urgent business and would not now be able to call until the morrow.

Deborah busied herself with her household duties until she learned that her brother was downstairs and she went off to find him. He was in the dining room, partaking of a late breakfast and looking decidedly grey. The look he threw at Deborah was a mixture of shame and defiance, so she forbore to question him on why he should be feeling so unwell. They both knew the reason for it, so she merely sat down at the table and said cheerfully that she would drink a cup of coffee with him.

She hoped his mood would soften, but a little while later, when she asked him how long Sir Sydney would be staying, Ran snapped back at her.

'For Heaven's sake, do not be worrying me with that now, Deb. Warslow knows he is welcome to stay here as long as he likes.'

'He is not welcomed by me,' she retorted and earned a glare in return.

Deborah sighed.

'Oh, Ran, let us not fight about it,' she said, reaching out to touch his hand. 'It is just that your health is never good when Sir Sydney is here.'

She jumped as his fist banged on the table.

'There is nothing wrong with me that a little more company wouldn't cure. I wonder that I allowed you to persuade me to come back here. Fallbridge must be the most unexciting place in the kingdom!'

Deborah knew it would be unwise to push him further so she held her peace and instead regaled him with an account of the altercation that had been going on below stairs.

'So you see, occasionally we do have some excitement here,' she said, smiling at him. She drained her coffee cup. 'Now, I had best go and see if Cook is yet ready to discuss dinner. Is there anything you would particularly like, love?'

Ran's answer was no more than a bad-tempered growl so she dropped a quick kiss on his cheek and went off, hiding her worries beneath a cheerful countenance.

Deb managed to avoid bumping into Sir Sydney for the rest of the day, and as she approached the drawing room just before the dinner hour the raised voices encouraged her to hope that perhaps Ran had fallen out with his guest. As she paused outside the door she heard her brother saying angrily, 'It ain't to be borne, Warslow. It's too close to home. I won't have it, I say.'

She entered quietly in time to see Sir Sydney raising his shoulders in a careless shrug.

'An oversight, Kirkster. There's no harm done.'

'No harm? When that damned note clearly came from here? I—' Ran broke off hurriedly when he saw Deborah in the doorway, but without a word he turned and went to the sideboard, where he began to pour wine into two glasses.

'Ah, Miss Meltham, your brother was just telling me you have been the victim of a fraud.'

'Yes, someone passed off a bad note on our housekeeper,' she replied, ignoring his outstretched hand.

She crossed the room and took a chair near the window, busying herself with the arranging of her skirts.

'Woodrow shouldn't buy off the market traders,' muttered Ran, handing a brimming glass to his guest.

'My dear brother, Mrs Woodrow has been shopping in the market for ever and is well acquainted with most of the farmers who bring in their produce.' She added, trying to make light of the incident, 'It is only a two-pound note, after all, and we shall all be much more careful in future.'

'An admirable point of view, Miss Meltham.' Sir Sydney smiled at her. 'I was suggesting as much to your brother when you came in.'

He deftly changed the subject, moving his attention back to Randolph, and Deborah was grateful that she was no longer required to take part in the conversation. She had kept herself busy all day, but still she had had far too much time to think of what had happened at Sollom Hall last night. Not that she regretted a single minute of it, but Gil's crying off today was disappointing. She was anxious to see him again, to reassure herself that she was not wrong and that he did truly care for her. For once when dinner was over and Deb retired to her room, the fact that she was leaving her brother alone with his so-called friend was not the foremost worry on her mind.

A restless night did little to soothe Deborah's nerves and when she learned that Ran and his guest had not gone to bed until dawn she received the news with mixed feelings. Much as she worried for her brother, she was relieved that she would not have to sit at breakfast with anyone. She wondered how soon she might expect to see Gil and was sorely tempted to fetch her spencer and bonnet and wander the grounds until he appeared, but the day was so overcast and blustery that it would be obvious she was waiting for someone and it would play havoc with the curls that Elsie had coaxed to fall so artlessly around her head. Instead she decided to go to the morning room and work on her embroidery. The fact that this would allow her to sit by the window overlooking the drive, where she could see anyone approaching, had nothing to do with her decision. Nothing at all.

Half an hour later Speke announced Mr Victor. Even though she had seen his tall figure striding along the drive, Deb felt unprepared for his arrival. With hands that trembled slightly she secured her needle in her work and put it aside to rise and greet her guest. She held out her hand, trying to smile politely, but fearing that her pleasure at seeing him must be shining in her eyes.

His lips barely brushed her fingers, but even that

light touch was like a burn on her skin and sent white-hot arrows of awareness shooting through her. Her blood was singing and it was all she could do not to throw herself into his arms and beg him to kiss her.

Instead they stood for a moment, looking at one another, silent and indecisive. It was Gil who spoke first, his voice polite, as if he was talking to a stranger.

'You arrived home safely, then, the other night.'

'Yes.' She added shyly, 'I thought you would call yesterday.'

'It was not possible. I beg your pardon.' He paused. 'You have no regrets?'

She searched his face for some sign of warmth, but could see none. She wondered if perhaps he was nervous. He was still holding her fingers and she clasped his hand between both her own.

'None at all.'

Their eyes met and held, his sombre, hard as slate and unreadable, but that did not stop her from smiling at him.

After a long, silent moment he disengaged himself and walked over to the window, staring out across the lawns and winding drive. Deborah invited him to sit down, asked him if he would take refreshment with her. She knew she was gabbling, but there was nothing she could do about that. There was so much she wanted to say, so much she could not. All she had at her disposal were the rituals of polite behaviour.

'No, thank you.'

Gil turned and walked towards the fireplace. He had come to say goodbye; he had spent yesterday rehearsing the words, but now they stuck in his throat.

She was standing before her chair and watching him intently, as if trying to read his mind.

He thought she had never looked more beautiful and he must say goodbye.

'You are troubled,' she said quietly. 'If you are concerned that I might expect something more of you after—after what occurred, then pray put your mind at rest. You owe me nothing.'

Her quiet dignity tore into him. He said, more roughly than he intended, 'You are wrong, I owe you a great deal.' Two strides would have taken him back across the room to her, but he willed himself not to move. 'At the very least I owe you an explanation for why I have to go away. Why we cannot meet again.'

'N-not meet again?' Her eyes flew to his face.

'No, it would not do...' He paused to draw a deep breath. 'That is why it is better that we part now, before it becomes too painful.'

She was staring at him, the colour drained from her face. Slowly she came towards him, standing so close he could feel the heat from her body. His own was crying out to close the small gap that separated them and take her in his arms. The faint trace of her perfume was heady as wine and it was weakening his resolve to leave.

'Must we part so soon, when we have only just found one another?' she said softly. 'I do not think it could become any more painful, but I am willing to take that chance.'

She was gazing up at him, her green eyes so innocent and trusting that the only way he could continue was to move away from her disturbing presence. He swung around and took a few steps towards the fire, but her reflection was in the mirror on the chimney breast. There was no escape from those green eyes, so he turned back to face her. This was proving even more difficult than he had thought.

'Is it the scars on my shoulder?' she asked him, her voice not quite steady. 'Perhaps I am too disfigured, too ugly—'

'No!' The word was torn from him. 'You are beautiful, never let anyone tell you differently.'

'Pray do not think you need to be kind—'

His hand flew up, cutting her off. He said stiffly, 'Please, Miss Meltham, you must trust me in this. It is better we part now. If I stay I shall only cause you more pain and I could not bear to do that.'

Deborah heard his words, but neither they nor his cold tone made any sense. She felt as if she was standing on the edge of shifting sands. She had asked for nothing, demanded nothing from him. Why, then, must he go? Why must they not see one another again?

'I am sorry,' she said, struggling to express her thoughts aloud. 'It was my first time. With a man. I do not understand these things. Did, did I not p-please you?'

He closed his eyes, as if her words pained him. Or perhaps he was embarrassed by her naivety.

'Exceedingly,' he said, still with that chilling politeness, 'but it is best we part now, before something occurs to spoil our memory.'

She frowned. '*Is* something likely to occur? I cannot think—'

She was interrupted by the soft click of the door opening and her heart sank as Sir Sydney walked into the room. When he saw her companion he stopped, his brows going up in surprise.

Deb glanced back at Gil, but he was immobile. He looked as if he had been turned to stone.

'Well, well,' drawled Sir Sydney. 'Viscount Gilmorton.'

Deb's brows drew together. 'Viscount?'

Warslow was still speaking. 'No need to introduce us, Miss Meltham. Gilmorton and I are old, ah, acquaintances.'

'Viscount?' she said again, her eyes darting between the two men. Her world was now feeling very unsteady. 'No, no. This, this is Mr James Victor.'

'Technically accurate,' replied Sir Sydney, still in that hateful, purring voice. 'James August Victor Laughton, ninth Viscount Gilmorton. Have I remembered it correctly, my lord?'

'Perfectly.'

'But…' Deborah struggled to understand what she was hearing. 'You are known by everyone here as Mr Victor.'

'Is he, by Gad?'

Warslow lifted his quizzing glass and gazed with cool insolence at Gil, who stared back, silent and impassive. Deb thought he might have been carved from stone, so unresponsive was he. Why did he not speak? She tried to think of some reasonable explanation, but there was none.

'*That* is why you said people call you Gil,' she murmured, beginning to understand at last.

And with understanding came anger.

'You deceived decent, innocent people like Sir Geoffrey and his family.'

You deceived me!

Inside she was screaming with pain and rage. Tears clogged her throat, but she forced them down. Bad enough that Gil had tricked them all, but she must not reveal the full extent of her own folly before the odious Sir Sydney, who had strolled across to stand beside her. She clenched her fists, digging her nails into the palms to stop herself from shaking.

'Now, my dear, why should a viscount be masquerading as plain Mr Victor? Shall we ask him?'

To beguile innocent maids. Deborah looked at Gil. His expression was closed, even a little haughty, but the tension in his cheek pulled on the scar so that it gleamed in a white, jagged line down his face. Surely a disfigured viscount would be considerably more acceptable in society than a mere gentleman. So why, if he was intent upon fixing his interest with her, did he hide his identity? Unless he thought she was angling for a husband.

Sigh no more, ladies...

'No need,' she said bitterly. 'Shakespeare expressed it perfectly when he said men were deceivers ever. Were you afraid I might try to trap you into marriage, *my lord*?' Her lip curled. 'I would not stoop so low.'

She saw him flinch, the merest flicker of his eyelids. If she had wounded him she was glad. It could not be a fraction of the pain she was experiencing. She had trusted him, given herself to him, only to discover he had been deceiving her from the start.

'It is not as it seems, Miss Meltham.'

Chaotic thoughts were chasing through Gil's head. What was Warslow doing here? He seemed very much at home in the house, and if he was the guest Deb had mentioned then it bore out everything Gil had learned about Lord Kirkster. By God, the fellow must be dissolute indeed to allow a dangerous villain like Warslow anywhere near his sister.

Warslow had been in the army for a short time, which was where Gil had become acquainted with him. He knew him for a cheat and a bully. A coward, even, but he had sold out before the rising number of allegations against him could be proven. Now he was standing here and Gil wanted to knock the smile off his face, but it was impossible. *He* was the one in the wrong and Deb was looking at him as if he was the greatest villain alive.

Which he was, to have hurt her so.

'Miss Meltham, if you will allow me a few minutes, in private—'

'Oh, no,' Warslow interjected silkily. 'I am informed that Lord Kirkster is indisposed, so in her brother's absence I will take it upon myself to say that it would be most improper for Miss Meltham to see you alone.'

Gil's jaw was clenched as he suppressed a furious retort. He looked at Deb. Her face was ashen, she looked stunned, only the green eyes were alive, sparkling with fury and unshed tears.

'There is nothing *Lord Gilmorton* has to say that I wish to hear,' she said icily. 'Please leave this house, my lord. Immediately.'

There was nothing he could say, no way to defend himself, even if Warslow had not been present. He would have to leave and let her think the worst of him.

With a stiff bow, he turned on his heel and walked out, knowing that her parting look would haunt him for ever.

Deborah watched him go, saw the door close behind him. Slowly she unclenched her fists and rubbed the palms against her skirts. She felt nothing. It was as if this was happening to someone else.

'How long has Gilmorton been in the area?'

'What?' She had forgotten Sir Sydney was beside her and struggled to marshal her thoughts. 'Oh, a little over a month, I think.'

A chill ran through her. She had thrown caution to the winds and would now suffer for it. How could she condemn her brother as weak-willed when she had given herself to a man about whom she had known so little? It was a lowering thought, but she very much feared her craving for Gil would match her brother's need for laudanum or strong liquor.

'Why did he come to Fallbridge, I wonder?' mused Sir Sydney, stroking his chin.

She shook her head, trying to clear the fog of pain and confusion that made it difficult to think clearly.

'He came here on business, I believe,' she said. 'And he was looking to buy a house here. Although why that should require such deception I do not know.'

'Do you not? I fear he was trying to ingratiate himself with you.'

The look he gave her brought the blood rushing to her cheeks. There was no point in denying it, but she tried to shrug it off.

'He dined here but once.'

'Oh, and what does your brother make of him?'

'They have little in common.'

She would not tell him how the evening had ended, that Ran had embarrassed her by drinking himself into a stupor.

He nodded, apparently satisfied.

'Well, he will trouble you no more. Now, what say you to a stroll in the gardens before dinner?'

He touched her arm and, suppressing a shudder, she moved quickly away, gracefully declining his invitation and saying that she must look in on her brother.

Miller met her at the door to Ran's chamber and told her in hushed tones that Lord Kirkster was out of bed now and getting dressed. Deb stayed only long enough to ascertain that he would be coming downstairs for dinner before she went off to her own bedchamber. If he had been too ill to leave his room she would have left Sir Sydney in solitary state rather than dine alone with him.

When she had brought Ran to live in Fallbridge she had dispensed with her elderly companion, ostensibly because her brother was all the chaperon she required, but in reality it was because Ran had not wanted anyone to know of his addictions. Now she realised how unwise that had been. A companion could have acted as chaperon when Ran was indisposed.

A companion might also have counselled Deborah to beware of plausible rogues.

She quickly shut her mind to such a thought, knowing it would depress her still further, but unfortunately she could not block out the memory of that last meeting with Gil. Learning of his deception had been devastating, made even worse by the fact that Sir Sydney had been present and they had had to pretend they were no more than acquaintances.

If they had been alone she would have ripped up at Gil, battered him with her fists. Her puny strength would have made little impact, but it might have given her some relief from the pain that racked her. Now she could only pace the floor, afraid to indulge in a bout of tears because that would leave her eyes red and puffy. Even if her brother did not notice, Sir Sydney might guess the cause of her distress.

Deborah fought down her unhappiness, summoned her maid and dressed with all her usual care. Looking in the mirror, the frivolous curls and ringlets that Elsie had worked so hard to arrange now mocked at her, but they must remain for the rest of the day. If she brushed them out now, it would be obvious that she had made a special effort for Gil's visit.

'No one must ever know,' she murmured as she made her way downstairs to join the gentlemen for dinner. 'No one must ever guess what a fool I have been.'

It was not to be expected that Sir Sydney would refrain from mentioning the Viscount's visit and Deb could only be thankful that he waited until the end of the meal, when the covers had been removed and the servants had withdrawn, before doing so.

'So, Mr Victor is in reality Viscount Gilmorton?' said Randolph, refilling his wineglass. 'Dashed peculiar, but never mind that. What think you of this claret, Warslow? It's some m'father laid down and I think it's pretty good now.'

'By Gad, Kirkster, ain't you concerned that the

fellow's been running free in your house under false pretences?'

'That has not been the case.' Deb corrected him with icy dignity. 'Mr—Lord Gilmorton has been inside this house on no more than three occasions.'

Sir Sydney inclined his head.

'I beg your pardon, Miss Meltham, but you cannot deny that he has imposed on you unpardonably.'

No, Deb could not deny it, but she would never confess just how much.

'Well, no harm done,' muttered Ran, shrugging. 'Unless Deb's lost her heart to him.'

Somehow she managed a derisive laugh.

'A man I have met only half-a-dozen times? Ridiculous.'

'There you are, then. You've sent the fellow packing, Warslow, so there's an end to't. Now, Deb m'dear, p'raps you should go off to the drawing room and Speke can bring in the brandy.'

For the first time in her life, Deborah felt thankful that her brother was more interested in his pleasures than in her welfare and she went off without another word. However, sitting alone in the drawing room the silence pressed in on her, taunting her with those final few moments with Gil. She found herself going over every word, every look. He had denied nothing, explained nothing.

It is not as it seems.

Deb closed her eyes and pressed her fingers to her temples. It was useless to go over and over everything he had said. It was all lies and deception. She was not the first woman to be betrayed in this way and she would not be the last. She must put it out of her mind and be thankful that no one else knew of it. This was her burden, she must live with it.

Chapter Nine

Gil was shrugging himself into his riding jacket when his valet came into the bedchamber.

'Where the devil have you been, John? I thought I'd have to pack up everything myself.'

Gil scowled. He sounded like the sort of contemptible fop he most disliked.

'Well, my lord, it isn't as if you ain't more than capable of doing so,' retorted Harris, not a whit put out by his master's ill humour. He stood, silently regarding the Viscount.

'So?' barked Gil, catching his eye. 'Come on, man, what is it?'

'Miss Meltham is below.'

'The devil she is!'

'That fool of a butler we have here was about to tell her you wasn't at home, but I managed to forestall him and have her shown into the parlour.'

'Hell and damnation, John, I would rather you had sent her away!'

Gil buttoned his coat, thinking rapidly. Yesterday, after his disastrous visit to Kirkster House, he had arrived back at Sollom Hall with his thoughts in turmoil. Part of him wanted to warn Deb of the danger Warslow posed to her, but how could he? Why should she believe anything he told her after the way he had acted? At that point he had been tempted to call for brandy and to drink himself into oblivion. Instead he had set the household by the ears, ordering everything to be packed up ready to leave the house first thing in the morning.

Viscount Gilmorton could have driven away and left his man of business to order everything, but Gil had discovered that it was not so easy for a mere Mr Victor to give up a property. There were accounts in Fallbridge to be settled in person and servants to be paid off. Thus it was that it was nearly noon and he had not yet quit the hall.

'You will have to see her, my lord.'

Gil glared at him, about to damn his impudence, but Harris met his eyes with a challenge in his own.

He said, 'It is the least you can do.'

He was right and Gil knew it. He said now, 'I would take that from no one but you, John.'

'Aye, my lord.'

'You warned me no good would come of my plan. I suppose now you will say you told me so.'

A rare smile glimmered in the valet's eyes.

'Nay, my lord, I ain't one to rub salt into a wound.'

Gil sucked in a breath, mentally squaring his shoulders for the meeting to come, then, with a nod to his man, he strode out of the room.

She was waiting for him in the little parlour where not so long ago he had welcomed her with wine and cakes. Now she was gazing out of the window at the travelling carriage that was being loaded with his trunks and bags. She did not turn as he entered and for a moment he allowed his eyes to dwell on her, trying to store in his memory how well her riding habit fitted across her shoulders and the way its mannish tailoring accentuated the dainty figure he knew lay beneath the layers of cloth. Resolutely he turned his mind away from those hidden delights.

He said roughly, 'Are you not afraid to be alone with me, Miss Meltham?'

She came away from the window and guilt cut through him when he saw how pale she looked. But she answered him calmly.

'You have done your worst with me.' She waved a hand towards the window. 'You are leaving.'

'Yes. There is nothing for me to stay for.'

'Because you have succeeded in your plans,' she suggested bitterly.

'On the contrary. I have failed, damnably.'

Her chin went up. 'What, because I am not left pining for *Mr Victor*, believing he had acted oh-so-nobly and was leaving me for my own good?'

'No, that is not it at all!'

He clamped his jaw shut upon the impulsive words that came to his tongue. He could not even say he had not meant to hurt her, for that had been precisely his intention in coming to Fallbridge. To ruin her. He moved back towards the door.

'I think it is best that you should go, Miss Meltham. It will serve no purpose to prolong this interview.'

She did not move.

'Yesterday, when Sir Sydney recognised you, you said things were not as they appeared.'

'That is true.'

'Then explain it to me, if you please.'

She gazed at him, a faint hint of hope in her eyes. The guilt sliced deeper.

'No.' He shook his head. 'I have acted very wrongly by you, madam, that is all you need to know.'

'Yesterday you wanted to tell me.'

'Yesterday I was not thinking rationally. There is nothing more to be said.'

'On the contrary, there is a great deal more to say.' Her hand went to her shoulder, a painful reminder to Gil of what she had already suffered. 'Will you tell me that what we did, here in this house, that what we shared, meant nothing to you?' When he did not reply, she came closer, pressing her bunched fist over her heart. 'I feel it, *here*. I thought it was the same for you. Can you deny it?'

She was so close he could smell the summery fragrance of her, a heady mixture of herbs and flowers that summoned up images of goodness and innocence. It also brought back the memory of how he had taken that innocence away from her. Somehow Gil managed to stop himself reaching out for her. He dragged his eyes away and moved towards the window.

'For heaven's sake, go home, Deborah. This is doing neither of us any good!'

He stared out at the view, seeing nothing, and held his breath, willing her to leave him. Instead he heard the whisper of skirts as she sat down.

'I will not go until you have told me everything.'

He swung around. She was perched on the edge of

one of the chairs beside the empty fireplace, hands clasped around the riding crop that rested across her knees. Her white knuckles belied the calm tone of her voice.

'Do not ask me, Deborah,' he begged her. 'I am trying to save you more pain.'

A shadow flickered across her face.

'Do you think it will be better for me to spend a lifetime imagining what it is that I have done to warrant this treatment?'

Her eyes, dark and troubled, were fixed on him, waiting for him to speak. Gil raked a hand through his hair, exhaling a long, hissing breath, then he reached into his coat and pulled out a gold locket. For months he had worn it around his neck, next to his skin, but he had removed it the night he had planned to seduce her. Since then he had not been able to wear it. He opened the catch and handed the locket to her.

'The two likenesses you see there are of my sister and brother. Kitty was fifteen, my brother Robin two years older when that was painted for me two years ago. It was a birthday present, I was on leave for a month prior to sailing for North America that June with my regiment and I was very glad to have it.'

Deborah stared at the tiny portraits. They were clearly the work of a master and the family likeness was strong. She wanted to comment, to tell him how handsome they were, but some instinct prevented her. Silently she handed it back. He looked at the pictures for a moment, then carefully closed the locket and put it back into his coat.

'It was the last time I saw either of them.'

Deb looked up quickly, but he had turned away from her.

'That November Kitty went missing from her school, a select seminary in a village near the port of Liverpool. Knowing I would be frantic with worry, but an ocean away and unable to help, Mama and Robin decided that I should not be told immediately. They thought she had gone to Gretna and they fully expected everything to be resolved before I returned. They thought the couple would turn up, married, and although it might not be the match we had hoped for, Mama would have accepted it and made the best of it.'

He stopped and Deb waited, knowing from the pain in his face that something dreadful was to come.

'Kitty *was* found eventually, the following April. She was in Liverpool. She was with child and had been abandoned by her lover. Robin went immediately to fetch her home, but Kitty was too ashamed of what she had done. She slipped away from him and threw herself in the river.'

Deb put up her hands to cover her mouth and stifle a small cry of horror. Gil was staring at nothing in particular, reliving the past as he continued to speak.

'However, before she did so, she told Robin everything. How she had been on an excursion to the local village with a party of her school friends and a fashionable gentleman—nay, a lord—had seen her. He contrived a meeting and then courted her in secret. She said he was charming, handsome and she fell in love with him. One dark night he spirited her away from the school. She agreed to elope with him, because he promised to marry her.

'Needless to say, the promise was never kept. He

set her up in rooms in Liverpool, but when he discovered she was carrying his child he left her, abandoned her without a word, and without a penny. She wrote to my mother, begging that she might come home, but by the time her brother reached her she was in such a pit of despair that nothing he could say could persuade her that her life was still worth living. Robin convinced them to record her death as accidental so he was able to bring her body home for burial in the family vault. However, as soon as the funeral was over, he went in search of the wretch who had destroyed his beloved sister.'

With an increasing sense of dread Deborah watched Gil pace the room. As his frown deepened the scar on his face grew whiter and more ragged, a vivid expression of his torment.

'Of all this I knew nothing,' he went on. 'My mother wrote to me, when Kitty was first discovered, and then again when she—when she drowned herself, but Bonaparte was on the loose again by then and we had already set sail for the Netherlands to join Wellington. By the time her letters reached me, Waterloo was over. I quit the army as soon as I could and headed home, but it was already too late. Robin had met with the scoundrel and been killed.' His lip curled. 'My brother was barely eighteen years old. No honourable man would accept a challenge from a boy, but this man did. He killed him.'

He stopped and stared down at her, his grey eyes dark and hard as slate.

'And the name of this "gentleman", this villain?' he bit out. 'Your brother Randolph, Miss Meltham.'

* * *

'No.' The room began to swim. Deb closed her eyes, fighting back the faintness and nausea that threatened her. 'Randolph would never do such a thing,' she whispered. 'There must be some mistake.'

'Do you think I did not make sure of my facts before I embarked upon this campaign?' he threw at her. 'I went to Kitty's school, spoke to the teachers and to her friends there. Those who had seen him described to me the handsome, fair-haired, fashionable gentleman who was courting my sister. There can be no doubt it was your brother, madam, and one or two of Kitty's closest friends even knew his name.

'But I did not leave it there. I went to the lodgings where Kitty and her lover had stayed. I saw the rent book, the rooms taken in the name of Lord Kirkster. The rogue made no attempt to cover his tracks. It was not difficult for Robin to find the family home in Duke Street and to challenge Kirkster to a duel. Believe me, madam, if I had been in England it is not *my* brother who would now be lying in his grave.'

'B-but duelling is illegal. To kill a man in a duel is murder. If all you say is true, why did you not inform the authorities and bring my brother to trial?'

'I have seen the way the law works in these matters, madam. By the time your brother had wheeled out his cronies to attest his good character, do you think any jury would convict him of murder? It would be manslaughter at best and the judge would let him off with a small fine and a few months in gaol. That was too small a price for him to pay. I decided he must suffer, as my family has suffered.'

Looking up into his hard, uncompromising face, Deb read murder in his eyes and she shivered.

'So that is why you came to Fallbridge,' she whispered. 'To be revenged upon my brother by seducing me.'

His lip curled.

'Exactly, Miss Meltham. Precisely.'

'Oh, Gil,' she whispered, staring at him with a mixture of horror and sadness. He looked away, shaking his head.

'It was a plan made in the white-hot heat of grief,' he told her. 'It made perfect sense, when I planned it all, but then I came here and met you.' He rubbed a hand across his eyes. 'If there is one thing I regret deeply, it is embroiling you in this.'

'And yet you still went through with it. You still took your revenge.'

'No!' His head went up. 'Believe me, Deborah, that is not how it was. I had decided to give it all up, to send you away, but then, when you disclosed your scars, I could not do it—'

She interrupted him with a cry.

'So you took me out of *pity.*' She wrapped her arms across her body, her right hand clasping the damaged shoulder. The pain she had felt then was nothing to the searing agony that was ripping through her at his revelation. 'To think you liked me, desired me enough to seduce me was bad enough, but now you tell me it was done out of compassion—dear heaven, that makes it even worse!'

'No! No, Deborah, you misunderstand! I—'

'Oh, do not try to scramble out of this mire, my

lord. There is nothing you can say now that would not make me despise you even more.'

She hunched in her chair, head bowed. She felt like a wounded animal, curling up against the pain. She knew he was watching her, could hear his breath, ragged and uneven.

'You wanted to know why I came to Fallbridge, I have told you,' he said at last, his voice low. 'It does not excuse what I have done, it was wrong of me and I am more sorry for it than you will ever know. It is small consolation, but no word of what happened between us will ever come from me. Your reputation at least is safe. Only my coachman and valet know what happened here and they will say nothing. If I could make reparation for the damage I have done to you, madam, I would, but you can see for yourself, it is impossible.'

'Quite impossible.'

Deborah pushed herself out of the chair, wondering if her legs would support her. They did, but she felt very unsteady as she crossed to the door. With her fingers on the handle she turned back.

'So,' she said quietly, 'we have both exposed our scars now, have we not? But yours, I think, are the more to be *pitied*.'

Gil stood with his head bowed, listening to the door closing behind her, the soft thud of footsteps in the hall, then the clatter of hoofbeats on the drive as she cantered away. Her words and the anguish he had seen in her face cut him to the core. He wanted to go after her, to beg her forgiveness, but the spectre of his dead sister and brother stood between them.

He sank down on a chair and dropped his head in

his hands. The pain was almost physical, like a body-blow. What he felt for Deborah Meltham was stronger than anything he had ever experienced before. Family ties, honour, even life itself were all eclipsed by it. An uncomfortable suspicion began to take root in his mind and he fought against it. This distress was merely his conscience, a dislike of breaking his own moral code of protecting civilians. It could not be love.

He did not believe in love.

Gil closed his eyes and was transported back to a dinner he had shared with fellow officers, shortly after Waterloo. Everyone was in high spirits, an antidote to the sheer horror of the bloody battle. Some of the men were looking forward to getting back to their wives.

'And you, Gilmorton. Who is waiting at home for you?'

'My family. My mother, sister and brother.'

'No little woman ready to welcome you into her arms?' asked one.

'Into her bed!' quipped another.

'No, and I have never seen the need to add another female to those who already worry about me.'

'Can't stop 'em, old boy,' remarked a dashing cavalry officer, prompting a burst of laughter around the table.

'Aye, Donegal's bed is never empty,' cried Gil's neighbour. 'He is always falling in love.'

'Love is merely a distraction,' Gil replied, reaching for the decanter.

'No, no, old boy it's what makes everything worthwhile,' argued Major Donegal, shaking his head.

'The Viscount is not to be persuaded,' laughed Gil's colonel. 'He does not believe in love.'

'Not the sort that you are describing,' Gil replied. 'Naturally I love my family, that is one's duty.'

'Duty!' Major Donegal was looking at him almost pityingly. 'I am not talking about *duty*, man, I am talking about passion. To see the glow in a woman's eyes and know she thinks you are the only thing in the world that matters—that is priceless.'

Gil's smile in response to that had been perfunctory. Let the others say what they would, he did not believe it. He had never expected to survive his years of soldiering and had always kept his mind fixed upon his duties. What he *had* experienced in those years—the brutal killing, the loss of friends—had taught him to keep his feelings shut down. As for women, they suffered worst of all. They lost their menfolk and sometimes their children, and many suffered horribly at the hands of marauding soldiers. It was the nature of war. He accepted it and did what he could to prevent innocents suffering, but he reserved all his affection for Mama, Robin and Kitty, waiting safely at home.

It was the very morning after that dinner that he received the letters from his mother and the news that only grief awaited him at home.

So, no. He did not, *would* not, allow himself to love anyone. Gil shook off the memories and sat up, dragging in a breath, drawing on his years of military service to give him strength. He was a soldier and would not give in to this. What he felt for Deborah Meltham was nothing more than a natural sympathy for a woman he had wronged. He had not acted honourably by her and he must live with the guilt of it.

Gil strode out of the room, barking out his orders. He would ride to Gilmorton Hall rather than sit in his carriage and allow his thoughts to prey upon him. And what of Deborah Meltham? Gil told himself it was not his concern. Deborah had her brother to protect her. A brother she refused to believe was as depraved as Warslow himself.

'Bah. It is not your concern!' he repeated, jamming his hat on his head and hurrying out of the house. 'She does not need you. She told you herself that she despises you. Better to leave the whole damn lot of them to their fate.'

The revelations at Sollom Hall had shocked Deborah and she rode back to Kirkster House in a daze, a welter of emotions boiling inside her. Her chest felt so tight that she could hardly breathe. She could not deny that Gil had used her in a most callous and calculating way, yet she could not forget his kindness, the night she had dined alone with him. He had been so gentle and caring and he had made her feel beautiful. Now she knew he had acted out of pity.

A wave of nausea swept over her at the thought that it had all been a sham and she was obliged to draw rein and slow her horse to a walk, fearing that she might lose her balance. But whatever Gil's intentions when he had taken her to his bed, her responses had been real. No one could deny her that.

Anger choked her again. Anger with Gil for what he had done and with herself for being so eager to fall into his arms. And yet...she could never forgive him, but she could understand something of his reasoning. His sister had been tricked into an elopement, just as Deb had been, but Kitty had suffered far worse than a scalded shoulder. Not only that, her younger brother had died trying to protect her. Gil believed Randolph was responsible and the death of two beloved siblings was enough to drive even the best of men to seek revenge.

When Deb reached Kirkster House her emotions were still in turmoil. She did not doubt Gil had done his best to discover the truth before he embarked upon his vengeance, but she could not believe what he had told her. Randolph was wild, yes, and under the influence of drink or laudanum he might act rashly, but he was not a cruel man and she was sure he would not deliberately set out to trap an innocent young girl. No more would he leave her to her fate. Something was wrong, if only she could work it out. Deborah slipped quickly into the house and up the stairs to the seclusion of her room, where she hoped a period of quiet reflection would help to settle the confusion in her mind.

Yet as she closed and locked her bedroom door she knew that there was no confusion about one point at least. Any connection between herself and the man she now knew to be Lord Gilmorton was at an end.

By the time Gil reached his family home his horse was in a lather, but even riding at breakneck speed, he could not outrun the demons at his heels. He left his exhausted horse at the stables and went into the house. He was thankful to learn that the Viscountess was in her room, for he could not face her questions tonight and besides, there was a letter he must write, immediately. It was one thing to say he would leave Deborah to her fate, but Gil hated to think of her alone and defenceless, with Warslow circling around like a vulture, waiting to strike.

The letter was soon penned, a civil note on the fine paper that bore his family crest, assuring Miss Meltham that if ever she thought herself in danger, if ever she stood in need of his help or assistance, he would do his utmost to serve her. The letter was addressed and sent off in haste.

The reply came express two days later, but when he broke the seal and unfolded the paper, his own missive tumbled out, torn into tiny fragments.

Deborah gazed out through the rain-streaked windows of the drawing room. Since her last interview with the Viscount all signs of approaching summer had disappeared, replaced by rain and blustery winds. It was as if the weather was reflecting her low spirits. Her only relief during the past seven days had been in tearing up Gil's letter and returning it to him. She had contemplated penning an angry response, but in the end she had decided a dignified silence would serve her better, although it did nothing to assuage the unremitting gloom that had settled around her like a damp cloak.

It did not help that life at Kirkster House was becoming increasingly bleak. All the improvement in Randolph's health and mood that she had seen over the past few months had been undone by the constant companionship of Sir Sydney Warslow. Deborah knew that her influence with her brother had waned to dangerously low levels, a fact that had been brought home to her earlier that day, when Ran had come down to breakfast and announced that they were removing to London.

'London!' She had almost dropped her coffee cup. 'But what is there for us in town?'

'Amusement,' he retorted, handing his ale glass to Speke to refill it. 'Excitement, Deborah, entertainment. I am bored to death in Fallbridge.'

They were alone in the breakfast room, Sir Sydney not yet having made an appearance, so she felt at liberty to speak freely.

'But, Ran, you know your health will not stand such a journey. Besides, you gave me your word—'

He waved aside her protests. 'I am stronger than you think, Deb. Warslow has agreed to accompany us and he will make all the arrangements, so you need not trouble yourself over anything.'

If anything was needed to put Deb against the scheme it was that. She pleaded with her brother, but he was deaf to it all.

'There is no point in arguing, I am decided. I have contacted the land agent to tell him this house is to be let and Warslow knows of a snug little property in town that we may rent and be very comfortable there.'

He accepted his refreshed glass from the butler and eyed her over the top of it.

'No! Ran, you cannot do this!'

'I have done it,' he replied sulkily. 'We leave in a sennight, as soon as the papers are signed.'

'This is Sir Sydney's doing,' she said. 'Randolph, listen to me. This is not wise—'

'Wise be damned!' His fist came down on the table, making the cups rattle in their saucers. 'I am master in this house, Deb, and it is about time you realised it.' He flushed when he saw the horrified look on her face and as he got up to leave the room he dropped a hand on her shoulder. 'I can afford a small allowance for you, Deb. If you want to hire lodgings in Fallbridge and remain here, then you are free to do so. In fact, it would be safer for you to do so.'

'Safer?' She looked up at him. 'What do you mean by that?'

He shook his head. 'I cannot say more, Deb, I am in too deep, but you—you should save yourself, while you can.'

He left her then, but her fears for the future grew ten-fold.

Deb had spent the day thinking about it but now, as the rain pattered against the glass and the familiar landscape faded in the dusk, she knew that she could not leave Randolph, not while there was the slightest chance of saving him from near certain destruction.

She heard the door open and turned quickly, thinking it would be the footman come to light the candles, but it was Sir Sydney Warslow.

'Ah, Miss Meltham. Do we dine alone tonight, perhaps?'

The hopeful note in his voice was not lost on Deb and it was all she could do not to shudder.

'Not at all. My brother will be here at any moment.' She spoke calmly, knowing that Speke and Joseph Miller would make sure Ran would join them very soon. The staff had been with the family since her father's time and she knew there was some tacit understanding amongst them that she should not be left alone with Sir Sydney for any length of time.

It would be different in London. Ran had informed her that all the staff at Kirkster House, except Miller and her personal maid, would remain to serve the new tenants, so the servants in London would be strangers, but she would face that hurdle when she came to it. Perhaps she would begin secreting one or two hatpins in her hair, in case Sir Sydney's attentions should become too persistent. He was watching her now, his smile almost predatory, and she coldly turned her shoulder to him.

'I trust you are not uncomfortable in my company, Miss Meltham.'

She was obliged to face him, but she said coolly, 'No, of course not.'

He came closer. 'I had hoped that by now we might be…friends.'

Deb stood her ground, although it was not easy. She would not give way to this man or show him how much she disliked him.

'I have no idea what you mean,' she said now. 'You are my brother's guest and will be treated as such.'

'Always so cold. Or perhaps you are merely shy. Because of your…'

Her brows went up. 'Because of what?'

'Your previous experience of, ah, gentlemen.' He moved a step closer, saying softly, 'Your brother has told me of your little *accident*. I assure you it makes no difference to me. In fact, I am quite eager to see it.' Before she knew what he was about, his fingers slipped beneath the muslin at her neck.

With a cry of outrage, she slapped his hand away and stepped back. 'If you touch me again, I shall have Randolph throw you out of the house!'

He laughed at that. 'That drunken sot!'

She stared at him. 'You dare to speak of him like that? He is your host.'

'Yes, I dare.' As the door opened he leaned closer to hiss at her, 'How long do you think it will be, madam, before your influence with him is nought?'

Randolph came in, followed by the footman who proceeded to light the candles around the room. Deborah watched in silent indignation as Sir Sydney stepped away and greeted her brother cordially, as if he had said nothing amiss.

Deb made up her mind to tell Randolph, but by the time the servant had withdrawn she had had an opportunity to gauge her brother's mood. His eyes were over-bright and his cheeks flushed. With a sinking heart she realised that if she forced a confrontation at this moment, she could not be sure that he would support her.

And if the situation was bleak here, in her family home, how much worse would it be in London? She needed help, but who could she turn to? Her friends in Fallbridge were good, honest people. If she told them her fears, they would urge her to inform the authorities, but Ran's words that he was in too deep convinced her that any recourse to law would end with his arrest. She needed someone who was prepared to work outside the law. Someone powerful and ruthless enough to stand up to Sir Sydney and remove him as a threat. By the time dinner was ended Deborah had come to a decision.

Chapter Ten

'Gilmorton!'

Gil started. 'I beg your pardon, Mama. Did you say something?'

The Viscountess looked at him with exasperated affection. 'My love, I have been addressing you for the past ten minutes. I might as well have asked these citrus trees to move themselves.'

Gil begged pardon again and gave her a rueful smile. 'I came into the orangery to help you arrange the pots and I have done nothing. Forgive me, my thoughts have been otherwise. What is it you said to me?'

She shook her head at him. 'Your thoughts have been otherwise since you came home a week ago.' She looked suddenly serious. 'You have said nothing about where you have been, save that you did not achieve your purpose of punishing Lord Kirkster.'

'Mama—'

'No, Gil, let me finish. I wanted to tell you that I am...' she paused, choosing her words carefully '... I am *relieved* your plan did not succeed. Robin and

Kitty are gone and nothing can change that. The grief of it will be with us for ever. I have accepted that and I would like to think that you have, too, and that you can now get on with your life. I am very glad to think you are no longer seeking vengeance. It will do you no good, my love, and there has been too much damage done already.'

'Even more than you know,' he muttered, so quietly that his words were lost as a sudden gust of wind rattled the door of the orangery.

The Viscountess was looking at him with a mixture of love and concern. She said softly, 'You were a soldier for so long, my son, that I am sure violence is not unknown to you, but you are a good man and I would not have you do anything dishonourable, even in the name of justice.'

Too late for that.

He looked away. She would be distressed beyond measure if she knew just how dishonourably he had acted. But that was his burden and he must bear it alone. He had at last faced up to the fact that his thirst for vengeance had been born out of grief and guilt that he had not been able to protect his family. And now the thought of how he had wronged Deborah Meltham was a constant pain, like a knife in his heart.

He heard his mother sigh and when he looked back she was tending one of the small potted citrus trees. She was still in full mourning, with a white linen apron tied over the gown to protect the black crepe while she was in the garden. The black-lace cap she wore accentuated the increasing amount of grey in her dark hair, but there was a serenity about her, a tranquillity that Gil envied. He sat down on a stone bench and watched her moving between the plants, nipping off an errant shoot or a dead leaf and tidying the soil in each pot.

'How do you cope, Mama?' The question burst from him. 'How can you be so calm with all you have had to bear?'

She straightened and looked at him for a moment, then she put down her trowel and came to sit beside him.

'You mean how do I manage to live without Kitty and Robin?'

'Yes. I cannot believe you do not still feel their loss.'

'Of course. I feel it terribly.'

'I beg your pardon. I did not mean to imply otherwise, it is just—' He raked one hand through his hair, sighing. 'When I came home and learned of what had happened in my absence I was consumed by grief. And rage, not least with myself, that I had not been here to protect them. I thought I had failed them in life, so I must try to make amends. I could think of nothing else and was desperate for action.'

'For revenge, you mean.'

A sigh escaped him.

'Yes,' he admitted, 'I wanted to exact retribution. I thought it would ease the pain.'

'My grief was assuaged, a little, with tears, Gil, and believe me I cried enough of them. But I could not let the loss of Kitty and Robin defeat me, that would only have added to the tragedy. Gilmorton needed me. The estate, the people, I could not leave everything to Saunders, even though he is a very good steward and knows our business as well as anyone. I have a duty to the family and in performing that duty I find some small consolation.' She squeezed his fingers. 'And it should be your duty too, Gil. This is your inheritance.'

'You never agreed with my plan for revenge, did you, Mama?'

'No, my son, you will recall I begged you not to go. I was afraid for your safety, but even more than that, I was afraid it would diminish you.' Her fingers clung to his. 'Promise me, Gil,' she said urgently. 'Give me your word you have relinquished this thirst for vengeance. It will not bring Kitty or Robin back, you know.'

She stopped there, but Gil saw the concern in her eyes, the worry that she might lose him, too. Well, he could make her that promise. Kirkster was so far abandoned to his addictions he was unlikely to live much longer and, in any event, having met the man, Gil doubted he was capable of anything like penitence now. Certainly nothing like the remorse Gil was feeling for his treatment of Deborah.

'You have my word, Mama. The past cannot be changed.' He drew in a breath, aware of a new resolution within him. 'I should look to the future. There is more than enough work here to occupy me.'

She raised her hand and cupped his cheek, giving him a misty smile. 'Gilmorton needs its master and I need my son.'

Catching her hand, he pulled it to his mouth and pressed a kiss on to the palm.

'Then you shall have him. There will be no more talk of revenge, Mama, I promise you. Now, where did you want me to put this lemon tree?'

Gil returned to the house an hour later, once the orangery was organised to his mother's satisfaction.

He entered by the garden hall and was already on the stairs when the butler came hurrying towards him.

'I beg your pardon, my lord, but there's a lady to see you.'

Gil halted, hope surging through him. 'A lady?'

'Yes, my lord. Veiled, my lord, and she wouldn't give her name, but she arrived in her own carriage.'

Gil could see the speculation rife in the older man's eyes, but not by the flicker of an eyelid did he show his own emotion.

'Thank you, Culver. Show her into the morning room, if you please, and tell her I will be down directly.'

He took the stairs two at a time and almost ran to his room, where he did nothing more than wash the earth from his hands and check in the mirror that his clothes were not dusty before hurrying back to the morning room.

Deborah was waiting for him. He had thought never to see her again; he had tried to tell himself he must forget all about her, but he could not ignore the powerful kick of attraction he felt at the sight of her. A thick travelling cloak hung around her shoulders, but beneath it she was dressed soberly in a plain cambric gown with a russet-coloured spencer and matching bonnet and half-boots. She had put back her veil and when she turned he could see the dark smudges beneath her troubled eyes. The blade in his heart twisted still further to think that any part of her current anxiety could be laid at his door.

She said without preamble, 'You said, if I needed help, I might come to you.'

His heart lifted to think that she had read his note

before she tore it up. But she looked as if she might bolt at any moment, so he must tread carefully. She allowed him to take her cloak and she untied the ribbons of her bonnet with fingers that were not quite steady. When he had laid her bonnet and cloak aside, he invited her to sit down. Her hair, he noticed, was once more dressed close around her head, but all he could think of was the way he had seen it fall in luxurious waves over her naked shoulders, the silky feel of it between his fingers. Driving those thoughts away, he cleared his throat.

'Would you like a little refreshment?'

'No, nothing, thank you.' She sank down on to the sofa, sitting on the edge of it, very stiff and upright. 'I had coffee at the Gilmorton Arms before coming here. I stopped there to bespeak a room. I must not be long; my maid is waiting for me in the chaise.'

Silently Gil lowered himself into a chair. The message was very clear: she wanted his help but she was not about to throw herself on his mercy.

Or into his arms.

Part of him wished she would do just that. He longed to hold her again, to kiss her and keep her with him, but he knew that would be disastrous. He dared not lower his guard where Deborah Meltham was concerned. Despite his resolve to give up any thoughts of revenge she was still Kirkster's sister. To let her get too close would make him vulnerable. Not only that, but a scandal would ruin her and he knew now her welfare was paramount with him. He must appear composed, indifferent.

'So how may I help you?'

Gil winced at the cold politeness of his words. Deb shifted a little.

'First, there are things I must tell you. About my brother.' He stiffened and she went on quickly, 'I have thought a great deal about what you said of your sister's seduction. I told you I could not believe Randolph capable of such villainy. This was not merely because I did not *want* to think my brother could act in such a way.' She twisted her hands together in her lap. 'Yes, Randolph was living in Duke Street when your sister was at school in that nearby village, but he was not well. And, whatever else he may have done, I *know* he could not have killed your brother. You see, I fetched him away from Duke Street last summer, to live with me at Fallbridge. For several weeks prior to that he had not left the house. And if he did not fight a duel, then neither do I think he seduced your sister.'

She glanced at him and a faint colour washed her cheeks.

'You look sceptical, my lord. Perhaps you think I would lie to protect my brother, but there is more you do not know. My brother has an addictive nature: gambling, drink. Laudanum.'

He interrupted her. 'You are mistaken. Miss Meltham. I had already realised that.'

Her small hand fluttered, as if to deflect a blow.

She said quietly, 'Ran was just eighteen when our father died. We were placed in the guardianship of an uncle, who paid very little heed to us. Our mother was ill, so I remained at Fallbridge to look after her and Ran joined us whenever he came down from Oxford for the vacation. When Ran attained his majority and control of his fortune he opened up the family house in Liverpool. He refused my suggestion that I should keep house for him and insisted I remain at Fallbridge. I knew he had been a little wild at Oxford, but I did not think it was anything more than the high spirits of most young men and, although I worried about how he was living in Liverpool, I did not then know the extent of his addictions. Whenever I saw him he was always on his best behaviour. Only later did I realise this was because I always gave him notice of my visits.

'Then, in the spring of last year I arrived and found him bedridden. It was then that I learned the truth from Ran's valet, who is devoted to his master. I discovered that he had so-called friends who encouraged him in all his vices. I wanted Ran to quit Liverpool then, but he would not do so, despite my pleading. I was sure his acquaintances were encouraging him in his dissolute ways, but nothing I could say would persuade him to drop them. But I did not give up. I fetched our own doctor to tend him and I made more frequent visits to Liverpool. However, it was not until May that Randolph could be persuaded to come home with me to Fallbridge.' She paused, raising her eyes to look at him. 'He was by then very ill, unable to hold a pistol, let alone fire one. Whatever else he has done, my lord, I am convinced he did not kill your brother.'

Gil knew she was waiting for a response but he said nothing. The proof he had collected told a different story, but he would not contradict her. Not yet. With a tiny nod she looked down at her hands again.

'I nursed him back to health and he promised me he would give up his errant ways, which he has always assured me hurt no one but himself.'

'And you, madam.'

She gave a twisted little smile.

'Yes. And me. I have always believed that Ran would not deliberately cause anyone harm, but your accusations made me wonder.' Another pause. Gil realised how difficult it was for her to tell him this, to reveal so much about her beloved brother. 'Earlier this week I called upon Dr Reedley. He has known Randolph since he was a child and after I discovered the true state of Ran's health he came with me to Liverpool on several occasions, so he is well acquainted with my brother's illness. I asked him about the possibility of—'

She broke off. Gil watched her take another breath to steady herself, then she raised her head and met his eyes.

'In the doctor's opinion, Ran was so riddled with strong drink and laudanum last year that he would not have been capable of organising an elopement and he was certainly not able to father a child.'

'But you cannot be sure of that,' he threw back at her. 'You were not living with him on a daily basis when this courtship took place. You cannot know with any certainty how incapacitated he might have been. Do you not think I did not ask these questions of my own doctor, once I realised the extent of your brother's dissipation?'

Her chin went up. 'You are right, of course, I cannot be certain, but you will allow me to know something of my own brother, my lord!'

Gil frowned.

'Are you asking me to believe that someone impersonated your brother, Miss Meltham? That some scoundrel was brazen enough to perpetrate these acts in his name?'

'Yes,' she said, her gaze steady and unflinching. 'Yes, I am.'

Gil pushed himself out of his chair and went over to the window, staring out, but not seeing the pleasant vista it offered. He wanted to believe her, but he could not. Confound it, did she think he had entered lightly into his plan for revenge? He had made exhaustive enquiries and there had been more than enough evidence to convince him that Kirkster had seduced his sister and killed his brother.

'Your silence tells me you think I am saying this merely to protect Randolph.' Her voice was low and not quite steady and Gil felt a flash of something that might well have been envy.

'I know how fond you are of your brother, madam. Would you deny that you would do anything to protect him?'

'I am not blind to his faults. He is not immune to female charms and he might flirt with a pretty woman, but I do not think him so dissolute that he would seduce an innocent maid. And he has been so ill these past two years that I do not believe he was capable of a sustained courtship.' She leaned forward, saying earnestly, 'I was present when Sir Sydney disclosed your identity to Randolph. He showed no sign of recognition. He could not have been so unconcerned, had he been acquainted with your sister.'

Gil shook his head impatiently. 'You do not need to justify your brother's actions to me. It makes no odds now. I have put the past behind me and no longer seek revenge for the wrongs done to my family. No, madam, if you need help, my offer is unconditional.' He added in a low voice, 'It is the least I can do, after—'

She jumped up. 'This has nothing to do with what happened between us,' she said coldly. 'I do not ask your help as some sort of, of *atonement* for what you did to me.' She turned away from him. 'I am perfectly willing to take my share of responsibility for what occurred.'

Gil saw her hand go to her cheek, as if to brush away a stray tear. He clenched his fists, keeping his arms at his sides as he waited for her to compose herself and speak again.

'I came here because I know of no one else who can help me. Who can help Ran. I believe—I am sure—my brother is in the power of someone who has embroiled him in a dangerous scheme. I dare not go to the magistrate because I am very much afraid that Ran would be arrested as a felon.'

'And you think this *someone* is also responsible for my sister's seduction?'

'Yes. I thought knowing that might make you more inclined to help me. I thought you might want him arrested and tried for his crimes. All I ask is that you spare my brother and let him go free. If that is possible.'

Deb clasped her hands together, the knuckles gleaming white as the silence continued. Only the direst necessity had brought her to Gilmorton Hall. For herself, she would rather suffer any fate than debase herself before this man. But she was doing this for Randolph. Gil's note had said he would help her, but his lack of response now showed otherwise. It was a lie, a sham, like all the rest. And now by her confession she had quite possibly earned Gil's contempt as well as placed Ran in even more danger.

'I should not have come,' she muttered, hurrying towards the door. 'It was foolish of me to think—'

'No.' Even as she grasped the handle he was behind her, catching at her shoulders. 'Stay,' he said gently. 'Stay and tell me everything.'

She froze, her body refusing to shake off his hands. Her spine tingled, he was standing so close she could even smell him, the enticing mixture of spices and leather that she remembered so vividly. But now there was something else, the fresh clean scent of lemons. It filled her head, making her dizzy and momentarily blocking all coherent thought.

'Come.' He turned her away from the door. 'Sit down and talk to me. I will help you if I can.'

Deb allowed him to take her back to the sofa and push her down upon the richly brocaded seat. He drew a chair close and sat down facing her.

'Tell me,' he said. 'Tell me who you think would be villain enough to entangle your brother in criminal schemes and use his name to cover his mischief?'

'You are acquainted with him. Sir Sydney Warslow. He was a frequent guest at my brother's house in Duke Street and the main reason I did not take up residence there when I discovered how ill Ran was. I knew I would have to take Ran away to Fallbridge. I thought there he would be safe from Sir Sydney, but it seems I was wrong. He is an evil man and he is destroying my brother, my lord, encouraging him to drink to excess and providing him with the laudanum he craves.

I think he is more than capable of using my brother's name for his own ends.'

She glanced up. Gil was frowning, his gaze abstracted.

'I agree with you,' he said at last. 'Warslow is a cunning devil and the sort of coward who would hide behind another's name. He is also a crack shot and would not cavil at taking up a challenge from a mere boy. He has a reputation for killing his man.

'He was a soldier when I met him,' he went on, reading the question in her eyes. 'Warslow was a scoundrel then and it was no loss to the army when he inherited the baronetcy a few years ago and sold out.' He said abruptly, 'Is he still a guest in your house?'

'My brother's house,' she corrected him. 'Yes, he is still there. I have begged Ran to dismiss him, but he refuses to do so. Or rather, he says he cannot do so. I believe Sir Sydney has some sort of hold over him.' She shivered and crossed her arms, as if she could in some way defend herself from her own thoughts. 'I am terribly afraid that Sir Sydney Warslow is dragging my brother to hell with him. He has persuaded Ran to take a house in London, for what purpose I do not know, but it cannot be for Randolph's benefit.'

Gil sat back and considered her words carefully. He had promised Mama he would not seek vengeance, but this was different. Deborah might suspect Warslow of seducing Kitty and killing Robin, but there was no proof and there was no denying that Deb would want to believe that. However, it was highly likely that Warslow was involved in something illegal and, if he could bring the fellow to justice and help Deborah in the process, then it might go some way to restoring his honour.

'Just what do you suspect?' When she hesitated, he added, 'Whatever you tell me will not go any further. You have my word.' It pained him that she looked so unsure and he said more roughly than he intended, 'If you want my help, madam, you will have to trust me.'

She blinked, those great green eyes reminding him of a wounded animal, and he realised then how desperate she must have been to come to him. He waited with as much patience as he could muster until she was ready to speak again and, when she did, he marvelled at how well she had collected herself.

'It was something my brother said, about Liverpool becoming unsafe for Warslow. That is how I managed to persuade Ran to come back to Fallbridge with me, because Sir Sydney was no longer in town. You can imagine my dismay when he turned up in Fallbridge. And then, the day after his arrival, I was told that a bad two-pound note had been discovered in the housekeeper's cashbox. It was a very good likeness and would easily have been missed without careful scrutiny, but when I looked into it, I learned that Sir Sydney's man had given Mrs Woodrow just such a note in exchange for coin to pay the postilions.' She shrugged. 'I have no proof, because there were other notes in the box, so it might have come from elsewhere, but Ran was very angry when I told him and I came upon him discussing it with Sir Sydney, and saying he would not have it—' She broke off, twisting her hands together. 'I am not privy to my brother's finances, but it has seemed to me over the past few years that his spending has been more lavish than the estate can afford. I believe there is very little of his fortune left. If, if he has turned to counterfeiting to pay his way…the punishment for such a crime is severe.'

'It is indeed, but I can well imagine Warslow might be mixed up in such a thing,' said Gil, considering everything she had told him. After a few moments' thought he nodded. 'Very well, I will make enquiries, but it may take weeks. In the meantime, it would be safer if you did not accompany your brother to London.'

'I have no choice. I must stay with my brother, to protect him.'

'But who is to protect *you*?'

Not you, said her look, more eloquently than any words.

She gave a little start when the ormolu clock on the mantelpiece chimed the hour and her lashes came down, screening her thoughts from him. She rose from the chair.

'While Sir Sydney has need of my brother he will not risk offending him by hurting me. Now, I must go.'

He made no attempt to detain her. She collected her hat and cloak and he accompanied her out to the waiting chaise.

'When do you leave for town?' he asked as he handed her into the carriage.

'At the end of the week. I do not know where we will be living. My brother tells me Sir Sydney has arranged it all.'

The idea of her being in Warslow's power chilled Gil. He did not like it one bit, but he knew that any protest would bring from Deborah a curt reminder that he had no right to dictate to her, so he merely nodded.

'Send word as soon as you know your direction, Miss Meltham. A message to Gilmorton Hall will find me, wherever I may be.'

'Thank you, my lord.'

She was in the carriage, but still clinging to his hand. For a heartbeat her clear green eyes stared into his without fear, without enmity, then the dark lashes swept down, gently she withdrew her fingers and sat back on the seat. Gil stepped away, the servant closed the door and the coachman whipped up his team.

Chapter Eleven

Deborah pressed her back against the squabs of the carriage and closed her eyes. It was an effort not to lean forward and peer out of the window, to see if Gil was still standing on the drive. It should not matter to her, after the way he had deceived her she was determined he would not hurt her again, but just seeing him had brought everything back with painful clarity. How they had talked together, laughed together. Lain together. How he had made her feel beautiful. Her insides liquefied just at the thought of his lips on her skin and it was useless to tell herself it had all been a lie. Whatever Gil's reasons for taking her to his bed, whether it had been for revenge or out of sympathy, he had made her feel more alive than ever before and the memory of the happy weeks they had shared provided a stark contrast to the living nightmare of her current situation.

Having shut her heart against Gil, all Deb's concern now was for her brother. He was the reason she had to come here today to beg for help. She felt exhausted, drained with the struggle to keep all her emotions in check, but it had been worth it, because Gil had agreed to help her. She believed him. With every fibre of her being she believed that Gil would do his utmost to save Randolph.

And Randolph was now her sole reason for living.

A week later, Deborah and her brother arrived in London, where the late spring weather was still distinctly unsettled. Their travelling chaise turned into Grafton Street at the end of a chill, wet day, but there was still sufficient light for Deborah to see that the street was lined with substantial mansions.

'Here we are,' said Ran as the coach came to a halt. 'Welcome to our new home, Sister.'

Deb stared at the impressive frontage with its stone pillars and a pediment surrounding the door. She put a hand on his arm as he was about to alight.

'Ran, surely this is far too expensive for us.'

Immediately his sunny mood vanished and he shook off her hand, saying curtly, 'That need not concern you. Come along!'

His reply did not reassure Deborah at all, and by the time she retired to her room that night, her anxiety was considerably increased.

They had brought only Ran's valet and her own maid with them from Lancashire, and although the servants were all perfectly polite, Deborah was not comfortable. She could not like Enfield, the butler, nor his wife, who was housekeeper. There was a coldness about them, and a wariness in their eyes, which she could not like.

'You are just being missish,' she told herself, thumping her pillow to try to make it more comfortable. 'They are London people and you are unaccustomed to their ways.'

But as the days went on, her uneasiness grew, especially after Sir Sydney joined them. He insisted he was merely a guest, but he seemed to be on excellent terms with the staff, and when Deb mentioned this to her brother at breakfast one morning, he shrugged it off with an impatient wave of a hand.

'Well of course, he saw to the hiring of them, after all.' He saw that Deb was not convinced and gave a huff of exasperation. 'Oh, come along, Deborah! You are feeling homesick for the north, that is what is wrong with you. Warslow thought you would be delighted with this house, being so near to Bond Street and the very best shops.'

Deborah said no more, but when she wrote to advise Gil of their direction she went out to post the letter herself, rather than giving it to a servant. She did not know if he would reply, but when three weeks had passed without word from him she began to suffer a twinge of doubt. Perhaps he had not meant what he said about helping her. She did not want to believe it, but it was increasingly difficult to ignore the insidious little voice in her head that told her she had been wrong before about the Viscount. Perhaps, now that she was no longer in his company, he had forgotten all about her.

Gil had been in Liverpool for two weeks and his enquiries about Sir Sydney Warslow had made little progress. He was again travelling as plain Mr Victor, having decided that a viscount asking questions would attract far too much attention, but even so he had learned nothing of import. He was reluctantly coming to the conclusion that Deborah's suspicions about Warslow were unfounded. Perhaps her affection for her brother had led her to imagine that the fellow was a villain. Whatever the truth might be, Gil decided there was nothing to be gained by remaining here any longer.

However, before leaving Liverpool he wanted to see Deborah's old family home. Despite the chill wind and an ominous blanket of low grey cloud covering the sky, Gil decided to walk to Duke Street.

It did not take him long and he soon reached a wide street lined with tall terraces, each doorway surrounded by an elegant portico. He located Meltham House and stepped across to the other side of the road to see it better. A thread of smoke rose from one of the chimneys, but the house looked closed up, with the shutters across the windows and the knocker removed. Gil regarded the building, trying to imagine it as the happy family home Deborah had described to him.

His valet had remarked that the young Lord Kirkster did not take his responsibilities seriously and Gil thought the house showed every evidence of this, with its faded paintwork and rusted railings. A wry, humourless smile twisted his lips. Who was he to criticise, when he had remained in the army and shirked his own family duties for years?

He re-crossed the road and stood, irresolute. He should go. There was nothing here for him. He was about to walk away when a homely-looking woman in a red cloak came bustling along the street and opened the gate to the area steps. She stopped, eyeing him with a mixture of curiosity and suspicion. He touched his hat to her.

'Good day to you, madam. Have I the right building? This is the house belonging to Lord Kirkster?'

'Aye, it is,' she said warily.

Gil smiled, glad she had approached from his right side, so his scar would not frighten her.

'I am a friend of the family.' This information did not appear to lessen the woman's suspicions and he continued in as friendly a manner as he could. 'That is, I am acquainted with Miss Deborah Meltham. My name is Victor, I met Miss Meltham in Fallbridge a few months ago.' He nodded towards the house. 'She told me she spent many happy times here as a child.'

The woman's frown lifted a little. 'Aye, that she did. This was a very happy house. In the old days.'

He could not help himself. He took a step closer.

'I wonder...' he shrank into his coat, as if to escape the biting wind and at that providential moment, fat drops of rain began to splash down '...could I step into the kitchen, until this shower passes?' He drew out his purse. 'I will, of course, pay you for your trouble.'

Her eyes widened, but after subjecting Gil to another searching look she gave a little nod and gestured to him to follow her down the steps. She opened the door into the basement kitchen. A quick glance showed him a clean and tidy room, at its centre a large well-scrubbed table. A cheerful fire burned in a grate, with a kettle hissing quietly over the flames and as they went in, a grey-haired man pushed himself out of a chair by the hearth.

'Mr Wallis, this gentleman wanted to shelter from

the rain,' said the woman, waving the old man back into his seat. 'He's a friend of Miss Deborah's.'

'Is that so?' said Mr Wallis slowly.

Gil removed his hat and smiled. 'It is indeed so. I was just passing and had a fancy to see Miss Meltham's old home. She has told me so much about it.'

'Well, you can't see upstairs,' said the old man. 'Everything's locked up. Me and the wife lives here to look after the place.'

'I perfectly understand,' said Gil, putting his hat and gloves upon the table and sitting down. 'But it is so cold and damp outside that I thought you might not mind if I took the opportunity to warm myself by your fire.'

He pulled a couple of coins from his purse and pushed them across the table. The woman's eyes widened as the silver glinted in the firelight and her manner softened perceptibly.

'P'rhaps you'd like tea, sir?' she asked him, smiling for the first time.

'I would indeed, madam, if it's no trouble.' He sat back while she bustled about. He must be careful not to appear too inquisitive. 'You have been in the family's service for some years, no doubt?'

'Aye, sir, that we have,' said the old man, tapping out his pipe and refilling it. As he held a taper to it he looked up, his eyes fixed on the scar on Gil's face. 'You a soldier?'

'I was. Cavalry.'

The old man nodded, apparently satisfied. 'I was in the navy for a time. Nothing like it for teaching a man discipline. I don't hold with these young fellows who've nothing to do but drink and gamble their lives away.'

The woman gave a little tut of disapproval and frowned at her husband, who lapsed into sulky silence.

'Does the family mean to return?' Gil asked his hostess.

'That we don't know sir,' she said. 'His lordship lived here for a while, then upped and went off to Fallbridge.'

'But that was no loss.'

Another sharp word from Mrs Wallis had her husband falling silent again. Gil pretended not to notice. He smiled his thanks as a cup of tea was put in front of him.

'This is a big house for a bachelor,' he remarked, stirring milk into his tea. 'No doubt it was much more lively when the old lord was here with his family.'

'Oh, aye, sir.' Mrs Wallis smiled reminiscently as she sat down at the table and picked up her own cup. 'Those was happy times, with the children laughing and causing such mayhem!'

'What, even Miss Meltham?' asked Gil, his brows raised in surprise.

'Oh, yes, she was quite as reckless as her brother.'

'Worse,' put in the old man, grinning. 'Many's the time her sainted mother came looking for her when she'd slipped out. Off on her adventures, Miss Deb would call it, when she came back from the fair or the market or wherever it was that she'd been.'

The old woman sighed. ''Course, everything changed when the mistress fell ill. Miss Deb gave up her flighty ways and settled down to nurse her. The family moved to Fallbridge then, for the mistress's health—and there Miss Deb has stayed ever since.'

'But young Lord Kirkster preferred to live here, did he not?'

Gil felt the change in the room as he asked his question. The couple looked at one another, but did not reply. He drank his tea and waited, knowing there was more chance of them confiding in him if he stayed silent. His instinct proved right.

'Aye.' The old man scowled into the fire. 'His lordship was here for a while, but it wasn't like the old days. His father, God rest his soul, would never have allowed such goings on here.'

'Young men are often a little wild, when they find themselves free of restraint for the first time,' remarked Gil. 'I saw plenty of that in the army.'

He smiled at the housekeeper, who was clearly fighting the temptation to share her grievances.

'Led astray, he was,' she burst out at last. 'Those wicked, wicked men who called themselves his friends! I blame them for it all. And Miss Deb, bless her heart, when she found out, well, it was too late for her to do anything about it, save to take the young lord away to Fallbridge out of harm's way.'

'But they have not sold this house,' Gil mused.

'No, but I think his lordship will sell before long,' replied the housekeeper with a sigh. 'He is already moving out some of the furniture. His sainted mother would have been happy to sell it years ago,' she said, leaning in confidentially. 'Lady Kirkster was better born, you see, and never comfortable with the fact that the family was in trade. She made the present lord's father give up the business, but he kept his shares in one o' the ships.'

'Aye, the *Margaret*,' put in her husband, puffing on his pipe. 'She don't sail to the Americas now, though. Keeps to coastal waters, delivering sugar all around the country. Quite a comedown for a fine, full-rigged ship like the *Margaret*. Why, his lordship's grandfather would turn in his grave if he could see her now, and if he knew how his grandson had turned out...'

'Aye, well, that's neither here nor there,' his wife interrupted him. She rose and looked pointedly at Gil. 'And now, sir, it looks to me like the rain's stopped, so you will be wanting to get on your way and we mustn't keep you.'

Gil left them and walked quickly back to the inn. There was still a hint of rain in the air and the cloud hung low and heavy over the streets, but he was barely aware of it, for he was thinking of what he had learned about Deborah. He had been right about her, that air of restraint and dowdiness was not natural. It went back further than the injury to her shoulder, too, although he had no doubt that incident had had its effect.

She had devoted herself to looking after her family, first her mother and now Randolph. The reserve and dull clothes were something she had adopted as a protection against the unwelcome attentions of gentlemen such as himself. And he had to confess that with her severe gown and solemn demeanour he would not have given her a second glance if he had not been bent upon securing her for himself.

Regret at what he had lost reared up in him again and he savagely pushed it away. There could be nothing between them. Deborah might believe her brother innocent of seducing Kitty, but Gil had revisited the school, talked again to anyone who knew of his sister's involvement with a rake. True, the description of the man could as easily be Warslow, but however much Gil wanted it to be the truth there was no proof and he had resigned himself to the fact that there might never be.

Deborah lay in her bed, listening to her maid's gentle snores. She had formed the habit of locking her bedroom door since they had come to London and on a couple of occasions now someone had tried the handle in the middle of the night. She had not mentioned the incidents to anyone, but they had coincided with the nights Sir Sydney was staying at the house, so she had had a truckle bed made up for Elsie in her own room as a precaution.

She and Ran had been in Grafton Street for almost a month now, and life at the house was proving a trial for Deborah. Randolph alternated between almost delirious happiness and deep gloom. He refused to tell her why they had moved to town, except to say he wanted more entertainment. He also refused to explain who was financing the move, because although Ran's name was on the agreement, Deb was increasingly convinced that Sir Sydney was paying for this house.

She felt she was mistress in name only and on several occasions she had been obliged to confront Mrs Enfield, who seemed to know very little of what was required of a housekeeper. Despite the severe black gown and cap, there was a blowsiness about the woman, and a familiarity in the way she looked at Sir Sydney, that made Deb wonder if she was perhaps his mistress. Not that it prevented him from trying to fix his interest with Deborah and her brother's increasingly erratic mood was worrying. The more she asked him to confide in her the more truculent he became, as if he were uneasy, guilty, even, about what was going on.

Sir Sydney's role as Ran's guest was little more than a veneer now, but he had not yet gone beyond the bounds of propriety, and Deb was thankful for the support of her maid and her brother's valet, both of whom had quietly pledged their help, if she should need it. And as spring gave way grudgingly to summer, she thought it a distinct possibility that she would need their assistance.

Ever practical, Deb began to wear a discreet but serviceable hatpin pushed into the hair coiled neatly at the back of her head. When she had sought out Gil to ask for his help she had told him that Sir Sydney would not risk offending Ran, but she was very much afraid that the time was rapidly approaching when Randolph would be powerless to protect her and she must be prepared for it.

Thinking of Gil only increased her feeling of loneliness. When she had written to advise him of her direction, she had asked him to direct any reply to the nearest post office, which happened to be the local apothecary. She had not said so in her letter, but she suspected the staff at Grafton Street would deliver any correspondence to Sir Sydney rather than herself.

It was impossible not to be disappointed that so far she had heard nothing from Gil. Perhaps his offer of help had been no more than lip service to a woman he had treated abominably. Her stomach twisted into a knot—a woman whom he pitied. She did not want to believe that and she had come away from their last meeting convinced that he was sincere. But she had to admit that all the evidence was against her and as time went on she was more and more inclined to think that her gut feeling about Gil was entirely wrong. She was coming to the lowering conclusion that Gil could not or would not help her.

Chapter Twelve

'Good morning, Miss Deborah.' Elsie came into the room with a cheerful smile and carefully placed a cup of hot chocolate beside Deborah's bed. 'Mr Miller said to tell you that his lordship intends to join you for breakfast. Now, what would you like to wear today?'

Deb sipped her chocolate while Elsie bustled around. The maid's seemingly innocent message conveyed the comforting news that not only was Ran feeling well enough to get up early this morning, but she would not be alone and obliged to make polite conversation with Sir Sydney at the breakfast table. That and the bright sunlight shining into her room was cheering. She decided to put on her lemon muslin and it was in an optimistic frame of mind that she made her way downstairs.

The mood lasted only until Sir Sydney announced that they were going to the masquerade evening at Vauxhall that night. When Deborah declined, he gave his sly, oily smile.

'But it is all arranged, Miss Meltham, is it not, Lord Kirkster?'

'It is,' said Ran, excitedly. 'It is a high treat, Deb. We will be taking sculls across the water rather than getting caught in all the traffic on the bridge.'

Deborah had only gone out on a few evenings since they had been in London and on each occasion she had been less than impressed with the company her brother and Sir Sydney were keeping.

There were soirées and parties in houses that she soon realised were on the fringes of society. The sycophantic behaviour of those they met did nothing for Deb's enjoyment. The women were heavily painted, the men loud and overbearing, but Ran accepted their overtures and when Deb remonstrated with him he merely shrugged and said she must accustom herself to society ways. The only pleasurable trip had been to the theatre, where they had had the seclusion of their own box, but the treat had not been repeated.

Sir Sydney gave a faint sigh at her hesitation.

He said, 'Lord Kirkster tells me you have never been to Vauxhall, Miss Meltham. You may think it a little vulgar for your tastes, but I am sure there will be something there for you to enjoy. There is the orchestra, of course, and the tumblers, or the mechanical spectacles. I would be delighted to show you all of them…and more especially the Italian Walk.'

Deborah disliked the implication in his last words and was about to give him a sharp set-down when Ran interrupted.

'Oh, do say you will come, Deb. We shall all be masked, after all, so there can be no impropriety.'

'It is the masks that encourage impropriety,' she told him.

'But I shall be there to look after you. You have my word.'

If Sir Sydney had not been involved, Deborah had to admit that she would have been happy, even eager, to go to Vauxhall. She looked at Ran, who was clearly keen for her to join them, so at last she capitulated.

'As long as you will escort me,' she said to her brother and earned from him a grateful smile and an assurance that he would take care of her.

Randolph's mercurial mood deteriorated during the day and by the time they reached Vauxhall he was sinking into the silent depression his sister knew so well. Their party was augmented by Mr and Mrs Wortleby, friends of Sir Sydney's. They were affable to a fault, smiling at everything and gushingly grateful to be included in the party. Deborah gave up her attempts to stop Mrs Wortleby addressing her as 'my lady' and instead she tried to direct their attention away from her brother. When they reached the supper box, she sat beside Ran and when he slumped dejectedly over the table she asked him quietly if he would like to go home.

Sir Sydney was engaged in responding to the Wortlebys' rapturous delight for the gardens, the supper box and the musicians, who were already playing in the rotunda, so Deborah took the opportunity to tell Ran that she was more than ready to leave.

'No, no, I am very well,' he muttered in reply. 'And we have not been here five minutes, how would it look if we walk away now? I wish to heaven you would leave me alone, Deb!'

She relapsed into silence and gave her attention to

listening to the orchestra and watching the throng of people passing by. There was no doubt the crowd was very colourful. There were dominos of every shade that covered a person from head to toe and some people were even dressed in fancy costume, but without exception everyone was masked. If she was allowed to sit here undisturbed all night, Deborah thought that the evening might pass quite pleasantly, but within moments of this thought Mrs Wortleby took a seat beside her and was determined to talk.

'Well, your ladyship, and this is a very fine treat, is it not? La, 'tis years since I was at Vauxhall and it doesn't change. It is still the place to find a beau. Why, even now we are being ogled by that gentleman over there in the purple domino.' She pushed her hood back and put a hand up to her improbably black curls, reminding Deborah very strongly of a bird preening itself before a prospective mate. 'Over there. Do you see him, standing in the shadow of that tree? I vow he has been watching us since we sat down.'

'No, I had not noticed,' replied Deb. 'I thought the reason for wearing a domino was to be incognito. The gentleman is most likely listening to the orchestra and not interested in us at all.'

Her neighbour was in no wise discomposed by this damping response.

'Well, if that is what he wants then he should not wear such a deep colour, it positively *reeks* of extravagance! I dare say you are probably not so accustomed to being ogled in this manner. I have been pursued by such creatures for years and it is no different now I am married, either. Quite forward they can be, some of these gentlemen!'

Deb pursed her lips in distaste, but instead of reading it as a sign of disapproval Mrs Wortleby took it as envy and gave a trill of laughter.

'There is no reason why it shouldn't be the same for you, my dear. There are beaux aplenty to go around. Of course, on a night like this, when everyone is masked and all our finery hidden beneath a domino, it can be more difficult, but if one uncovers one's head, the mask is very little disguise. Here, let me help you.'

She reached across and twitched Deb's hood back.

'There, you see?' She sighed. 'It is a pity that you dress your hair so plainly, for you do not do yourself justice, my dear. And the colour, it is such a nondescript brown. But that need not be a problem, these days, you know. I use a mixture of tree barks and roots for mine, but most likely you would prefer to make it fairer and more like his lordship—La, but it is a sin that your brother has such flaxen locks while you have ended up with mouse, but there it is! I have a friend who uses a very efficacious mix. St John's wort, saffron, celandine roots and I do not know what else, but I would be only too pleased to beg the receipt from her if you would care to try it.'

Deborah declined with a smile and was thankful when the lady's husband caused a diversion by enquiring what time they would be having supper.

'It will be served at ten o'clock,' Sir Sydney informed them.

'Oh, capital!' cried Mrs Wortleby, clapping her hands in delight. 'That will give us time to see the cascade, which is unveiled at nine, is that not so, Sir Sydney?'

'It is indeed, ma'am, as you say.'

Deborah had heard much about this spectacle, which the advertisements declared gave the illusion of a working mill with real running water, so natural that audiences were amazed at its genius. She thought the mechanical aspect of it might appeal to Randolph, too, but although he had agreed to accompany her, she noted with alarm that he was sinking deeper into gloom and when at length Mr Wortleby declared that they were going off to find the cascade, Randolph told his sister morosely that he would wait for her in the supper box.

'But, Ran, you promised to come with me!'

'Perhaps, Miss Meltham, you will allow me to escort you?'

Sir Sydney was standing up and offering her his hand. Deborah cast a last despairing glance at Ran, who hunched even lower over his glass.

'There you are, Deb, Warslow will take you. Off you go now.'

Deborah bit her lip in silent frustration as she pulled her hood up over her hair. She accepted Sir Sydney's escort, but not his arm, and they set off after the others. It was clear that a large number of people were intent on seeing the spectacle, for the crowds grew considerably thicker as they approached the cascade and Deborah soon lost sight of the Wortlebys. She was obliged to remain close to Sir Sydney who, to his credit, managed to secure a place near the front of the crowd, where Deborah had a clear view when the curtain was drawn up.

People were still jostling for places behind Deborah, but she barely noticed, entranced by the spectacle. It was a pretty country scene of a miller's house and a water mill complete with turning wheel and what appeared to be a waterfall cascading down, the water then foaming around the wheel before gliding away. She was well aware that it was all done with metal sheets, turning screws and clever lights, but the noise and the effect drew gasps of admiration from the crowd.

She turned to remark on it to her escort, but found they had been separated by the pushing crowds. At that moment, someone caught her hand and a deep voice murmured close to her ear, 'Come.'

Her head snapped back, but only in time to see the back of a purple domino. The man was holding her hand in a vice-like grip and he began to lead her away through the crowd. She said nothing as she squeezed her way between the crush of bodies, but when at last they were free of the press of people and he pulled her into a secluded walk she begged him to stop. The suspicion that had started to grow as the tall figure half-dragged her out of the throng was making her heart drum heavily against her ribs. As soon as he halted she stepped in front of him and pushed back his hood, revealing the thin strip of black silk covering his eyes, and beneath it, running down his cheek, the thin line of a scar.

'Lord Gilmorton. It *is* you!'

Deborah could not prevent the smile curving her lips. She should hate him, but all she felt now was indescribable relief. His eyes glittered through the slits in his mask and her thoughts tumbled out into speech before she could stop them. 'I was afraid you had washed your hands of me.'

'You think me so fickle?'

His growled words sent a delicious tingle running down Deb's spine and she had to fight against the temptation to lean against him and draw comfort from his presence. Instead she quickly drew away from him, knowing her defences were close to collapse. She wanted to throw herself into his arms, but she must be strong. She did not want to give him any more cause to pity her.

And yet. She had only to gaze into those slate-grey eyes, look at the curve of that sensuous mouth and she forgot everything save how much she wanted him. It shocked her. He had lied to her, tricked her, but her body reacted strongly to his presence, the tug of attraction so great it made her feel weak, breathless.

'I have been in Liverpool,' he said, his voice deep and low, wrapping around her like a soft woollen blanket. 'When I finished my investigations there I came directly to town. To see you.'

To see her! Deb knew she must not read too much into that. She was in danger of succumbing to his charms all over again. Steeling herself, she dragged her eyes away from him, trying to speak rationally.

'How did you know we would be here?'

'Ever since you sent me your direction I have had your house watched. From your letter, I inferred that it might not be safe to write to you, so I thought it better to come and meet you.'

He took her arm and led her to a shadowed arbour a little way along the path, where he invited her to sit down with him. They stayed very close, so that anyone seeing them would think it was a lovers' tryst. Just the thought of that made Deborah want to cry, but she resolutely turned her mind to more practical problems.

'And what have you discovered, my lord? Have you learned anything that would prove my brother innocent?'

'I am afraid not, but I do think that your suspicions were correct and that Warslow is in some way involved in a counterfeiting scheme. But all I have so far is conjecture, based upon what I know of the fellow and his connections in Liverpool. I learned that counterfeit notes have been passed there and that has attracted the attentions of the Bank of England inspectors. I am sure Warslow is involved, but I cannot yet prove it.'

Deborah gave a little gasp of dismay. 'Then the bad note in Fallbridge was not a coincidence.'

'No, I do not think it was.' He reached for her hands and she snatched them out of the way, as if his touch might burn her. It was too dark to see his face clearly, but she thought she heard a faint sigh before he continued. 'Releasing the note in Fallbridge was, I believe, a mistake. In such a small place, it was always likely that whoever passed it on might be discovered. In London tracing such notes would be much more difficult.'

'And that is why he has persuaded Ran to come to town.'

He said urgently, 'Warslow is playing a dangerous game and you will be tainted by association. You should leave London. Go back to Fallbridge, you will be safer there.

'No. I must stay. As long as Ran needs me.' She sought wildly for some crumb of comfort, 'You say you have no real proof. Perhaps we are both wrong and Sir Sydney is not involved in any illegal dealings.'

'I wish it were so, but we are not the only ones who

are suspicious. A Bank inspector was already making enquiries at your house in Liverpool when I was there.'

'You went to Duke Street?'

'I wanted to see where you had lived.' He stopped, pulling back a little as if he had not intended to say that. He continued gruffly. 'Where your brother had lived. It was necessary to discover what I could about his activities in the town and his connection with Warslow.'

'Of course.' The sudden rise in her spirits was immediately halted. It was foolish to think he had any interest in her. Save pity. Only pity.

'The Bank's people are very tenacious,' he warned her. 'They will show no mercy if they find your brother is involved in forging banknotes.'

'But nothing like that took place in Duke Street!'

'Possibly not, but I fear they may seek out your brother here, in London.'

'And if any notes are traced to Grafton Street, it is Ran's name on the lease,' she muttered. 'It is Ran who employs the staff, even though Sir Sydney took care of all the arrangements.'

'Did he now?'

She nodded. 'He hired the staff and I have ascertained that they are all recently come to London, with no family or friends that they might gossip with. The exception is the Enfields, who appear to know Sir Sydney well. They act as butler and housekeeper, but I do not trust them, and I do not think they were ever in service before. From something Mrs Enfield said I think her husband was in the army.'

'And if we dig a little into his past I have no doubt we will discover that he was under Warslow's command,' Gil muttered. 'And that possibly goes for some of the other servants, too. You must be very careful.'

'Thankfully I have my maid and Miller, my brother's valet. I confess I should not be happy there without them.'

'You should not be staying in that house at all!' he exclaimed. 'Deborah, I—'

In her dreams she heard him calling her name, but now the sound of it upon his lips brought only shaming memories of the night he had taken her to his bed out of compassion.

She put up her hand, saying in a tight little voice. 'You will call me Miss Meltham, if you please. As befits mere acquaintances.'

He jerked away as if she had slapped him and almost immediately he rose from the bench.

'I should take you back to your friends.'

Had she offended him, would he walk away from her now, leave her and Randolph to their fate? She tried to read his expression as she stood up beside him, but the shadows were too deep. However, his next words were perfectly calm, if not encouraging.

'I have not yet found a way to extricate your brother from this coil, nor, I must tell you, anything that convinces me he is as innocent as you think him to be.'

'As I know him to be,' she said with some vehemence.

He inclined his head politely. He did not believe her, she thought, her heart sinking. But that did not matter, as long as he was prepared to help.

'That is why I needed to speak to you,' he continued, 'to discover if you have seen or heard anything untoward.'

He indicated that they should walk along the path and she fell into step beside him, thankful that she could turn her thoughts to more practical matters.

'Sir Sydney spends a great deal of time in Grafton Street,' she said slowly. 'But he is mostly with my brother in his study. I have come upon him talking to Enfield on several occasions, but I have heard nothing one could call suspicious.'

'Warslow has taken up residence with you?'

'No, he does not live with us all the time. Ran insists a room is kept in readiness for him, but he has a lodging nearby.' She clasped her hands tightly before her. 'I think he is keeping a distance. I think, if charges were to be brought against Randolph, Sir Sydney would plead ignorance of it all.'

'Very likely. Your brother provides a convenient front for him.'

'And more than that,' she added. 'I believe he is using Randolph to gain entrée into more wealthy society. Not the *haut ton*, but those scrambling for gentility.' She could not help a little huff of distaste. 'Types Ran would once have described as toadying mushrooms.'

'Such as the couple sharing your supper box?'

'Yes.' She nodded. 'They are overjoyed to be going about in the company of a lord, even if my brother is merely a baron. Consequently they are very free with their money. But I do not understand, that may gain Sir Sydney new acquaintances, perhaps there will be new people he may impose upon, but it is not unlawful.'

'But as you say they are wealthy and I don't doubt some of them are in trade. They would accept Warslow as a gentleman, giving him the opportunity to spread his forged notes without suspicion.'

'And the chance to ruin their lives...' Deborah sighed '...as he is doing to my poor brother!'

His breath hissed out. 'Perhaps I should force a quarrel upon Warslow and make an end of him.'

'But you said he is a crack shot.' She shuddered at the thought.

'So, too, am I considered a deadly opponent.'

She clutched his arm, saying impulsively, 'I pray you will not do anything so dangerous.'

He turned his head. 'Afraid for me, Miss Meltham?'

Quickly she removed her hand. She dared not look into his face, but she was sure there was a trace of laughter in his voice. How dare he tease her. Not for the world would she have him think she cared a jot!

'Not at all,' she said crossly. 'I should be delighted if you were to kill each other. But if he has embroiled Randolph in his horrid schemes it might leave my brother in even more danger.'

'Quite so, ma'am. I shall therefore continue to make enquiries and keep you informed of my progress.'

'But how will you do that? I dare not ask you to send a note to the house save in the direst emergency. You might leave word at the post office, which is situated at the local apothecary's.'

'But would it not arouse suspicion for you to be visiting his shop every day?' he replied. 'I have a better idea, ma'am. You are but a step from Green Park; I am convinced a daily walk between the reservoir and the Lodge would be of benefit to you.'

'Why, yes,' she said, almost smiling in spite of the heaviness in her heart. 'I shall endeavour to do so after breakfast each morning. Or to send Elsie on an errand in that direction.'

Deborah could now see the lights from the promenade and the supper boxes ahead of them and she stopped.

'We should part here, in the shadows. I do not want anyone to see us together and become suspicious.'

Gil halted beside her, reluctant to bring the encounter to an end, but knowing it must be so.

'Very true.'

He reached out to pull the hood of her domino a little further forward over her head. It was not really necessary, but it was the nearest he could come to touching her.

'Off you go then,' he said. 'I have people watching Grafton Street day and night. If you discover anything you may send a message to the Running Man tavern just around the corner, addressed to John Harris.' He added softly, 'Send word there, too, if you need me. I will come for you.'

She did not move. Her face was turned up towards him and through the slits of her mask her eyes shone in the dim lamplight, glittering like emeralds. Did she, too, feel the pull of attraction? Was she even aware that her lips were slightly parted, inviting his kiss? No, she hated him and with good reason. Biting back his own desires, he reached out and turned her away from him.

'Go,' he said roughly. 'Your party will be growing anxious for you.' Beneath the cloth, the bones of her shoulders felt as delicate and fragile as porcelain, arousing every protective instinct within him and for a moment his fingers tightened their grip. 'Be careful, Deborah.'

Her hand came out, but whether it was to touch him, or in that gesture she used when she was nervous, reminding herself of her scars, he dared not wait to discover. Using every ounce of will power he released her and turned away, striding back into the shadows without another look.

Randolph and the rest of the party were in the supper box. Deborah compelled her unwilling feet to carry her towards them, but added to the leaden weight of her brother's predicament was her own desperate unhappiness. Seeing Gil again had brought back all the pain of his treachery. He had deliberately sought her out and courted her until she fell in love with him and he was only helping her now because he had wronged her.

She was an obligation, she thought miserably, a debt of honour he needed to pay before he could forget her. In other circumstances she would rather die than accept anything from this man, but she needed him. She had neither the wealth nor the influence to save Randolph and Gil had both. Reminding herself of this, Deborah walked towards the supper box, schooling her face into a look of unconcern.

Sir Sydney looked up and saw her approaching and soon they were all exclaiming with relief that she had returned. As she murmured reassurances that she was perfectly safe and had merely got lost in the crowds, her wayward thoughts returned to her meeting with Gil. She could not forget the memory of his hands on her shoulders, the reassuring strength of his arm when she had clutched at it. His words, that were burned into her heart.

If you need me, I will come for you.

Chapter Thirteen

Remembering Gil's suggestion, Deborah incorporated a morning walk into her daily routine, no one in the household thinking anything amiss in an energetic young lady wishing to take the air. Neither her brother nor Sir Sydney—when he was staying overnight—ever quit their rooms much before noon and she was left very much to herself to enjoy her exercise with only her maid for company. But almost a week passed without seeing Gil in the park and she was beginning to lose hope when her thoughts were given an unexpected turn.

Elsie came in one morning to help her dress and was clearly big with news. The maid checked there was no one listening outside the door before she began, coming close to speak to her mistress in low, conspiratorial tones.

'Miller bumped into Lord Gilmorton's man yesterday,' she said, her eyes shining with excitement. 'He says you are to expect an invitation today from—now what were his words? Miller said 'twas important I tell you true—from a *toadying mushroom* with whom you are acquainted. His lordship says 'tis important you accept.'

Deb's heart began to race. 'But who? Where? Oh, why does the man have to be so obscure?'

The maid's eyes twinkled and her round face creased into a beatific smile. 'I think 'tis very romantic.'

Deb felt herself blushing and said crossly, 'It is nothing of the sort. I need the Viscount's help, not puzzles that set my head in a spin!'

But the day did seem a little brighter, for all that.

Deborah was in the morning room a few hours later when she was informed she had a visitor.

'Mrs Wortleby.'

Gil's message immediately jumped to her mind as she invited her guest to sit down.

'Thank you, my lady, I don't mind if I do, even though I can only stay a minute, for I have an appointment with my dressmaker soon and I daren't be late, she is in such demand with all the most fashionable ladies that I was lucky that she could find time for me! La, ma'am, what a lovely room this is! You have made it quite your own.'

Deborah curbed her impatience while Mrs Wortleby continued in a similar vein and after several minutes her visitor broke off, saying with a laugh, 'But I am sure you must be curious to know why I should call upon you unannounced.'

'As a matter of fact, ma'am, I am. Very curious.'

Mrs Wortleby beamed at her.

'Well, ma'am, I have come with an invitation! I have two tickets for a concert given by Signora Maranella tomorrow evening. I obtained them quite by chance, for they were all sold out weeks ago and I had not even thought of going! Dear Wortleby cannot come, so I thought, why not ask Miss Meltham if she would like to join me? It is for a good cause, too, the Foundling Hospital. Everyone will be there, lords, ladies, possibly even a duke or two!'

Deborah felt a little kick of excitement. This must be Gil's invitation from a toadying mushroom, but even if she had not received his message she thought she could not have turned down the opportunity to listen to the celebrated opera singer.

Her acceptance was received with obsequious rapture, but almost immediately Mrs Wortleby rose to take her leave.

'I shall call for you tomorrow, Miss Meltham. Now, I beg your pardon for flying away so quickly but I must keep my appointment with Madame Sophie. Such a tyrant, she is, but I must have my new gown for the concert, whatever the cost. Until tomorrow, my lady!'

Randolph said nothing when Deb told him of her forthcoming treat, and if Sir Sydney was surprised by her sudden change of heart about keeping company with the Wortlebys he said nothing, merely nodded approvingly when he heard of it.

She felt her excitement growing as the concert drew near. Gil had not said he would be there, but she hoped he would be. She thought it would not arouse suspicion if she shed her usual plain style for the concert. She decided to wear a new frock of white Persian gauze trimmed with silver filigree and persuaded Elsie to dress her hair *à la grecque*. Gloves of French kid and a white-crepe fan completed the ensemble, and as Deborah arranged the blush pink shawl of Norwich silk around her shoulders her maid gave a gusty sigh of appreciation.

'Ooh, mistress, I don't think you have ever looked finer.'

Deborah studied herself critically in the looking glass, then she laughed.

'I have no doubt I shall be quite cast into the shade by Mrs Wortleby!'

But as she went downstairs to await the carriage she hoped that Gil would be there tonight, to appreciate her efforts.

The concert was being held in the drawing room of a rich society hostess and even Mrs Wortleby was awed into silence by the opulence of her surroundings and the company. She recognised at least two dukes, but when she applied to her companion to identify more of the august society, Deborah could not help her.

'I regret my acquaintance in town is very limited,' Deb told her, apologetically.

'Ah well, it doesn't matter,' remarked Mrs Wortleby, sighing. 'I had hoped…but never mind, we shall enjoy the concert. And what a tale I shall have to tell dear Wortleby in the morning!'

The seats were filling up fast and they slipped into an empty row, where Mrs Wortleby was soon in conversation with the bejewelled matron beside her. Deborah was still arranging her skirts when the next seat was taken and she jumped when she heard a deep, familiar voice bidding her good evening.

'No, no, do not look at me,' Gil murmured, his eyes fixed upon his programme. 'Your companion has no idea who I am and it is better if she remains in ignorance.'

Deb's nerves were fluttering, but, following his lead, she opened her programme and pretended to study it.

'How did you arrange this?' she hissed at him.

Risking a glance from the corner of her eye, she saw him smile.

'By the simple expedient of making a large donation to the Foundling Hospital,' he murmured. 'I guessed your mushroom would not be able to resist the lure of such an event. I had only to arrange for tickets to come in her way and my contact planted the seed that Miss Meltham was the very best person to accompany her.'

'You would have looked nohow if her husband had decided to come with her.'

'There was no possibility of that. I had arranged other equally tempting entertainments for him.'

She choked back a gurgle of laughter. 'You are quite reckless.'

'Sometimes that is best,' he murmured. 'Hush now, Signora Maranella has arrived.'

The soprano was warmly applauded as she took her place before them and the musicians struck up for the first melody. Deborah was sufficiently familiar with Italian to understand most of the words and normally she would have been entranced, oblivious of everything except the music, but tonight that was impossible. She could not quite relax, could not forget who was sitting beside her. She realised how much she had longed to see him tonight. As she had gone about her daily business she had imagined meeting him, talking to him, even—oh, heavens!—the touch of his lips as he kissed her hand in greeting. She had spent the day with an almost unbearable lightness within her, an aching void that she longed for him to fill.

And all day she had told herself it was foolish to think about him in that way. He could never be anything to her. He was not even a friend.

She kept her hands clasped tightly about her fan, lest she should impulsively reach out for Gil as the music swooped and soared at its most moving. He was resting one hand lightly on his knee and she noticed that it twitched occasionally, as if he was fighting a similar temptation. Quite a ridiculous idea, she was well aware of that, but still the feeling persisted and it warmed her, like a secret candle flame burning deep inside.

The tingle of awareness did not diminish as the concert continued. Deb could feel the heat of his leg, so close to her own, his arm against her sleeve. The curl of desire became a physical ache between her thighs and she was so on edge she thought a mere touch would ignite her.

Deborah kept very still, enjoying every delicious moment of the music, the words and the guilty pleasure of sitting beside Gil. She wanted it to go on for ever, but a glance at the programme indicated that they had reached the final song of the first half of the concert. She heard the Viscount addressing her as the room erupted into enthusiastic applause.

'There is a corridor, behind the staircase. Come to me there.'

Deb's heart kicked against her ribs. Come to him?

Surely it was too dangerous to meet. How could she leave her companion? How could she escape notice? But before she could protest Gil had disappeared into the press of people slowly making their way out of the room.

Dazed, she turned towards Mrs Wortleby, only to find her preparing to accompany her neighbour to the dining room for refreshments. Deb followed them out to the anteroom, but then she hung back. The double doors leading to the landing were thrown wide, but everyone was heading in the opposite direction. Fanning herself, Deborah moved slowly out to the landing, as if in need of a little air. There was only one corridor, a shadowed opening beneath the rise of the stairs and framed by velvet drapes drawn back on either side.

Cautiously Deb approached, glancing around to make sure she was not observed before entering the passageway. Almost immediately a hand shot out around her waist and pulled her into the shadows. She lost balance and cannoned into the hard wall of a man's chest.

'Steady.'

Deb knew she should be reassured by Gil's voice, but he had his arms about her and her heart was beating so fast and hard she feared it might burst. She was angry with herself for her lack of control and even more angry with Gil for making her feel this way. She pushed herself away from him.

'I am perfectly able to stand,' she told him crossly. 'Now why was it necessary that I should be here tonight? What news have you?'

'None, I am afraid.'

His tone was regretful, but she had the distinct feeling he did not mean it. She peered up, trying to read his face in the gloom. It was impossible, but just standing so close, within touching distance, was making it difficult to breathe. She tried to step away, but immediately he caught her and swung her around.

'That white gown of yours will stand out in the gloom so we must keep you out of sight.'

Now he was between her and the light. Her back was to the wall and he was towering over her, as black and menacing as a predator. And far too close. He filled her senses and she was now almost trembling with need. Deb swallowed and tried to concentrate.

'You asked me to come here for no reason at all?'

She wanted to sound indignant, but feared her voice was shaking too much.

'I thought you might enjoy the concert. You told me you like fine music.'

'I do, but think of the risk we are taking.'

That was better. She was the one in control and talking sensibly.

'I also wanted to make sure you knew how to contact me.'

'Yes, yes, the Running Man, and Green Park, where I have walked every morning, I might add!' she said, with a fair assumption of irritation.

'And you are looking much better for the daily exercise. Quite radiant, in fact.'

She felt herself blushing, anger, laughter and desire warring inside her. What was left of her defences was crumbling and she said hastily, 'We agreed it all. I should get back.'

'And...' his hands shot out, landing on the wall on either side of her '...I wanted to see you.'

She did not doubt his sincerity now, but she could not allow it to make any difference. They could not even be friends, their previous encounters marred by too much mistrust and betrayal. Her head knew it, but her body had developed a will of its own and heaven help her if Gil felt the same strong tug of attraction!

There was barely any space between them and her breasts tingled, pushing up against her gown as if trying to reach him. The memory of how it felt to have him make love to her was like a physical force, pushing her towards him. She closed her eyes, but it did not help at all. She could feel his presence. Smell him.

Since she could not back away, she put her hands against his chest to hold him off. One hand landed on his waistcoat, smooth and cool against her palm. The other rested against one side of his fine wool evening coat and she found herself hooking her finger through a buttonhole.

'This is madness.' Her words were little more than a sigh.

'I know.'

His breath was warm on her cheek, as if he had lowered his head. She could not help it, she turned her face up, lips parted, inviting his kiss. It did not come. Her nerves were taut as bowstrings and when she opened her eyes and saw how close he was, the finger hooked into his coat curled tighter, closing the gap between them and at the same time she eased herself on to her toes and feathered her lips against his.

He took her face in his hands, cupped it with infinite tenderness and for a heartbeat—or a lifetime—neither of them moved. Then his lips captured hers, demanding, insistent, and she responded eagerly, hungry for his kiss. As if they were lovers reunited after a long absence.

The thought made her whimper, but still she clung on, unable to break away. He slipped one arm around her back, pulling her closer while his mouth plundered hers, drawing out her very soul. Desire burned inside Deb. She was aware of it smouldering somewhere deep and low in her body, but when Gil's hand moved to her breast it burst into life; she was consumed by heat and sensations she could not control. She broke off the kiss because she could no longer breathe. She dragged in great, shuddering gasps of air, her body trembling like a frightened animal. She clung to him, her fingers gripping his coat as if her life depended upon hanging on to him. His mouth was on her ear, her cheek, her jawline. She tilted her head back and he trailed kisses down her throat to the very edge of her gown and all the time his hand was caressing her breast, drawing up the desire from somewhere very deep inside her.

She could feel the heat of his skin through the gauze of her bodice. It aroused such a need in her that she pushed against it, giving a little animal cry as his finger and thumb found the nipple and massaged it slowly through the gossamer-thin material. She reached for him, drawing his head towards her again that she might kiss his mouth, explore it, plunder it. He matched her kiss for kiss, their tongues twisting and dancing. Her senses took flight, carrying her higher and higher until she thought she would die of pleasure. Gil was still in possession of her mouth so her cry was muted, but her body convulsed like a wild thing. Gil gathered her into his arms and held her tightly as wave after wave rose up inside and battered her until she was too exhausted to do more than lean against him.

She felt dazed, bruised by the experience. It had lasted only a few minutes, but it felt like a lifetime. He had carried her to new heights with only a kiss and a touch. Dear heaven, but he was dangerous.

Gil held her in his arms, cradling her while her ecstatic shudders diminished to nothing. Still she clung to him. He rested his cheek on her hair, breathing in the fondly remembered essence of her. He smiled ruefully to himself. It had been madness to arrange this meeting. If they were seen together, if Warslow realised he was in town, then all might be lost, but he could not help himself. Seeing her again at Vauxhall had stirred up the longing he had tried so hard to suppress. Snatching meetings in Green Park, where they would barely be able to acknowledge one another and certainly not be able to touch, would be torture. He wanted to see her, to kiss her. But even now he had done so he knew it was not enough. He turned his head a little to kiss the top of her head.

'Hell and damnation,' he murmured into her hair, 'you will be the ruin of me.'

He was aware of her steady intake of breath, the straightening of her shoulders as she pushed herself out of his arms.

'This was foolish beyond words, my lord, and it is quite unforgivable to take such advantage of me.'

'Can you tell me truthfully you did not want it to happen?' he asked her.

'What I *want* and what must be are irreconcilable,' she told him. 'I cannot deny the attraction, but that does not mean it is *right*.' She stopped, lifting her head as a sudden swell of sound came from the anteroom. 'The interval is ended. I must return to my seat.' She threw him a hard, angry look. 'I pray you will not indulge in any further nonsense such as this, Lord Gilmorton. It does neither of us any good.'

There was a note in her voice that told him tears were very close.

'I had not intended—' he began. 'I wanted only to see you, to hear your voice. The *nonsense*, as you call it, was a mistake, I admit that, but the temptation to have you to myself, if only for a few moments, was irresistible. You said yourself there is a special bond between us.'

'I was mistaken,' she said coldly. 'It is not so much a bond as a burden that will drag us to disaster if we do not fight it. We can be nothing to one another. All that can happen at such encounters as this is that I realise just what a fool I have been! Is that what you want, to prolong and increase my misery?' She pushed him away and began to straighten her gown, shaking out her skirts with sharp, angry movements. 'I am ashamed of my weakness, but I am not afraid to admit to it. I pray you will not contact me again, sir, unless you know something that might help my brother.'

'As you wish, madam.'

'And all future meetings must be in public, with my maid in attendance.'

With that she turned and swept away from him across the landing and out of sight amongst the crowd milling in the anteroom. Gil fell back against the wall, exhaling as he turned his head to stare at the shadowed ceiling. She thought of him as her weakness, her shame, and he could not blame her.

But he could blame himself. What had happened to his iron will and military discipline? He should never have arranged this meeting, never have given in to the temptation to see her again, to kiss her. Whatever her brother's faults, Deborah deserved better than this. She deserved a good man who would cherish and protect her. Marry her. Love her. He wished with all his heart that he could be that man, but marriage was out of the question. He could not take her to wife believing—knowing—her brother had destroyed his family. And as for love, he was no longer capable of it. The pain of losing his brother and sister was too much and he would not risk his heart any further.

As he stepped from the shadows he glanced down. His cravat was disordered and the front of his evening coat was creased where Deb had gripped it. Nothing that could not be rectified by Harris with a little water and a smoothing iron, but if he returned to the concert it was sure to be remarked upon by some sharp-eyed acquaintance. He turned and headed for the stairs. He would go home. That at least would relieve Deborah of his shameful presence for the rest of the evening. And in future, he would ensure they kept their meetings formal.

'My dear Miss Meltham, where *have* you been? I looked for you at supper. Did you have the headache, is that it? Yes, yes, I can see that you are not looking quite yourself. But you must not think I was lacking in company. Lady Gosling and I found much to talk of. Such a treat, you know, to be sitting next to a perfect stranger and discover our minds are so alike. I shall be paying her a morning call tomorrow. But come along now, we must take our seats and quickly, for the *signora* is about to sing again!'

Deborah smiled and nodded as Mrs Wortleby chattered on. She heard only one word in ten and understood none of it, her brain still reeling from that encounter with Gil. Surely everyone must see how shaken she was, everyone must know that she had been kissed to within an inch of her life, but, no, a quick glance showed her that no one was paying her any attention at all. She sat down beside Mrs Wortleby and composed herself for the second half of the concert.

As she joined in the applause to welcome the singer back on to the dais she glanced at the space beside her. No doubt Gil would return to the concert at the last moment. But the seat remained empty and a chill little cloud of loneliness settled over Deb's spirits.

Chapter Fourteen

A night's repose did much to restore Deborah's equilibrium. She had been at fault to go in search of Gil. Any lady should know the dangers of being alone in the shadows with a man and her previous experience with Viscount Gilmorton should have warned her of what might happen.

A little tremor ran through her. She had *wanted* it to happen. She could not deny she had wanted him to kiss her. That the kiss would lead to such an earth-shattering explosion of feeling on her part was unexpected and went to show just what strain her nerves had been suffering recently.

Gil had left the concert without another word to her, but Deb was as sure as she could be that he would not withdraw his help, so the next morning she was up early and walking in Green Park, as usual.

She recalled his comment, that the daily exercise was doing her good. There was no doubt that she enjoyed her walks and felt the better for being out of the house. She had quickly become familiar with Green Park, noting that the most crowded walks were at the eastern side of the park, near the reservoir, where the guards paraded every morning. She chose to stroll towards the less popular areas to the west, where shrubs and trees provided a degree of privacy, should it be required.

For two mornings after the concert she looked for Lord Gilmorton in vain, but on the third, when she was beginning to worry that perhaps she was wrong and he had abandoned her and Randolph to their fate, she saw him striding towards her from the western end of the park. She caught his glance for a moment before turning on to one of the more secluded walks.

She had not gone very far before Gil was beside her and try as she might, Deborah could not quell the relief she felt at seeing him again. She nodded to Elsie, conveying with a look that the maid should drop back to a respectful distance. They walked along the path, in step, but never touching, both looking straight ahead.

'I kept my word,' he said. 'I promised you I would not seek you out unless I had news.'

Her step faltered but she recovered quickly.

'Go on, my lord.'

'I think we have something.'

Anxiety immediately ousted all other emotion and it only deepened when she heard the grim note in his voice.

'Tell me.'

'I have discovered a pattern to your servants' going out. Enfield or one of the footmen goes each night to a certain eating house in Wardour Street where they meet up with women.'

Deb's mouth twisted into a little moue of distaste.

'I am not so innocent that I am not aware that such things go on, my lord. I certainly do not condone it, but I know it is far from unusual.'

'But it is not only prostitutes they meet up with. In fact, most of the women are in respectable trades. They are flower sellers, hawkers, milliners, domestics, all of them poorly paid wretches who would very likely be willing to take forged notes to busy markets and buy some small item, receiving their change in good coin. They get to keep a tiny fraction of what they exchange, the rest goes back to their master.'

'Sir Sydney,' she said.

'Not necessarily.'

She stared at him. 'You still think my brother could be involved in this?'

'I *know* he is involved,' he corrected her. 'What I cannot be sure of is how deeply.'

Deborah shivered. Ran's own words to her suggested he was not wholly innocent.

'Tell me truthfully,' he said. 'Do you think your brother is aware of what is going on?'

Her spirits sagged. 'I believe so. His whole demeanour has changed recently. I think he believes he is implicated too deeply to withdraw.' She twisted her hands together, ending bitterly, 'And he finds solace in laudanum.'

'Encouraged in his addiction by Warslow, no doubt.'

Deborah put a hand over her mouth, sick with misery and fear for her brother.

Gil ached with frustration at Deb's unhappiness. He felt so helpless, unable to comfort her as he would wish. He was afraid for her, too. He leaned closer.

'Deb—Miss Meltham, I earnestly beg you to move out of Grafton Street. If you need funds, I will help. You have my word that whatever I may think of your brother, I will do my best to keep him out of this, but there is no need for you to take the risk.'

'No. I cannot leave Ran. He is all I have to live for.'

Her words were like a physical blow to the gut. Her anguish was evident in the downward curve of her mouth, the tension in her jaw as she tried not to cry. He wanted to hold her, to protect her, but he had forfeited any right to do that. He could not even offer her his arm in such a public place. They strolled on in silence and after a while she began to speak again, as if she thought it was necessary to explain about her brother.

'Mama became ill soon after Randolph was born and there was no one but me to look out for him. When he was eight years old he fell from a tree. He suffered nothing worse than bruises, but my hugs and kisses eased the pain. I was his big sister, always there to love and comfort him, until he was sent away to school, where it seems to me that he learned only how to drink and gamble and spend money. But whenever he came home he curbed his wildness and was a loving son.' She stopped, as if reliving the past. 'Then Papa died and Mama retired to Fallbridge. I was too busy looking after her to see that he was getting himself into trouble. But after she had died, I should have gone to Liverpool more often. If only I had been there with Ran, to protect him, to help him.'

'We can all look back and think *if only*, Deb.' The words were coming from his heart and Gil realised with a shock that he was speaking to himself as well as her. 'There is nothing we can do to change the past. We can only live for the future.'

He knew now that his thirst for revenge had been as much about his own guilt as anything else. He had not been there to protect his family when they needed him, but instead of acknowledging those feelings of guilt he had allowed them to fester into an all-consuming rage that had merely buried his grief, not assuaged it. He knew it was too late to mend the damage he had done. Deborah would never forgive him for trying to exact his revenge through her, but perhaps he could redress the balance, just a little.

'I give you my word I will rescue you, and your brother, from this coil.'

'How do you propose to do that?'

'I do not yet know, but it must be soon. It is too dangerous for you to remain much longer in Grafton Street. If I have been able to discover Warslow's scheme, then the Bank inspectors will soon know of it.' He frowned. 'We must try to find something, anything, that will incriminate Warslow rather than your brother. Perhaps you could leave a door unlocked one night and I could search the house.'

'There is no need for that. I can do so much more effectively.'

'You must not put yourself in danger.'

She did not answer, but the determined set of her chin told him she would not heed his warning. She would do anything to save her brother. A memory stirred.

'Tell me,' he said, 'what do you know of a ship called the *Margaret*?'

'Randolph is part-owner,' she responded, surprised.

'It is our last remaining link with the family business. I think Papa kept it because it was named after his mother, our grandmother. Why do you ask?'

'Something I learned in Liverpool. I believe it is bringing some furniture to London for your brother.'

'And why not? If it comes by water it is more likely to reach us in one piece than if it were transported on an ox cart. You do not think...? No, no, I would personally vouch for the captain. He was a personal friend of my father's and an honest man. He would never carry an illicit cargo. *If* he knew of it.' She gave a little gasp of dismay. 'Oh, heavens, perhaps forged notes would be hidden inside the furniture.'

Gil waved a hand dismissively, wishing he had not spoken. 'I am merely speculating. Pray to not let it worry you.'

But Gil knew it would worry her. Fighting the temptation to keep her with him any longer, he used his cane to indicate the fork in the path just ahead of them.

'We should part here. It is not wise to spend too long together.'

'No. I agree.'

So we must not meet again until I have some news for you.

'So I shall meet you here tomorrow.' Gil closed his eyes briefly as he realised what he had said, knowing it was madness.

'Very well.' They stopped and for the first time she looked up at him. 'Thank you, my lord.'

Her green eyes were shadowed with anxiety and she looked so forlorn that his arms ached to pull her close and kiss away her worries, but that would only send her flying from him and he might lose his opportunity to help her, so he contented himself with raising his hand and running the backs of his fingers along her cheek. It was smooth as satin to his touch and immediately desire flared within him. He stamped it down, but dragging his hand away was like pulling against a magnet.

'Do not look so worried, D—Miss Meltham. I will save your brother, if I have to knock him over the head and carry him away.'

She sighed. 'We both know even that will not save him. Nominally it is Ran's servants who are passing on these counterfeit notes. And if you are correct about the *Margaret*, then that, too, would point to Randolph being involved. Sir Sydney has done everything he can to make sure the blame will land upon my brother, if their scheme is discovered.'

He could not deny it. If Warslow was caught he would have no hesitation in implicating Kirkster. Even if the boy turned King's evidence he would still face transportation, a gruelling sea journey that would probably kill him.

'It will not come to that,' he said, with more confidence than he felt.

He was rewarded when the faint crease on her brow disappeared and she gave him a brave little smile.

'I know you will do your best, my lord.' With a little nod she turned to go on her way, but he put a hand on her arm.

'Deborah—I know you have no reason to trust me, but—'

Her head came up, the shuttered look returned to her eyes.

'I am doing this for my brother's sake, my lord, and I believe he is innocent, even if you do not.'

And with that she turned and walked briskly away.

Deborah did not return directly to Grafton Street. Instead she spent an hour in New Bond Street, making several purchases while she considered all that Gil had told her. Her blood ran cold to think that Warslow was distributing his forged notes from Randolph's house, and although she hoped it might not be true she really did not doubt it. The risks to her brother and herself were huge and it made her feel so angry that she wanted to go back and challenge Sir Sydney immediately, but she knew that was far too dangerous. She must find a way to remove Randolph from London, or trust Gil to do so. And the strange part was she *did* trust him.

'But that does not mean I shall ever forgive him,' she muttered as she set off for Grafton Street. She would allow him to help her, but then, for her own peace of mind, she decided it would be best if she never saw nor heard of Viscount Gilmorton again.

Nevertheless, when she found Gil waiting for her on the path the following morning she could not deny the rush of pleasure she felt at the sight of him. It was quickly followed by anger at her own weakness and she resolved to put an end to it.

'You should not be here,' she said, when he told her he had no news. 'It is too dangerous—what if we are seen and word reaches Sir Sydney?'

'But you might have something for *me*,' he reasoned.

'Then Elsie would bring word to the Running Man,

as we agreed. I have searched most of the house, but cannot find anything suspicious. However, I have not yet had the opportunity to search my brother's study and that is the most likely place to find something.'

'I wish you would not do anything that will put you at risk.'

The concern in his voice was like a caress. It sent a flutter through her body, as if someone had opened a net full of butterflies in her chest. She recalled how he had made her feel loved, cherished, and she was dismayed to find he still had that power, even though he was most likely quite unaware of it. The only way she could combat the longing it roused within her was with anger which, even to her own ears, sounded half-hearted.

'Meeting you here every day is putting me at far greater risk!'

'Then tomorrow we will meet somewhere else. The circulating library in Piccadilly, perhaps. What do you say to that?'

Just the sound of his voice was like the touch of velvet on her skin. It distracted her and made it difficult to concentrate.

'No. Yes.' She shook her head, trying to clear the contradictory thoughts that were crowding in. 'No. I will not be there.' She closed her lips, knowing this was the safest, most sensible thing to do. But then, just as he was preparing to leave her, she burst out, 'Unless I have something useful to tell you.'

'Of course, Miss Meltham.' He touched his hat. 'Until tomorrow, ma'am.'

His voice was grave, but there was a warm smile in his grey eyes that brought the colour flooding to her cheeks. As if he knew perfectly well how much she wanted to see him.

She hunched one shoulder and hurried away.

'Conceited man,' she muttered. 'Hateful, *odious* creature!'

'I beg your pardon, miss, did you speak to me?'

Elsie was almost running to keep up with her and Deb moderated her pace, but her indignation was still growing and she could not help giving vent to her feelings.

'Lord Gilmorton is the rudest, most objectionable man I have ever met. I wish we never *had* met! I should have known he was a villain the moment I saw his hideously scarred face.'

Deborah bit her lip, appalled that her temper had caused her to say such a dreadful thing. She had never been repelled by his scar and now she barely noticed it, but she had wanted to strike out and hurt him in order to relieve her own pain. Blinking back tears of mortification, she hurried on with her maid walking beside her.

Elsie cleared her throat. 'Well, if you will pardon me for saying so, miss, I think his lordship has a very nice face. Despite that nasty scar. Handsome, I'd say.'

'You, you would?' said Deborah in a small voice.

'Why, yes, ma'am, I would,' replied Elsie. 'And it ain't like you to take against a person for their looks. *And*,' she went on, much more confident now, 'if his lordship wasn't trying to help us then I don't know where we'd be and that's a fact!'

But you do not know him, Elsie. You do not know that he stole my innocence!

Deb bit her lip even harder. No, he had not stolen

anything from her. He had promised her nothing. She had been perfectly aware of what she was doing and had gone to him willingly, given herself willingly. That he had had an ulterior motive for seeking her out and taking her to his bed had hurt her, terribly, but she understood his reasons and pitied him for the grief and pain that he must have been suffering. She also conceded that he might have been telling her the truth when he said that he had planned to send her away on that fateful night. After all, what choice did he have, when she had practically undressed before him? She acknowledged now that if he had rejected her at that moment she would have been desperately hurt and humiliated.

Not that she would ever forgive him, of course.

'You are right,' she said now. 'I should not have spoken in that way of his lordship. Pray forget I said anything, Elsie.'

The maid chuckled. 'Lord, miss, I've been with you long enough to know you don't mean the things you say when you're in a taking. I have to confess it don't happen so much nowadays, but when you was a child you was always in high dudgeon about something or other. To my mind, it's good to see you still have some of that fire in you.'

They had reached Grafton Street by this time and as they came to the steps of their house the maid took a deep breath and declared with the force of one who had been silent for too long, 'I know it ain't my place to say so, miss, but all those years looking after your sainted mama, and now running yourself ragged over Lord Kirkster, it's about time you thought about yourself a bit more!'

Deborah stared at her maid and felt a sudden rush of affection for the woman who had looked after her since childhood.

'How lucky I am to have such a friend as you, Elsie! Perhaps I shall have a little more time for myself, once this is all over.'

Impulsively she kissed Elsie's cheek before running up the steps to the house, where the butler was holding open the door.

'Ah, Enfield. Where is his lordship?' Deborah paused in the hallway to strip off her gloves while Elsie carried her purchases up to her bedchamber.

'Lord Kirkster had gone out, but he will be returning with Sir Sydney in time to take dinner.' Enfield gave an obsequious little bow. 'After which, his lordship informs me he has taken a box at the opera and hopes you will be able to join them.'

Deborah inclined her head and walked towards the stairs.

'And what answer shall I give his lordship?'

Deborah stopped and turned, her brows raised.

'I shall give Lord Kirkster my answer at dinner,' she announced, in a voice designed to depress pretension.

She saw a flicker of anger cross the butler's countenance and felt a momentary spurt of satisfaction. She was aware of how little power she had in this house, but Enfield could not challenge her outright. At least, not yet.

Randolph was in good spirits at dinner and accepted her decision not to accompany them to the opera with a good grace. Sir Sydney expressed his disappointment, but she was relieved that neither of them pressed her to go. She saw them off and returned to the drawing room to read her book, but after an hour, when she rang the bell, she was informed that the butler had gone out.

Deborah dismissed the footman and waited for a few moments before leaving the room. The hall was deserted and she paused at the bottom of the stairs to light one of the bedroom candles, listening and looking around her. When she was sure she was alone, she crossed the hall and slipped into Ran's study. This was where Sir Sydney and her brother spent most of their time together and she was sure that if there was any clue to their activities, she would find it here.

She moved over to the desk and put down the candle. The top was remarkably tidy. There was the usual ink stand and pens and a small pile of visiting cards on the desk, plus the journal she had given Ran years ago, in the hope that it might amuse him to keep a diary. He had never used it, but had always kept it on his desk, as if to placate her.

She moved around and sat down at the desk, drumming her fingers on the polished wooden top. It was most likely that anything of importance would be in the drawers. She was not surprised to find the centre one was locked, but she dared not force it open so she moved on to the others. Despite having been in town for only a short time, they were crammed with bills, letters and invitations, but nothing out of the ordinary.

Deborah closed the final drawer and sat back. Somehow, she would have to persuade Ran to let her have the key to that locked drawer, but in the meantime, where else should she look? The room was lined with cupboards and bookcases, but most of the furniture had been hired with the house and she thought it unlikely that they would hold any secrets. However, to be sure she would have to go through them all, but not tonight. She was about to get up when her eyes fell on the journal again and she noticed a folded paper had been slipped between the pages. She drew the book towards her and opened it carefully. The paper was a letter, addressed to her brother. The seal had been broken so she spread the sheets, turning them towards the candle to read the contents. Almost immediately she knew she had every reason to meet Gil the next morning.

Chapter Fifteen

⧼⧽

The circulating library was crowded. Gil browsed the shelves, avoiding the flirtatious glances of a dashing matron who was standing before the Gothic romances. He moved towards the religious tracts and histories, where he could keep watch upon the doorway, and took a book off the shelf at random. Would she come?

He knew he had angered Deborah yesterday, but she had looked so delightful with that blush upon her cheeks that he could no more prevent himself from teasing her than he could stop the sun from shining. Whatever she might say, she could not hide the fact that she still felt something for him, her responses at the concert proved as much. It could never come to anything, he knew that, but it was enough to know she did not hate him.

He spotted Deborah as soon as she walked in with her maid. She was dressed with quiet elegance in a dark green spencer over a gown of pale green cambric muslin. With a word to her maid to wait by the door, she approached him slowly and when she was close he nodded towards the dark green bonnet that covered her soft curls.

'No veil, Miss Meltham?'

She did not look at him, but ran a finger along a row of books as if deciding which one to choose.

'That would only draw more attention,' she murmured, pulling out a slim volume and pretending to read. 'You will note that no one else is concealing their face.'

'That is very true.'

Her cool response filled him with tender admiration. He wanted to take her in his arms, but instead he moved around the corner, from where they could talk to one another without appearing to converse.

He was unable to resist saying quietly, 'I take it you did not come here this morning merely for the pleasure of seeing me?'

He felt a tiny kick of satisfaction when his words brought the tell-tale colour to her cheeks.

'No, of course not. I found something last night, in Ran's desk.' She kept her eyes on the open book. Anyone watching would think she was mouthing the words from the page. 'It was a letter from the captain of the *Margaret*, advising my brother that he had set sail for London.' For the first time, she betrayed agitation and her eyes flickered briefly upwards. 'There was something else.'

'Tell me.' He was on the alert now, no longer tempted to tease her.

'A bill of lading for three large pieces of furniture from the house in Duke Street. If...' She ran her tongue nervously over her lips. 'If they wanted to move a quantity of bank notes, storing them in the locked compartments of two sideboards and an Italian commode would be one solution.'

'It would indeed.'

'I dared not remove the papers, but I memorised them. The captain writes in his letter that he hopes to dock at Wapping early next week.'

'Thank you, I will look into that.'

'Perhaps I should ask Randolph about the furniture. I might be able to discover when he expects it to arrive.

'No,' he said quickly. 'I would rather you did not. If Warslow thinks you suspect anything at all he could become dangerous.'

'He is already dangerous.' She spoke calmly, but as she replaced the book on the shelf Gil saw that her hand was not quite steady. 'What you said yesterday, about carrying Ran away, abducting him. Is that true? Could you do it?'

'It *could* be done, yes.'

'I spent a great deal of time thinking of it last night, after I found those papers. Randolph is clearly implicated in Sir Sydney's plans and I do not see any other way to save him. I think Ran knows that, too. Perhaps I could take him to France, or Italy. Now the war is over we could be safe there.'

'To live in exile.' An icy hand clutched at Gil's heart. 'To leave everything you know. So far from all your friends.'

So far from me.

'Randolph would be safe and that is what matters.' She gave up all pretence of looking at books and turned towards him, her hands clasped before her. 'I have read in the newspapers about a poor woman who was convicted of possessing just two counterfeit bank notes. She was transported. Transported! Ran could survive a sea crossing to France, I think, but not to the other side of the world. I am sure his valet and my maid will help me. They might also wish to come with us, because they are more like family than servants. So, so I think that would be the best solution, do not you?'

Gil stared at her. She would be lost to him for ever. He swallowed, forcing himself to admit it was for the best. The attraction between them was too strong to be denied and if she remained within reach he knew without a shadow of a doubt that sooner or later he would take her to his bed again. He had risked her reputation once but he must not do so again.

Tell the truth, man, an inner voice mocked him. *Is it not also that you are afraid you will grow to love her and then risk the agony of losing her, as you lost Kitty and Robin? No wound received in battle has ever cut as deep as that.*

'I know I am asking you to help him escape the law,' she said, misreading his hesitation. 'If you feel you cannot help, then all I ask is that you do nothing to prevent me from spiriting Randolph away.'

He shook off his own selfish concerns to say quickly, 'Of course I will help you. It will take me few days to arrange everything, but I will do it, trust me.'

'I do.' She tried to smile and it tore at his heart when it went awry. 'I do trust you, my lord.'

More customers were crowding in and Gil shifted closer.

'Continue your walks in Green Park. I will send you word once I have made arrangements to spirit you and your brother from the country.'

He was rewarded with a faint smile and a speaking look from those green eyes before she turned to go. She left the shop and Gil browsed along a few more shelves, resisting the temptation to follow her out of the door. After a judicious amount of time he made his way to the street and strode off towards Gilmorton House. There was much to be done.

The next few days tested Deborah's nerves to the limit. She avoided Sir Sydney's advances and did her best to prepare Randolph by telling him an aunt was sending her a parcel of dress fabric and she depended upon him to go with her to collect it from the carrier. Her brother was patently uninterested, but agreed to accompany her when the time came, and with that she had to be satisfied.

As she had hoped, when she mentioned her plans to Elsie and Joseph Miller they were both determined to accompany them, even though Deborah made it plain that there would be little money to spare for wages. Deborah could not deny she was relieved by their loyalty, for she was more than a little daunted by the prospect of travelling alone with her brother to a foreign land, but she had no doubt that once out of danger and away from Sir Sydney's pernicious influence, Randolph would make some sort of recovery.

It was on the third morning, when she was making her usual circuit of Green Park, that she spotted the Viscount. An early shower of rain had reduced the number of people strolling in the park and it was easy to pick out his tall figure as he approached, walking with his usual firm stride. She immediately turned off the main path to stroll amongst the trees. She heard his brisk, familiar tread approaching and did not turn as he caught up with her.

'It is all arranged for tomorrow,' he said without preamble. 'There will be a carriage waiting for you at the White Horse in Piccadilly at ten in the morning. Can you have your brother there?'

'Yes, if I have to carry him,' she said vehemently. 'Sir Sydney has gone back to his own lodgings for the past few nights and I hope he will do the same tonight, because Ran is always better when he is not there. Miller and my maid are to accompany us out of the country. It is already agreed that they will leave the house before us, ostensibly with bags of clothes for the poor, but in fact that will be our luggage. Whatever we can pack in them must suffice until we can buy more.'

They were strolling along side by side. She thought suddenly that to a casual observer they could be discussing something as innocuous as the weather.

'And have you thought how you will live?' he asked her.

'Yes. I know Ran will not have an opportunity to make arrangements before we leave, so we are unlikely to be able to use what is left of his fortune. But I have my pin money for this quarter, which is untouched, and I asked my brother to draw some funds for me, which he has done. He thinks I need to pay my dressmaker.'

She fell silent, trying to block out her worries for the future.

'Perhaps we should go to Brussels,' she said. 'I understand one can live there for very little.'

'Not that little,' he growled.

'Well, we shall see. I am not sure if Ran will ever

be able to call upon his bank once we are abroad, but I have some jewellery that Mama left me, which I will sell if I have to, and when that is gone, I can always look for work. I might perhaps teach English.'

'Oh, for heaven's sake!' He ran a hand through his hair. 'As a teacher you would earn barely enough to keep yourself, let alone your brother.'

She was aware of that and it frightened her, but she was not prepared to admit it to Gil.

She said stubbornly, 'We shall manage.'

He stopped and caught her arm, obliging her to face him.

'Deborah, if you need funds you must write to me. I want you to give me your word on that.'

She tore herself from his grip, panicked by the way his touch brought back all the memories. The aching need...

'You owe me *nothing*, Lord Gilmorton,' she flashed.

'I am not doing this through any sense of obligation,' he exclaimed as she tore herself from his grasp. *'I love you!'*

Deb stared at him. Gil's face was white and he looked stricken, even more shocked than she was at his outburst. She swallowed.

'You, you do not mean that.'

He rubbed a hand over his eyes. 'I cannot bear to think of you living in poverty.'

Deborah felt the colour drain from her face. He had not denied it, yet it could not be true. He must be teasing her again, but when she looked at him there was no hint of a smile in his eyes. Instead she could see only pain and truth and torment.

He recollected himself and tried to smile. 'I beg

your pardon. You have made your feelings very plain and I realise a declaration is the very last thing you wish to hear from me. Pray try to forget I said it. My man will be waiting at the White Horse in the morning, he will have with him everything you need for your journey, travel papers, letters of introduction and money—not a great sum, but you will need it, if you are to travel in any degree of comfort.'

She was too stunned, too shaken to think clearly and barely heard his words. Love. How could he love her? When he reached for her hand she did not pull away and he carried her gloved fingers to his lips.

'This is the last time we shall meet. I wish you a good journey, Deborah. God bless you.'

She watched his dark head dip over her hand, felt the pressure as he squeezed her fingers, then he was gone, striding away from her. For ever.

Deborah walked back to Grafton Street like an automaton. All she could hear was Gil's voice, saying he loved her. All she could see were his eyes, near black and tortured. It could not be true. It *must* not be true. There was a time when her greatest desire had been for him to say those words, but not now. She would never see Gil again and she had resigned herself to that, but she could not bear the thought that he, too, might suffer from their parting.

'Of course it is not true,' she told herself, as she approached the steps of the house. 'If it were so, why would he tell me to forget it? It was a mistake, an, an aberration, caused by the heat of the moment. He had been at pains to show his indifference, from the moment I asked for his help. Whatever he may say, whatever I may *wish*, Lord Gilmorton sees me as an obligation, nothing more.'

And fighting back a sudden desire to weep, Deb straightened her shoulders and entered the house.

Randolph was in the dining room, alone. He was looking very pale and hollow-eyed, and when she came in he gave her a baleful look.

'Where have you been?' he demanded pettishly. 'I make the effort to come down for breakfast and you are not here.'

'Certainly not at this hour,' she said with a cheerfulness she was far from feeling. 'It is nearly noon. But I am here now and I shall sit down and take a cup of coffee with you.' She waited until the footman had set a fresh cup before her, then smiled at her brother. 'What are your plans for today?'

'I have no idea,' he snapped. 'Warslow is gone off somewhere and I—' He broke off and rubbed one hand over his white face. 'I beg your pardon, Deb. I feel hellish, but I should not take it out on you.'

She could not help a little spurt of irritation.

'Perhaps you would feel better if you did not drink so heavily of an evening. And as for the laudanum, I cannot believe it is doing you any good.'

Ran's fork clattered on to his plate and he exclaimed wrathfully, 'Hell and confound it, do not preach at me! I know perfectly well what I *should* do! Drinking helps me get through the evening and the laudanum—it helps me forget...' He put his elbows on the table and dropped his head in his hands. 'You should leave me, Deb. You can do no good here. Go back to Fallbridge, anywhere, but get out of London.'

'Only if you will come with me.'

He looked up at that and she saw the naked anguish in his eyes. Her heart went out to him, but she knew from bitter experience that it would not do to press the matter, so she refilled her coffee cup.

'Tomorrow I am expecting the package from Aunt Filey to arrive at the White Horse,' she remarked. 'Do not forget you promised to escort me.'

'I do not know. I must see how I feel.'

Deborah said nothing more. She finished her coffee and went upstairs to change her gown. She must not be downhearted at Ran's lacklustre response. There was a plan in place to rescue him from this nightmare and saving her brother was all she had ever wanted.

But deep inside, not quite buried, was the memory of Gil's outburst. He had said he loved her. It comforted her, even though she knew it was merely a manifestation of the guilt and remorse that he felt for the way he had treated her. She was convinced now that the Viscount was a good and honourable man, pushed beyond the limits by grief over the loss of his siblings. She of all people could understand that. But that he should utter those words—the very words that she had hoped, prayed, he would one day say to her, when she had given her heart to him back in Fallbridge—how could it fail to bring back thoughts of what might have been, if it had not been revenge that brought them together? If they had been free to love one another?

But they were not free. Even if there had been the slightest truth in his words there was too much between them that could be neither forgotten nor forgiven, so it was too late for her to realise now that she would much rather remain in London with Gil than fly to the Continent and never see him again.

'Good morning, my lord.' Harris opened the shutters, allowing the sunlight to flood into Gil's bedroom. 'Looks like a fine morning for a drive to the coast.'

'Do you have to be so damned cheerful?'

Gil buried his head in the pillow. Perhaps he should not have had so much brandy last night.

'I beg your pardon, my lord, but you told me to wake you before I set off.'

'Aye, well, perhaps I have changed my mind about that.'

Harris chuckled. 'Not you, my lord. Just a little bit top-heavy after last night is my guess, having seen the empty decanter downstairs! Now, I've brought your coffee. Do you want me to help you dress?'

Gil struggled to sit up, wincing a little at the early morning sunlight.

'No, no, you go off about your business. I can fend for myself. And, John...' he met his man's eyes '...see them safe aboard the packet before you come back.'

'Aye, my lord, you can depend on me.'

When Harris had departed, Gil leaned back against the pillows and closed his eyes. It was out of his hands now, Deb and her brother would soon be in France. Gil had insisted that his man go in person to Dover to make all the arrangements, for he wanted no incriminating letters left behind, and John could be relied upon to use his old army contacts to good effect. And now he was off to Kilburn to collect the travelling chaise purchased to carry Deborah and her brother to the Continent.

Gil had done everything he could to make their flight as comfortable as possible. Deborah's pride might balk at it, but she would accept his help for her brother's sake. And everything he did to help her flee the country was driving another nail into the coffin of his own happiness.

He was just tying his neckcloth when a footman informed him he had a visitor.

'A Miss Meltham, my lord. I have shown her into the drawing room.'

'What the devil—?' Gil glanced at his watch. It was not yet eight o'clock.

Dismissing the servant, he quickly shrugged himself into his coat and made his way downstairs.

Deborah had not removed her cloak and was pacing back and forth on the Aubusson carpet. When he entered the room she moved towards him, her hands held out.

'Thank heaven you are here!'

He pressed her gently into a chair, and dropped down beside her, pulling off her gloves to chafe her trembling hands between his own.

'Now,' he said, 'tell me what this is about. It must be something important to bring you here.'

'Oh, Gil, our plans are all undone.' Her fingers clutched at his, her green eyes dark with worry. 'The *Margaret* has already docked, and Sir Sydney has taken Randolph off with him to fetch the counterfeit notes.'

'You are sure of this?'

She nodded. 'I heard Ran arguing with Sir Sydney late last night.' She frowned, struggling to remember it accurately. 'It was almost midnight and word had just come that the *Margaret* was in port. Ran said he wanted no more to do with the business and that he would not have any more notes issued from his house because it was too dangerous. And then Sir Sydney said in that case Ran must go to Wapping with him and they would deal with the matter there.'

'On the ship?'

She shook her head. 'Sir Sydney mentioned Katherine Street. Ran owns a warehouse there, I have seen it mentioned in letters from our man of business. He urged Ran to sell it, because it has not been used for years, but as far as I know, Ran has never made any attempt to do so. I did not hear anything further; Enfield was prowling around and I was obliged to retire to my room.' She looked away, a flush of mortification staining her cheeks. 'Oh, I have been so foolish! Everything is lost!'

He squeezed her fingers. 'I doubt that. Tell me it all.'

'I thought they were planning to go to Wapping later today and, since they are in the habit of sitting up until dawn and then sleeping 'til past noon, I thought we should be able to get Ran to safety before Sir Sydney left his room. Instead, Elsie woke me an hour ago to say that instead of going to bed they had fetched a cab and gone out, and taken Enfield with them. Miller also told Elsie that he had watched from an upstairs window as they were leaving. They had b-been obliged to help my b-brother into the carriage, because he was so intoxicated he could barely stand...'

'And you think they have gone to the docks?'

'I am sure of it. I looked in Ran's study before leaving Grafton Street. The bill of lading is gone.'

'And if the bill is in your brother's name then Warslow will need him to sign for the goods,' said Gil.

'I thought as much. That is why I came directly to tell you. Even if Randolph returns to Grafton Street within the next hour or so I do not think I can take him out again this morning without arousing suspicion. And even worse…' her voice dropped to a whisper '…after last night's argument, I am afraid Sir Sydney will not allow him to return at all.'

He saw the sheen of tears in her eyes and made his decision.

'Then I must go and fetch him.' Gil jumped to his feet and reached for the bell-pull. 'Now, this is what we shall do. You must go directly to the White Horse and wait there for Harris to bring the travelling carriage. Send word to your maid and your brother's man to join you. I hope to be there with your brother before Harris arrives, but if not, you must explain what has happened and tell him to bring the carriage to Katherine Street.'

'But you cannot go alone.'

'There is no time for anything else.' He added in a bracing tone, 'Do not worry, if necessary I shall merely hold them all at the warehouse until Harris arrives.' He pulled her to her feet. 'Trust me, we shall come about. By nightfall I hope you will all be safely in France.'

'Gil—'

'Quickly now. We must summon a cab to take you to Piccadilly.'

He strode to the door and held it open for her. As she passed him she paused, her eyes searching his face.

'You will be careful, my lord?'

Unable to resist, he touched her soft cheek with his fingers.

'Of course. Go now. Your brother will be with you soon.'

Chapter Sixteen

Katherine Street was deserted. One side was bounded by the plain wall of the London dock while on the other, the early morning sun had not yet risen above the run-down wooden warehouses. Long shadows stretched across the road, but even against the light, Gil could see that the buildings were all in poor condition and most likely had not been used for decades. That would account for the lack of traffic, thought Gil, moving along the road as slowly as he dared. He was dressed in dark, plain clothing and he hoped anyone seeing him would think him a trader. He had no idea which building belonged to Lord Kirkster, but he guessed it might be the one at the end, where the double doors opening on to the street showed signs of recent and hasty repairs. Glancing up, he saw a new rope dangling from the hoist that jutted out above the opening to an upper floor. He walked around the corner, then slipped into the alley that ran around the back of the warehouse. In one section, the planks that formed the walls were hanging loose. For a moment he was shaken by doubt. The silence and desolation of the place was unsettling and the building was now so run-down he wondered if it could be secured to store anything at all.

Perhaps the furniture had been taken directly to Grafton Street. If so, where were Warslow and Kirkster? At that moment Gil heard a rumble, like distant thunder, or heavy furniture being dragged across a floor. It was faint and was gone in an instant, but it was enough. He made his way back to the weaker part of the wall and eased himself between the loose boards.

Inside Gil stood for a moment, allowing his senses to adjust to the gloom. There were no windows at ground level, but sunlight slanted between the warped and weathered boards and as his eyes grew more accustomed he could see that the ground floor of the warehouse was clear save for the odd empty crate. He was standing directly below an upper floor that stretched across half the building and the murmur of voices filtered down to him through the wooden flooring. Pulling a pistol from his pocket, Gil made his way cautiously across to the stairs.

He had his foot on the first tread when he felt a sharp prod in his back and a rough voice behind him said, 'Well, well. On the sneak, are we?'

Gil froze.

'I'll take that barker, if you please.'

Gil did not resist as a hand came from behind him and plucked the pistol from his grip.

'Who is it, Enfield?' Warslow's sharp voice came from above. 'Well, well, Viscount Gilmorton.'

Gil looked up just as the man himself looked over the rail at the edge of the upper floor.

'Do come up, my lord, but I advise you to keep

your hands in sight. I have no doubt that you have the second of those exquisite duelling pistols secreted in your pocket. Make no mistake, my lord, Enfield will not hesitate to shoot you if he thinks it necessary.'

'I am surprised he has not despatched me already,' said Gil as he began to climb the stairs, aided by another sharp prod in the back.

Warslow gave a silky laugh. 'Since you have come this far it would be a shame if you were to die before you have seen what is going on here.'

Gil stepped on to the upper floor, where the morning sun pushed its way through the grime on two small windows and lightened the gloom. The man behind him quickly moved around, keeping the pistol firmly pointed at Gil's chest. So this was Enfield, the butler from Grafton Street. Gil thought the fellow looked very much at home here, dressed in dark homespun with an old kerchief tied around his neck, more like a dock worker than a gentleman's servant.

Making sure he did not obstruct Enfield's aim, Warslow stepped up and searched Gil's pockets.

'As I thought,' he murmured, pulling the pistol from Gil's coat. 'I saw you use those duelling pistols during my army days and always admired them. Since you will not be requiring them any longer I think I shall appropriate them.' He put out an imperious hand and Enfield gave him the second weapon.

Gil said nothing. A quick glance showed him three pieces of furniture. An elegant bow-fronted commode and pair of sideboards stood in the centre of the floor, doors and drawers open and a series of leather bags lined up in front of them.

A movement took his eyes to a shadowed corner of

the room where Lord Kirkster was sitting on a chair, head drooping and an open wine bottle clutched in his hand. Gil thought he would not prove a hindrance.

At a word from Sir Sydney, Enfield pushed Gil on to an empty chair and tied his hands behind his back. Gil cursed him roundly, earning a blow to the face that rattled his teeth and split his lip. He cursed him again and took a fist in the stomach. Enfield would have followed up with even more blows if Warslow had not ordered him to stop. But the distraction had worked. The knot at Gil's wrists was not nearly as tight as it should have been.

'You had best go and look outside, Enfield,' Warslow barked. 'Gilmorton would be a fool to come alone.'

Yes, thought Gil, as Enfield clattered away down the stairs, he had been a fool, but he was not prepared to show it. He stretched his legs out before him as if he was completely at his ease as he looked around. He nodded towards the pieces of furniture.

'I have interrupted you. Counterfeit notes from Liverpool, I take it.'

'Very clever of you,' sneered Warslow. 'I knew when we met in Fallbridge that you were not there by coincidence. You were after Kirkster, were you not? You wanted to make him pay for what happened to your sister.'

The familiar black rage rose up in Gil. He fought it down, knowing only a cool head would help him now. He looked across at Randolph, who was sitting with his head in his hands.

'It seems to me he is paying dearly for his association with you, Warslow.'

'Can I help it if the boy is a drunkard and an opium eater?'

'But you encouraged him in his habits, did you not?'

'But of course. To have a lord at one's beck and call adds greatly to my reputation, I have gained no end of connections through it. He is very useful to me.'

'But no more!' Randolph shouted, the words slurring into one another. 'I told you this is the last time.'

He slumped back, the wine bottle dropping from his fingers. Gil threw Sir Sydney a contemptuous glance.

'I cannot admire your choice of accomplice, Warslow.'

'No, I had hoped he would be more use to me today. We should have been gone from here by now if he had been able to help pack the bags and Enfield has already arranged for the first batch to go out.' A flicker of impatience crossed his face. 'I begin to think Kirkster has outlived his usefulness. And I have to admit his conscience is becoming troublesome.'

Gil froze. A question now might prompt Kirkster to confess, but the last thing he wanted to hear at this moment was how Randolph had seduced Kitty and slain Robin. That might well make Gil forget his promise to save him. He addressed Warslow again.

'Was it Kirkster's idea or yours to use his house as a base for your intrigues?'

'He needs my money to disguise the fact that he has used up his own fortune, so he could hardly object when I put this scheme to him.'

'And you are using his servants to distribute forgeries to the poor wretches you have persuaded to do your dirty work.'

Warslow spread his hands. 'They all make something from it, Gilmorton.'

'But not as much as you.'

'No, not as much as I.'

The reply was smug, complacent, and Gil strained against the ropes binding his wrists. There was some movement, but his fingers could not yet work on the knot. He must keep Warslow talking.

'You see, Gilmorton, the secret is to spread the notes between dozens of utterers, men and women who pass them off on unsuspecting tradespeople. That way there is no pattern that the Bank inspectors can trace. It has taken me months to organise everything, persuading Kirkster to move to London, hiring servants I could trust to keep their mouths closed and setting up the gangs of utterers throughout London, mostly respectable but poor working people, desperate to earn a little extra money.'

'And everything can be linked to Kirkster, but not to you,' said Gil, his lip curling. 'Despicable.'

'But ingenious, you must admit.'

'Hiding behind that poor wretch?' Gil jerked his head towards Randolph. 'Such conduct is not worthy of a gentleman. But then you never were that. Even in the army you were a coward.'

The barb hit its mark. Warslow's face darkened, he stepped forward, hand raised, and Gil prepared himself for a blow. It never came. There was the creak of boards and Gil heard Enfield's voice as the man came quickly up the stairs.

'It's as quiet as the grave out there. It seems the Viscount came alone after all.'

'Did he, now?' murmured Warslow, regarding Gil with contempt. 'How singularly inept.'

'Aye, ain't he just?' said Enfield, advancing upon Gil. 'I'll get rid of him now, shall I? Then we can get on.'

Warslow waved him away.

'No, not quite yet. I want Lord Gilmorton to dwell a while longer on just how badly he has failed his family.' He took out his watch. 'Some of our, ah, customers will be waiting for you at the fish market. You had best take one of the bags and go there now, we do not want to disappoint them. Afterwards you can come back here and help me to dispose of the Viscount.'

Enfield hesitated, his fists clenched. The look he gave Gil showed clearly that he would enjoy inflicting more punishment.

'If you are sure, Sir Sydney…'

'Of course I am sure, cloth-head! The sooner the utterers get those notes the better. I will pack up the rest while you are gone.'

'And where are you going to store them, if Kirkster will no longer have them in the house?' Gil enquired.

'Oh, they will go to Grafton Street, whatever Kirkster might say. It's that damned sister of his I blame for this sudden attack of conscience, but I shall soon have him back under control.'

'By feeding him laudanum until he is too befuddled to think clearly!'

Warslow scowled, but did not respond immediately. He waited in silence while Enfield picked up two of the leather bags and hurried away, then he turned back to Gil, his teeth bared in a vicious smile.

'Always so honourable, are you not, Gilmorton?

Even in the army you were always ready to condemn me, always happy to show me up in front of the other officers. But what good has it done you? You were too busy winning your battles and taking care of your men to look after your own family.'

Gil's brows snapped together.

'What the devil do you know of that?' he demanded.

Warslow's evil smile grew wider.

'It must gall you, my lord, to think that you were not there to protect sweet little Kitty and defend her honour. Oh, yes, I can see that it does. And I think it will gall you even more to know the truth. It wasn't that drunken sot who seduced your pretty little sister, it was I! And you will choke on this, Gilmorton, she did not think me a villain. She was besotted. So much in love that she was willing to run away with me.'

Gil fought down a growl of rage and strained his fingers to pick at the knot. It was loosening, but not enough yet for him to escape. Warslow's eyes were shining with cruel triumph.

'Oh, yes, sweet little Kitty. I came upon her quite by accident, you know, but having discovered she was your sister I could not resist the opportunity to repay you for spoiling my chances of promotion, for making my life hell in the army. It was absurdly easy. She was such an innocent, you see, it was amusing to see how she doted on me.'

Gil's rage was barely contained as he listened to this, but mixed with his fury was relief for Deborah. Her brother had not seduced Kitty. His fingers were sore, his muscles ached with the strain, but Gil was sure that he would soon be able to slip the rope from his wrists. He would need to choose his moment to give him the best possible advantage. Now, more than ever, he wanted to bring Warslow to justice.

He needed to keep Warslow talking, to distract him and learn as much as possible.

'And you used Kirkster's name for your evil plans.'

'Why not? It added a certain...elegance to the deception.'

'What's that?' Randolph raised his head and peered across the room. 'Who used my name?'

'Your *friend* Warslow,' barked Gil, keeping his eyes on Sir Sydney. 'While you were at home, sleeping off the effects of the laudanum he feeds you, Warslow was seducing an innocent girl in your name!'

'No.' Randolph shook his head as if trying to clear it. 'That's not right. Couldn't have been Sydney.'

'He was posing as you, Kirkster. Fouling your good name,' Gil went on. 'And when she was with child he abandoned her. She was so ashamed that she drowned herself.'

'No. S-Sydney wouldn't do that.'

'Would he not? Did you not think it odd that her brother should come to Duke Street, demanding satisfaction?'

Randolph shook his head again. 'I don't know anything about that.'

'No, of course you don't.' Warslow walked across to Randolph, holding out a small bottle to him. 'You are not thinking clearly, my lord. Here, take a little more of this.'

'No, I don't want...' but Randolph's hand was already going out towards it.

Gil watched him tip up the bottle, swallowing the liquid and sinking back on the chair with a sigh.

Warslow waited until his eyes were closed again, then he turned back to Gil.

'Since you are not going to leave here alive, Gilmorton, there is no reason why you should not know the truth. In fact, I want you to know it. Yes, your brother came to Duke Street to demand satisfaction, but he was denied admittance, so he wrote to Kirkster instead.'

'What?' muttered Randolph, rubbing his eyes, 'I never received any letter.'

'No, you drunken fool,' retorted Warslow with a contemptuous sneer. 'The letter came into my hands and *I* arranged to meet him.'

'The devil you did,' exclaimed Gil.

Warslow laughed. 'Just another thought to take to your grave with you, Gilmorton. It should have been *you* defending your sister's honour, not a schoolboy. But you won't worry over it for long, you will be dead before morning, and your body will be found floating in the river.'

'No.' Randolph struggled to his feet, but fell back against his chair. 'That, that's murder. I won't be party to murder.'

'You already are, Kirkster,' Gil told him. 'Warslow has been using you for his own ends and when he's finished he will destroy you with as little compunction as he destroyed my sister and brother.'

Gil had no idea if he heard him, for Randolph had collapsed on the floor, his eyes closed and his breathing ragged.

'You are wasting your time, Gilmorton, the fool is too full of opium and wine to understand you.'

'And you keep him that way, so you may use his house and his name for your own purposes.'

'Why not?' Warslow laughed. 'What else is the fool fit for? He has proved to be a convenient tool for me, first in Liverpool, where I used his identity to cover my tracks, and now here in London. You would not believe how many rich men and their wives are ready to toady up to a man just because he is a lord. He has been my entrée into another world, one where I can disperse even more of my counterfeit notes. No one would ever think to suspect Lord Kirkster and his good friend of anything untoward. But you are right, the fellow is becoming unreliable. He will have to go, but not yet. I need to keep him sweet for a little longer, at least until I can get his sister in my bed. The puritanical Deborah is proving very elusive, but the prize is always better for being hard-won, don't you think, Gilmorton?'

Only by supreme force of will could Gil remain impassive as Warslow looked at him, a triumphant smile on his face.

'You had an interest there yourself at one time, did you not, my lord? When I came to Fallbridge there was some talk that you were trying to fix your interest with Miss Meltham, but no doubt it was all part of your attempts to get closer to her brother. Fortunately for the lady, I queered your pitch there.'

Gil taunted Warslow with a laugh. 'Do you think you will fare any better?'

'I am sure I shall, because if she will not come into my arms willingly, then I shall use other methods—' He broke off, raising his head at the sounds of movement below. He moved towards the rail and looked down. 'Ah, Miss Meltham herself, we were just talking of you. How did you…ah, but I suppose Enfield left the door unbolted. Well, you had best come up, my dear.'

Gil's blood froze. He was not yet free. He did not want Deborah to walk into danger while he was unable to protect her.

'No!' he shouted down to her. 'Leave here now, madam. Go!'

'You will stay!' Warslow screamed over him. 'If you wish to keep your brother alive!'

Gil did not need to see the man's self-satisfied look to know that Deborah would remain. She would protect Randolph at all costs. He heard her light feet on the steps.

'That is right, my dear,' purred Warslow. 'Do come and join us. Ah, and you have brought your brother's valet. That was very thoughtful of you.' He weighed Gil's duelling pistol in his hand before casting a swift, sneering glance towards Gil. 'Who knows, I may even have the chance to try out this little beauty.'

Gil schooled his features to stony indifference as Deborah reached the top of the stairs, praying she would follow his lead and pretend they had not met since Fallbridge.

'What is going on here?' Deborah demanded. 'Where is…?'

Her eyes widened when she saw Gil tied to the chair and since Warslow was not looking at him, Gil risked a little shake of his head. There was a heartbeat's hesitation before she continued.

'I want to see my brother.' A groan from the shadowed corner caught her attention. 'Randolph!'

She flew across to him. Miller, the valet, hesitated, until Warslow indicated by a jerk of the head that he should attend his master. Gil watched as they struggled to help Randolph on to the chair, Deborah murmuring to him and gently pushing the hair from his forehead. Warslow strolled over, as if to observe them, and it was only at the last moment that Gil realised what he was about to do. He called a warning, but it was too late, Warslow brought the handle of the pistol crashing down on Miller's head and he crumpled, unconscious, to the floor.

Deborah gave a cry and jumped aside, staring aghast at the valet's inert form.

'He will survive,' Warslow told her, dropping the pistol into his pocket. 'But the odds were stacking up against me and I could not risk being overpowered.'

Casting him a look of loathing, Deb turned back to her brother. His head had rolled back, his eyes half-closed as he muttered incoherently. She scooped up the little bottle and sniffed at it. 'Laudanum!' She glared at Warslow, her eyes flashing. 'You devil, to feed him such stuff when you know it will kill him.'

'Eventually, perhaps, but not yet.'

'Fiend!' She threw the flask on the floor and took a step forward, her hands clenching into fists at her side. 'You have used him, embroiled him in your monstrous schemes!'

'Yes, I admit it.' Warslow laughed and moved towards her. 'You are both enmeshed so surely now that you have no choice but to continue. The law takes the manufacture of forged notes very seriously. It is a hanging offence, madam, you will not want to risk that. But if you show me a little kindness, my dear, I will make sure you are well rewarded. Who knows, if you please me, I may even spare your brother.'

He reached out and grabbed Deb's wrist, pulling her towards him. Deb swung her free arm up and caught him a resounding slap, but Warslow's response was merely to laugh again as he caught her hand.

'Damn you, let go of her!'

Gil's outburst merely brought more laughter. 'Ever the gentlemen, eh, Gilmorton? Well you couldn't save your own sister and you won't save Miss Meltham. But you might enjoy watching, to see how one tames a reluctant woman.'

Still laughing, he dragged Deborah into his arms, tearing away her cloak and ripping her gown in the process. She fought him violently, but was no match for his strength and could only turn her face to avoid his mouth. Gil's fingers worked at the knot binding his wrists. It was loosening, almost enough. And all the time Warslow was overpowering Deborah. He caught her face, determined to kiss her. Gil saw that she had one hand free and she reached up to her hair. The light flashed on the steel of the hatpin she pulled out and stabbed into Warslow's neck. He screamed and she managed to wrench herself out of his grip.

Gil felt the rope burning the skin as he dragged his hands free. He leapt at Warslow even as Deborah staggered away. Gil brought one fist back and landed a crashing blow upon his opponent's jaw, sending him sprawling, unconscious, to the floor.

Quickly Gil turned to Deborah. She was crouching against the sideboard, shaking.

'Oh, my poor love!' In a stride he was beside her, helping her to her feet. He said unsteadily, 'Confounded woman. Why did you not do as you were told and stay at the inn?'

Her hands clung to him. 'I c-could not. I had to come—' Her wandering gaze moved past him and she gasped, her fingers digging into his arms. 'Gil, look out!'

He was already turning. Warslow was on his feet and reaching into his pocket, but before Gil could move, Randolph shot past and with a cry of rage launched himself at Warslow. He ran full-tilt into him, the force of it carrying both men against the railing. It splintered under the weight and they plunged down to the ground below.

'Ran!'

Deborah shrieked her brother's name as she saw him disappear. She ran forward, but Gil caught her before she reached the broken railing, holding her back. Carefully they approached the edge of the platform and peered down into the shadowy space beneath them. To Deb's relief Randolph was pushing himself to his feet and she called down to him. He looked up, swaying slightly.

'Nothing broken, I think.'

Satisfied that he was not hurt, Deborah quickly turned back to Gil. She was already clutching his coat, holding it tightly, as if her fingers never wanted to let him go again. Now she reached up to touch the freshly grazed skin on his cheekbone and the cut on his lip.

'Oh, Gil, I am so sorry,' she said contritely. 'I should never have involved you in our troubles.'

'They are my troubles, too.' His arm tightened around her. 'You were right, Deb. Warslow confessed it all to me, how he masqueraded as Randolph to woo my sister and kill my brother.'

'Oh, Gil.'

Just for a moment he allowed her sympathy to warm him, then he frowned at her. 'But what are you doing here, why did you not wait for Harris?'

'It was not yet nine when I reached the White Horse, I could not bear to wait for him. I left Elsie there to give him your message, but I was so anxious I had to come and find out what was happening.'

'And put yourself into grave danger,' he retorted. 'If ever there was anyone so foolish!' He stopped and his face lost something of its hard, angry look. 'I do not know why I should be so surprised. I know you would do anything for your brother.'

She caught the faintest trace of wistfulness in his voice, saw the bleak look in his eyes and her hand, which had slipped to his shoulder, lifted, ready to cup his face.

'It wasn't only for—'

'Deborah.'

There was an urgency in Randolph's voice that cut across her words. Gil released her and they turned again to look down to the lower floor. Ran was kneeling beside Warslow's body.

'I landed on top of him,' he said now. 'He broke my fall, but I think I killed him.'

Chapter Seventeen

Warslow's contorted figure lay sprawled on the ground like a broken rag doll. Kneeling beside him, it took Gil only a moment to confirm that he was dead. There was a trickle of blood on his neck where Deborah had stabbed him and the hatpin had fallen on to the dusty floor close by.

Randolph leaned heavily against his sister. 'I never meant to kill him, Deb, you must believe me.'

'No, it was an accident, I know that.' She was standing with one arm about her brother, helping to steady him, but her voice broke as she whispered, 'But who will believe it?'

The door banged open. Gil's head snapped round, but he relaxed visibly as Harris came in.

'You have the travelling carriage outside?'

'In the alley alongside here, yes. And not a moment too soon, my lord. There is a party of men making their way along Katherine Street, checking every warehouse.' He added grimly, 'They looks mighty like the Bank inspector and the Bow Street Runner we saw in Liverpool.'

'The devil it is,' exclaimed Gil.

'We must get you out of here, now,' he said to Deborah. He looked up to see the valet coming down the stairs. 'Miller, come and help your master. You and Harris must get Miss Meltham and Lord Kirkster away from here. You will find a couple of boards loose in the back wall over there, if you leave that way you will not be seen. Go now, get them away to Dover and on to France as quick as you can.'

Deborah watched him pick up the hatpin and thrust it into his pocket.

'What about you?' She caught his arm. 'You must come with us.'

He was tense, like a man going into battle. His eyes were blazing with energy and she thought he was not really seeing her.

He said, 'If they find Warslow's body here, in your warehouse, there will be an immediate hue and cry. I will delay them. Give you time to get away.'

'But you can't.' She stared at him, horrified. 'If they find you here, they will think…'

'That is not important now. We must get you to safety.'

'No.' The word was no more than a whisper, her throat clogged with fear. 'You cannot do this. They will hang you!'

He looked at her. The blaze in his eyes softened for a brief moment.

'We will worry about that once you are safe. Now go. Harris, get them out of here.'

'I can't leave you.' Deborah felt as if her feet were nailed to the floor. 'Let Miller take Randolph to France. I want to stay here, with you!'

She saw the shadow cross his face, then he was smiling, running a finger along her cheek.

'There is nothing you can do here, Deb. Go and look after your brother.'

His face hardened. He looked over her head and barked an order to his man.

'John, take 'em away. Now.'

I want to stay. I want to be with Gil.

Deb felt a touch on her arm and heard Harris say quietly, 'Mistress, let us go.'

Her brother or her love.

Deborah hesitated, but Gil had turned away and was retrieving his pistols from the dead man's pockets. She put a hand to her mouth, feeling sick as Harris hurried her away.

They had just reached the loose boards at the back of the warehouse when Deb heard the heavy crash of the door being flung open and the confused noise of many feet and voices. Harris pushed her through the opening and followed her out, hurrying her away towards the waiting chaise.

After the dusty gloom of the warehouse the sunlight was glaring. Deborah breathed in, clearing her lungs and her head. Miller was half-carrying, half-dragging Randolph along the street, but Deborah stopped.

'You must go back,' she said to Gil's man. 'You must help your master.'

Harris shook his head. 'His lordship wouldn't thank me if I did that, Miss Meltham. He charged me with getting you and Lord Kirkster away safely and that is what I must do.'

He took her arm and almost hustled her towards the

carriage. A footman was holding the horses' heads and a second, sitting on the box, jumped down to open the door as they approached. There was something about their appearance that struck her as odd. Their livery was straining at the seams and they looked more like pugilists than footmen. When Harris stood back to allow her to climb into the carriage Deb caught his arm.

'You could take your hirelings back to the warehouse and free the Viscount,' she said urgently. 'We will wait here—we might all escape!'

'And we might all end up at Bow Street.' Gently Harris eased her fingers from his sleeve. 'That's not what they was hired for, Miss Meltham, and not what his lordship would want. He made me swear that I would get you out o' the country, whatever happened. In you get now, we will collect your maid from Piccadilly and get you to Dover as quick as we can. Once you are all safely aboard the packet I'll come back and look to his lordship. Trust me, madam, the Viscount has a full purse with him; he won't come to no harm for a day or two without me.'

With that she had to be satisfied. She climbed in beside her brother and his valet, Harris scrambled up on to the box and they set off at a smart pace. Deborah stared out of the window, her thoughts bleak. The charges were serious; counterfeiting notes was high treason and carried the death sentence, as did murder. Gil's rank and money would buy him a modicum of comfort while he was in gaol awaiting trial, but in the end, it would not save him from the executioner.

She closed her eyes, knowing now with a blinding, heartbreaking clarity that Gil loved her. It was for her sake that he had sacrificed everything—his good name, his honour, his freedom, his very life—to protect her and Randolph. She had thought no one could ever love her, but Gil was proving she was wrong. With his life.

They drove back to the White Horse to collect Elsie and Deborah ordered Miller and her maid to fetch several flasks of water from the inn.

'We need to flush the laudanum from Lord Kirkster's body, if we can,' she told Harris as they waited for the servants to return.

'We must crack on if we are to reach Dover this evening, so I was planning only to stop to change horses,' said Harris. 'However, if you want me to stop more often I can do so.'

'On no account,' she replied quickly. 'The sooner we are out of the way the sooner you can return to the Viscount.'

'But Lord Kirkster—'

'We shall look after him, but he shall have no more of that poison, nor wine or spirits while I have him in my charge.' She saw Harris glance at Randolph and she added, with far more confidence than she felt, 'My brother has the constitution of an ox. He will recover from this addiction, given time and good nursing.'

She clung to that thought for the rest of the day, as the carriage rattled on for mile after mile and Randolph came out of his stupor, demanding that they return to London. When it was explained to him that they could not go back he was by turns resigned, maudlin or angry. She encouraged him to drink the water or to take a hurried cup of tea or coffee from the various posting houses where they stopped to change horses. It was then that Deborah was most thankful for the help of their two devoted servants in preventing Randolph from obtaining anything stronger to drink from the inns.

As the day wore on Ran became more desperate and they were obliged to physically restrain him to prevent him from jumping from the moving carriage. He screamed at Miller, damning him to hell and dismissing him from his service. When Deborah tried to apologise for her brother, Miller merely shook his head at her and smiled grimly.

'Nay, miss, we've seen this before, when his lordship has partaken too heavily of laudanum. I don't take any notice of it. And you know as well as I that this mood will pass.'

Deborah did know it, but when her brother's anger faded she found his self-pity just as wearing. They stopped to dine at Canterbury, where Harris arranged a private parlour for Deborah and her brother.

Ran picked at his food, finding fault with everything, and she began to wish they were eating in the main dining room along with the servants. When she refused to allow Ran to drink anything other than small beer he slumped in his chair, muttering. Suddenly Deb could stand no more.

'Stop it!' she cried, almost dropping her tea cup in its saucer. 'For heaven's sake, Randolph, you are not the only one who is suffering! None of us wishes to go to France, I can assure you, and if you knew the damage your addiction has caused—!'

She broke off, clapping her hands to her mouth, horrified at her outburst. Ran looked up and frowned at her, a gleam of understanding brightening his dulled eyes.

'I beg your pardon,' she said, hunting for a hand-kerchief. 'I should not have spoken.'

She turned away, wiping her eyes, and heard Ran give a shuddering sigh.

'Don't cry, love. Please don't cry.' he said quietly. 'I have been a crass fool, but one day I will make it up to you, Deb. I will make you proud of me, I swear it.'

'Yes, of c-course you will, my dear.' Deb blinked back her tears and tried to sound cheerful, to tell her-self they might be happy again, once they were settled abroad, but she knew now it was too late. Her heart would remain in England.

Gil was taken to Bow Street, where he maintained his innocence of forgery and insisted that Sir Syd-ney Warslow's death had been an accident. Unfor-tunately, the Bank inspector recognised him as Mr Victor, whom he had seen coming out of Lord Kirk-ster's Liverpool house.

'And don't think of denying it,' the inspector con-tinued, when Gil did not respond immediately. 'There can't be too many men with a scar like that on their face. Now you tells us you are not Mr Victor, but a viscount, and you have been found standing over a dead man, in a warehouse containing a quantity of forged bank notes. Things is looking pretty black for you, my lord.'

Yes, thought Gil. Things looked black and, once it was discovered that Kirkster had fled the country, they would look even blacker.

* * *

News of Deborah and Randolph's flight reached Gil in the early evening. He learned from one of the gaolers that the Bank inspector, scenting that his quarry might escape him, had sent officers to check the ports. Gil could only hope that Deb and her brother would be safely out of the country, but until Harris returned to London he could not be sure, so he clung tenaciously to his story and refused to add anything to his previous statement.

A meeting with his family lawyer the same evening brought Gil little comfort. The man told him bluntly that unless he laid the blame for Warslow's death squarely upon Lord Kirkster and confessed everything he knew of Kirkster's involvement in the counterfeiting scheme there was no possibility of acquittal, but Gil was adamant that he would not say anything to incriminate Randolph.

Eventually the lawyer went away, shaking his head at his client's obstinacy and hoping that a night's reflection would bring the Viscount to his senses.

Left alone to consider his fate, Gil realised his prospects were bleak indeed. His spirits sank lower as he tossed and turned restlessly on the hard bed, watching the darkness turn into a grey and windy dawn. If this weather had blown in from the south there was every possibility that the packet had not sailed, so he could not even be certain that he had achieved his aim of keeping Deborah and Randolph safe.

Chapter Eighteen

Gil stirred and opened his eyes, looking up towards the square of light where the sun struggled to shine through the small window set high in the wall. His first thought was for Deborah. Was she safe? Had John managed to get them to Dover in time for the evening packet, or perhaps they had sailed at first light. That is, if they had avoided the law officers sent out to bring them back to London for questioning. He lay still for a moment, calculating how soon he could expect Harris to get back to London and tell him. If his man had not been arrested along with the rest of the party.

He closed his eyes again, finding solace in the last look he had seen on Deb's face. There had been no hatred for him then. True, there had been sorrow, but there had also been concern. It might not be love, but it was certainly a confirmation of the bond he had always felt existed between them. That alone made it worthwhile. He could never regret meeting Deborah Meltham, and not only because she had taught him what loving someone really meant.

If they had not met, if he had not agreed to help

her, Deborah and her brother would even now be here in Newgate, awaiting trial at the next sessions. He prayed now, as he had never prayed before, that they were safely abroad. That the pain his disgrace would inflict upon his family, and in particular his mother, would not be in vain.

'All for love,' he muttered, quoting Dryden's most famous play. 'And it is indeed the world well lost.'

Forcing away such dismal thoughts, Gil sat up and stretched. His rank and wealth had enabled him to secure a room to himself with a few basic amenities, but a straw mattress was no substitute for his own feather bed. He called for the gaoler, demanding hot water for shaving, and at the same time he reached into his pocket for his purse. One could get anything in Newgate. For a price.

The square of sunlight moved across the wall, indicating that the morning was advancing. With the discipline borne of years of military service, Gil made his bed, then washed, shaved and dressed himself in the clean clothes he had ordered to be fetched from his house. Whatever the day brought forth, he would look his best. He was just putting the finishing touches to his cravat when he heard the door open and a rough voice invite someone to enter. At last, Harris had returned. Now he would learn the truth!

He turned, expecting to see his man, but the vision that met his eyes stopped his breath. Deborah stood in the doorway, her dusty travelling cloak around her shoulders. She held her bonnet in her hands, turning it nervously between her fingers. The gaoler was looking on with interest and Gil knew he should remain indifferent, treat her as a mere acquaintance, but it was beyond him to hide his smile at the sight of her and he knew his eyes were shining with all the love that would not be denied.

Her anxious look faded, she ran into his arms, saying with a sob, 'I could not go. I could not leave you.'

Gil held her tight and rested his head on her hair, closing his eyes. He had dreamed of this moment, but given up hope that it would ever happen.

'Forgive me,' she murmured against his chest.

'There is nothing to forgive.'

He threw a coin to the gaoler, waited until the heavy wooden door was closed and they were alone before putting his fingers beneath her chin and tilting her head up for a kiss. It was as sweet as he remembered, the shock of desire striking through him with as much intensity as it had the first time.

She did not resist. Her hunger matched his, the kiss was full of longing and desire and regret for the time they had wasted. Gil did not want it to end, he wanted to lose himself in her, but she fluttered in his arms and immediately he lifted his head, although he could not bring himself to release her. She looked up at him, her eyes beseeching.

'Ran has gone on to France. He is implicated so deeply in Sir Sydney's plans that he will almost certainly face execution if he is caught. I could not insist he come back with me, can you forgive me?'

He put a finger against her lips. 'Hush now. We know Randolph never intended any harm. If he is safe in France now, then we shall be thankful for it. Tell me instead how you come to be here.'

He guided Deborah to the bed where he sat down with her, still holding her hand. She placed her bonnet carefully on the bed before clutching at his fingers again. She leaned against him, as if she was as desperate as he not to break contact.

'We had reached Canterbury before I realised I could not leave you to carry the burden for us all. Harris took my brother and Miller on to Dover and Elsie returned with me on the night mail.'

'Then where is your maid now?' He frowned. 'She should be here. You do your reputation no good being here alone with me.'

She looked up at him, a shy, teasing smile in her eyes. 'I was afraid you might not kiss me if I had my maid with me.'

'You are wrong. Nothing would have stopped me kissing you!'

She blushed adorably at that and nestled against him with a sigh.

'We reached town very early this morning,' she said. 'I was so fatigued that we took a room at a nearby inn. Elsie is there now, waiting for me.' Her smile disappeared as she turned her head to look at him, suddenly serious. 'I was not sure if you would wish to see me.'

'Oh, my dearest heart!' He kissed her again. 'I *should* have sent you away,' he muttered, holding her close. 'I told the Runners I hardly knew you.'

She gave a soft chuckle. 'Impossible to deny it now, my love.'

My love. His heart lurched.

'Is that true?' He cupped her face, gently raising it so he could look into her eyes, hardly daring to believe what he was hearing. '*Am* I your love?'

The glow in her eyes told him it was so.

'I did not want to love you,' she said, smiling mistily up at him. 'But from the moment we first met I felt the connection. Nothing could break it.'

He kissed her again, gently this time. His heart was thudding so hard against his ribs that he could scarce speak.

'For me also,' he confessed. 'It was not a choice, you are a part of me, as necessary as breathing.'

'My dear love!' With a sob she buried her face in his coat. 'This is all my fault. I should never have asked for your help. I have embroiled you most disastrously in our affairs.'

He rested his cheek against her hair, his mouth twisting into a wry smile. 'I was *embroiled* from the first moment I saw you, at great cost to yourself. And my actions against you were wholly unjustified. I can never forgive myself for that.'

'But if you had not come seeking revenge, we would never have met. And until I met you I did not think I could love, or be loved, ever again.' Her arms tightened around him. 'If only...'

'Yes. If only.'

She sat up. 'I will speak for you,' she said. 'I will tell them what really happened. That Sir Sydney coerced Randolph into helping him.'

'And will you also tell them that your brother killed him?'

'It was an accident.'

'Oh, my darling, do you think anyone will believe that?'

'They will, when I explain it all,' she said fiercely. 'I will convince them that you are innocent.'

He shook his head. 'And do you think, when word

gets out that you have been here with me, that a jury will believe we are not all involved in this? No. The best we can hope for is to keep you out of this scandal.' Reluctantly he let her go and went to the door. 'If you leave now we may yet succeed.'

'I am not going.' He turned to stare at her and she put up her chin, saying obstinately, 'I shall remain here with you.'

'Impossible.'

'Not at all. I have seen women staying with prisoners in the other cells. The gaoler told me it is perfectly possible. There is a charge, of course, but that is not an insurmountable problem.'

He swore under his breath. 'Deb, you cannot stay here. Those other women…'

'I know exactly what they are and it does not concern me.'

'Well, it should,' he exclaimed wrathfully. 'You are a lady.'

'I am your lover—!' She broke off, colour rushing to her cheeks. She looked shocked by her own words, but it was quickly followed by uncertainty. 'It was only one night and perhaps it did not mean so much to you.'

Her eyes were large and luminous in the dim light and he felt the rush of desire heating his blood.

'It meant everything to me,' he said, his voice low and shaking with raw emotion. 'That is why you must go. Perhaps, when the trial is over, we could meet. We could start again.'

She gave a little huff of exasperation.

'I have told you before I am not a child, Gil. I know as well as you what the outcome of your trial is likely to be. I want to be with you, here, now. For as long as I can.'

She moved towards him and pressed her hands against his chest. His heart reacted to her touch, pounding as if it would break through the ribs to reach her. He closed his eyes, clenched his fists at his sides to stop himself taking her into his arms again.

'No, Deborah. Don't do this.'

'Why?' Her voice was so close, caressing, like silk against his senses. 'We have a little time left together, Gil. Time to make up for the months we have lost.'

She put her arms around him and rested her head against his shoulder. He could smell her perfume, fresh and light with the subtle hint of summer flowers. It transported him away from Newgate, out into the fields and rolling hills around Fallbridge where he had walked and ridden with Deborah. Where he had fallen in love with her.

'Please, Gil, do not deny me the comfort of being with you, of loving you. Even for the short time we have left.'

Deborah closed her eyes and prayed he would not send her away. Pressed against him, she knew his body wanted her, but he was holding back, resisting. She waited, clinging to him, listening to the thud of his heart, the ragged breathing that gave the lie to his silence.

'You should go now, Deborah.'

With an angry cry she pushed herself away from him.

'How can you say that?' she demanded furiously. 'You are perfectly ready to sacrifice your pride, your honour and your family name to save my brother. You tell me it is for my sake, that you are doing this for my happiness, but do you not see that the only happiness I have is with you?'

She dashed a hand across her eyes. This was no time for tears, she must fight for what she wanted and fight hard.

'You are a foolish, stubborn man, Lord Gilmorton,' she told him. 'But you will not be rid of me that easily. You think I haven't considered what it would be like to live with you in here, as your mistress? To be scorned and mocked? Believe me, I have thought of little else on my journey back to town, and I am quite prepared to suffer the jibes and taunts and the gossip if it means I can share a little more time with you.

'But if you insist on sending me away then I shall come back, every day. They say money can buy almost anything in this place, well, I have a little money and I will spend it all, if necessary. I will bring your meals, fetch you water for washing, run your errands. I will camp outside your door, if they will let me, and I am sure if I pay them well enough they will do so. And I shall attend your trial, testify to your good name, even if it does no good at all. You taught me to love again, Gil. You taught me that there are still good men in this world, men to be trusted. And I want this world to know how much I love you, my lord, even if you refuse to acknowledge it!'

She turned from him, hunting for her handkerchief and biting her lip hard in an attempt to stop herself from weeping with frustration. Beyond the door, the passageway rang with the sound of footsteps and loud voices as the gaolers went about their business, exchanging banter with each other and their prisoners. Inside the cell, there was only silence.

'We could buy a feather bed,' he said at last. 'I could get a special licence. Make an honest woman of you. If this is what you truly want.'

Relief flooded through Deborah. She exhaled, feeling the tension ease. This was no Gothic romance like Mrs Radcliffe's novels. Deb knew there could be no happy ending, but she and Gil could give one another a few more memories, a little comfort. She turned slowly and walked back to him. Gil immediately enfolded her in his arms and she laid her head on his shoulder.

'Oh, yes, Gil,' she whispered, 'there is nothing I want more.' She thought suddenly of the quotation that had been in her mind upon waking, and she murmured softly, *"'All for love and the world well lost.'"*

'For me, perhaps, but when I am gone—' his arms tightened '—you will be left to fend for yourself and the world can be very cruel.'

'I have been looking after myself for years,' she told him. 'But we will not think of that now.'

'No.' He kissed her, smiling down at her in a way that made her heart flip over. 'If you will not change your mind about this foolishness, then we must send to the inn for Elsie to bring your bags. And I will pay her shot there until...' He swallowed, unwilling to say the words. 'For as long as is necessary—' He broke off as the door rattled open. 'Well,' he said irritably, 'what the devil is it now?'

Turning, he was surprised to see Harris there, looking curiously uncomfortable.

'It's Lord Kirkster, my lord. He's at Bow Street.'

He heard Deborah's soft moan. 'They caught him!'

Harris shook his head. 'Nay, ma'am. He insisted on coming back. Said he could not let another man take the blame for his crimes.'

Gil said sharply, 'I thought I could rely upon you, John, to get him on the packet.'

'Ah well, my lord. In the end he didn't want to go and with Miller to back him up, I had no choice but to drive 'em back to London.'

'It's my guess you did not try too hard.'

Harris gave him a long, considering look. 'Well, no, my lord, not once I could see his mind was made up.'

Deb's hands went to her cheeks and Gil stepped up close behind her, his hands sure and sustaining on her shoulders. 'Oh, Deb—'

'No,' she said quietly. 'It is as it should be. He said he would one day make me proud of him and I am more proud of him now than I have ever been.'

'And I'm here to tell you that you are free, my lord,' said Harris, allowing himself to smile at last. 'The magistrate sent the order back with me. It seems…' He screwed up his eyes, as if trying to recall the exact wording. 'The Bank wishes to apprehend the felons who are forging counterfeit notes. They aren't interested in those unfortunate enough be caught up on the periphery of these crimes and will not be bringing any action against them.'

Gil's fingers tightened on her shoulders. 'And that includes Miss Meltham?'

Harris's smile widened. 'Aye, my lord. It includes Miss Meltham.' He looked around the room. 'I have a carriage outside, my lord, and I will send someone from Gilmorton House to collect up your belongings.'

'Then let us remove from this place immediately,'

declared Gil. 'We shall go directly to Bow Street, to offer your brother all the assistance we can.'

'Are you sure?' She glanced up at him. 'When you have but this minute gained your freedom?'

'He is your brother, Deborah. You will not be happy if we did any less. We are as one now, my darling.'

'Are we?' She was very still. 'You need not marry me, Gil. I will not hold you to that, now you have your life back.'

He caught her hands and stared down at her, his eyes dark and intense.

'I have no life without you, Deborah. You taught me that it is worth risking everything for love. So, will you marry me, my darling, to live as man and wife for as long as Fate allows us?'

'Oh, yes, Gil.' Mistily she smiled up at him. 'No more doubts, no more fears. We will face everything together. My love.'

Epilogue

Five years later

The giant beech tree at Gilmorton had provided shade for generations of Laughtons and the latest addition to the family lay on a blanket beneath its spreading branches, chortling as the leaves moved and whispered gently above him.

'Baby Randolph is a very contented child,' remarked the Dowager Viscountess, reaching out a finger towards the baby, who gripped it in one chubby fist and pulled it towards his mouth.

'And so he should be.' Deborah smiled at her mama-in-law. 'He is very much loved. As is this little man.' She pulled four-year-old James on to her lap and cuddled him.

Her elder son endured this treatment for a few moments, until something new caught his eye and he struggled to escape from his mother's arms.

'Papa, Papa!'

Gil was walking from the house and the boy ran towards him as fast as his sturdy little legs would carry him. Gil swept him up, laughing as he threw his son into the air before settling him comfortably on to one arm. As he came up to the little group beneath the tree, Deborah could not prevent the smile that pushed its way out from inside her. Gil had been in London for three weeks and she had missed him terribly. She wanted to follow James and run into Gil's arms, but she restrained herself. He would come to her, once he had acknowledged the rest of his family.

He set little James upon his feet, stooped to plant a kiss upon his mother's head and greeted the baby with a gentle touch on his cheek before throwing himself down upon the blanket beside Deborah and pulling her close for a deep and lingering kiss. She felt the familiar desire sparking inside her, as strong as ever, and her body pressed towards him, momentarily oblivious of her children and her mama-in-law. They were all watching this display of affection with undisguised interest, and when at last Gil released her, she felt the blush flaming her cheeks. She sought for something to say that would cover her confusion.

'You look very pleased with yourself,' she observed at last.

'I am glad to be home,' he said simply, sitting very close and holding her hand, as if he could not bear to be parted for another minute.

'How was the coronation?' asked the Dowager.

'Too long, too hot, and very tedious.' He grinned. 'It was as grand as Prinny—I beg your pardon—*his Majesty* could make it.'

Deborah shuddered. 'I am relieved I had the excuse of the baby not to go.'

'And, of course, I was obliged to remain and look after your wife since you were duty bound to attend,' added the Dowager, her twinkling eyes belying her serious tone.

Gil shook his head, saying sadly, 'I am desolated that the ladies in my life are so averse to pomp and grandeur.'

'The newspaper accounts were enough for us,' said Deborah. 'I understand the Queen was turned away from the Abbey.'

'Yes, the officials shut the door in her face.' His mouth twisted. 'A farce and I am glad to leave it all behind.'

'I feel sorry for the Queen,' remarked the Dowager. 'It must be horrid to be married to a man one cannot love, or even respect.'

'Yes, I think so and I thank heaven that is not the case here,' said Deb, smiling at Gil.

He leaned in to steal another kiss and once again she felt a wave of gratitude for her good fortune.

'Oh, and I almost forgot.' He reached into his pocket. 'I arrived at the same time as the post and there is a letter for you. From Sydney Cove.'

Immediately her eyes lit up. 'Randolph!'

He laughed and handed it over. 'Who else should it be from? I am now so familiar with his writing that I know it instantly.'

'It is so long since we heard from him,' said Deb, eagerly breaking the seal.

Five years ago she had not dreamed things would work out so well. By telling the authorities all he knew of Warslow's counterfeiting schemes Randolph had avoided the hangman, but Deb had thought fourteen years' transportation would prove a death sentence. However, with the help of his faithful valet he had not only survived the long sea journey, but he had thrived, overcoming his addictions and using his education and considerable intelligence to make himself useful to the government officials.

Gil watched her with tender amusement as she scanned the closely written lines.

'With sea voyages taking half a year, is it any wonder?' he murmured.

'You will wish to read it in peace,' said the Dowager, rising.

Deborah looked up immediately. 'No, no, ma'am, there is no need to go, I assure you.'

'Of course there is,' said her mama-in-law. 'How can you concentrate on your brother's news if you have the little ones clamouring for your attention? I shall take them off to pick flowers.' She lifted little Randolph into her arms and held a hand out for James. Come along, darling. Let us go and see what pretty flowers we can find to put in the nursery.'

They walked away and Deborah returned to her letter.

'Well,' said Gil after a moment, 'what does he say? It cannot be dreadful news, because you are smiling.'

'Oh, Gil, just listen! He writes that he is being hailed as a hero, having helped to rescue passengers and goods from a ship that sank in the bay. Because of that and his exemplary service to the colony he has been given a full pardon and has been granted one hundred acres in, now what has he written here? I *think* it is an area called Airds.' She looked up, her eyes glistening with unshed tears. 'He says that being transported was the best thing that could have happened to him. With Miller to look after him he not only survived the voyage, but he also defeated his craving for laudanum and strong drink. And he maintains that the climate there suits him very well and he has discovered he has a talent for business.' She folded the letter and put it down. 'Who would have thought it would all work out so well?'

Gil touched her hand. 'Are you sad that he is so content without you?'

'No, not really.' She saw the troubled look in his eyes and smiled. 'I was there when he needed me, but he is his own man now. And I have a life of my own, too. A very good life.'

'Truly?' Gently he pushed her down on to the blanket. 'You have no regrets?'

She reached up and ran one finger lightly over his scarred cheek.

'Only that it took so long to find one another and we hurt each other so badly along the way.'

'I was a damned fool,' he muttered. 'What did you do to me that I did not deserve? Whereas you—'

'Hush now.' She put her fingers to his lips. 'If you had not sought me out to wreak your vengeance, I might have lived my whole life without finding true happiness. I shall be eternally grateful to you for that, my love.'

His grey eyes were warm with love as he gazed down at her and said softly, 'You are the best thing that ever happened to me, my dearest Deborah.'

She smiled, aware of the familiar desire pooling

deep within. She pushed her fingers into his silky hair and drew him closer.

'Then stop talking and show me, my lord.'

* * * * *

LET'S TALK
Romance

For exclusive extracts, competitions
and special offers, find us online:

- 📘 facebook.com/millsandboon
- 🐦 @MillsandBoon
- 📷 @MillsandBoonUK

Get in touch on 01413 063232

For all the latest titles coming soon, visit
millsandboon.co.uk/nextmonth